W9-CAF-378

LITTLE,
BROWN

LB

LARGE
PRINT

ALSO BY JAMES PATTERSON

SUMMER NOVELS

Now You See Her (with Michael Ledwidge)

Swimsuit (with Maxine Paetro)

Sail (with Howard Roughan)

Beach Road (with Peter de Jonge)

Lifeguard (with Andrew Gross)

Honeymoon (with Howard Roughan)

The Beach House (with Peter de Jonge)

A complete list of books by James Patterson is at the back of this book. For previews and information about the author, visit JamesPatterson.com or find him on Facebook or at your app store.

Second Honeymoon

James Patterson

AND

Howard Roughan

 LITTLE, BROWN AND COMPANY

LARGE PRINT EDITION

Little, Brown and Company
Hachette Book Group
237 Park Avenue, New York, NY 10017
littlebrown.com

First Edition: July 2013

Little, Brown and Company is a division of Hachette Book Group, Inc. The Little, Brown name and logo are trademarks of Hachette Book Group, Inc.

The publisher is not responsible for websites (or their content) that are not owned by the publisher.

The Hachette Speakers Bureau provides a wide range of authors for speaking events. To find out more, go to www.hachettespeakersbureau.com or call (866) 376-6591.

ISBN 978-0-316-21122-2 (hc) / 978-0-316-21121-5 (large print)
LCCN 2013932889

10 9 8 7 6 5 4 3 2 1

RRD-C

Printed in the United States of America

For my wonderful parents, John and Harriet Roughan—H.R.

PROLOGUE

THINGS THAT GO BANG
IN THE NIGHT

One

THE BOY WOULD be famous around the world one day, but there was no way he could imagine that now. What little kid could predict the future, or begin to understand it? Seven-year-old Ned Sinclair reached out in the darkness, his hand blindly feeling for the wall as he stepped outside his bedroom. He didn't dare turn on a light in the hall. He didn't dare make a sound. *Not even a peep. Not yet.*

Slowly, Ned tiptoed down the long, narrow hallway, the chill of the hardwood floor in the dead of an Albany winter reaching right up through his footed Superman pajamas. He was shaking, ice cold, his teeth on the verge of chattering.

Searching for the railing at the top of the stairs, Ned's arm waved back and forth like a delicate branch caught in the wind. He felt nothing...still nothing...then—*yes, there it was*—the smooth curve of the lacquered pine against his fingertips.

He gripped the railing, white-knuckled, all the way down to the first floor, one quiet step at a time.

Earlier that day, Ned almost forgot how terrified he was of the night. His big sister, Nora, had taken him to see the new movie in town, a sequel, *Back to the Future Part II*. He'd been too young to see the original four years earlier.

Sitting in the dark theater with a big bucket of buttered popcorn in his lap and an RC Cola, Ned was completely and wonderfully transfixed by the film, especially that DeLorean car.

If only I could travel through time, he wished afterward. *I don't want to be here anymore. I don't like it here.*

He wouldn't care where he went, just so long as it was away from his house—and the terrible bogeyman who haunted it late at night. He and Nora would make their great escape and live happily ever after. A new town. A new house. And in the garden of the new house? Nothing but yellow lilies, Nora's favorite.

He loved his sister so much. Whenever the other kids on the block made fun of his stutter—*Ne-Ne-Ne-Ned,* they would cruelly tease—Nora always stood up for him. She had even fought for him. Nora was as tough as any boy. Maybe wherever they went it would be okay to marry your sister.

But for now, he was still stuck in his house. A prisoner. Trapped. Lying awake each horrible night waiting for the sound he prayed would never come...but always did.

Always, always, always.

The bogeyman.

Two

NED TURNED RIGHT at the bottom of the stairs, his hands still guiding him in the darkness as he made his way through the dining room and den, covered in beige shag carpeting, before stopping at the door to his father's library, where he wasn't allowed inside, not ever.

He froze as the baseboard heating gurgled and then clanked a few times, as if it were being hit hard and fast with a hammer. The noise was followed by the sound of a river of water rushing through the old, rusty pipes. But nothing more than that. There were no other footsteps, no voices in the house. Just

6

his own heart pounding madly against his chest.

Go back to bed. You can't fight the bogeyman now. Maybe when you're bigger. Please, please, please, go back to bed.

Except Ned no longer wanted to listen to that voice inside his head. There was another voice talking to him now, a much stronger one. Bolder. Fearless. It told him to keep going. *Don't be afraid! Don't be a scaredy-cat!*

Ned walked into the library. By the window was a mahogany desk. It was lit by the hazy glow of a small electric clock, the kind with those flip-style numbers that turned like those on an old-fashioned scoreboard.

The desk was big, too big for the room. It had three large drawers on the left side of the base.

The only drawer that mattered, though, was the bottom one. It was always kept locked.

Reaching across the desk with both hands, Ned gripped an old coffee mug that was used to hold pencils and pens, erasers and paper clips. After a deep breath, almost as if he were counting to three, he lifted up the mug.

There it was. The key. Just as he'd found it weeks before. Because curious seven-year-old boys can find most anything, especially when they're not supposed to.

Ned took the key in his hand, pinching it between his thumb and forefinger before easing it into the lock on the bottom drawer.

He gave the key a slight twist clockwise until he heard the sound. *Click!*

Then, ever so carefully, slowly, so as not to make a sound, Ned pulled open the drawer.

And took out the gun.

Three

OLIVIA SINCLAIR SHOT up in bed so fast it made her a little dizzy. Her first thought was that the heat had come on, that god-awful clanking noise from the pipes that would practically shake the house.

But that's why she always wore the wax earplugs when she went to bed, so she could sleep through it all. The earplugs always worked, too. Not once did she remember waking up in the middle of the night.

Until now.

If that noise wasn't the heat and the pipes, what was it? It had to be something.

Olivia turned to her left to see the time. The clock on the nightstand said 12:20 a.m.

She turned to her right to see the empty pillow next to her. She was alone.

Olivia took out her earplugs and swung her legs off the bed, her bare feet quickly finding her slippers nearby. The second she flipped on the light, she was jolted by another noise. This one she recognized instantly. It was a horrible scream, just awful.

Nora!

Bursting out of the bedroom, Olivia sprinted down the long, narrow hallway toward her daughter's bedroom, where the light was on.

When she turned the corner at the doorway, she felt worse than dizzy. She felt sick to her stomach.

There was blood everywhere. On the floor. On the bed. Splattered on the pink-painted wall between posters of Debbie Gibson and Duran Duran.

Olivia's eyes pinballed around the rest of the room. She took in a breath. The smell of the gunshots was still thick in the air. In one quick and utterly horrifying moment, she realized what had happened.

And what had been happening for more than a year.

Oh, my God! My daughter! My sweet and innocent daughter!

Nora sat curled up in the tiniest ball by the headboard of her bed. Her arms were wrapped tightly around her knees. She was naked. She was crying. She was looking at her brother.

Across the room in the corner, Ned, pale as the winter's snow outside, was standing frozen like a statue in his Superman pajamas. He couldn't even blink.

For a second, Olivia stood frozen, too. The next second, though, it was as if she'd suddenly remembered who she was. These were her children.

She was their mother.

Olivia rushed over to Ned and kneeled down to hug him, her arms squeezing him tight against her chest. He started to mumble something, repeating it over and over and over. "The bogeyman," it sounded like.

"Shh," Olivia whispered in his ear. "Everything's okay. Everything's okay, honey."

Then, very carefully, she took the gun out of his hand.

Slowly, she walked over to the door, looking

back one more time at the room. Her daughter. Her son.

And the "bogeyman" lying dead on the floor.

Moments later, she picked up the phone in the hallway. She stood there holding the receiver for a long moment, then she dialed.

"My name is Olivia Sinclair," she told the 911 operator. "I just killed my husband."

BOOK ONE

THE STRANGE CASE OF THE O'HARAS

Chapter 1

ETHAN BRESLOW COULDN'T stop smiling as he reached for the bottle of Perrier-Jouët Champagne chilling in the ice bucket next to the bed. He'd never been happier in his whole life. He'd never believed it was possible to be this happy.

"What's the world record for not wearing clothes on your honeymoon?" he said jokingly, his chiseled six-foot-two frame barely covered by a sheet.

"I don't know for sure. It's my first honeymoon and all," said his bride, Abigail, propping herself up on the pillow next to him. She was still catching her breath from their most daring lovemaking yet. "But at the rate we're going," she added, "I definitely overpacked."

The two laughed as Ethan poured more Champagne. Handing Abigail her glass, he stared deep into her soft blue eyes. She was so beautiful and—damn the cliché—was even more so on the inside. He'd never met anyone as kind and compassionate. With two simple words she'd made him the luckiest guy on the planet. *Do you take this man to be your lawfully wedded husband?*

I do.

Ethan raised his Champagne for a toast, the bubbles catching a ray of Caribbean sunshine through the curtains. "Here's to Abby, the greatest girl in the world," he said.

"You're not so terrible yourself. Even though you call me a girl."

They clinked glasses, sipping in silence while soaking everything in from their beachfront bungalow at the Governor's Club in Turks and Caicos. It was all so perfect—the fragrant aroma of wild cotton flowers that lingered under their king-size canopy bed, the gentle island breeze drifting through open French doors on the patio.

Back on a different sort of island—Manhattan—the tabloids had spilled untold barrels of ink on stories about their relationship. Ethan Breslow, scion of the Breslow venture-capital-and-LBO empire, onetime bad boy of the New York party circuit, had finally grown up, thanks to a down-to-earth pediatrician named Abigail Michaels.

Before he'd met her, Ethan had been a notorious dabbler. Women. Drugs. Even careers. He tried to open a nightclub in SoHo, tried to launch a wine magazine, tried to make a documentary film about Amy Winehouse. But his heart was never in it. Not any of it. Deep down, where it really counted, he had no idea what he wanted to do with his life. He was lost.

Then he'd found Abby.

She was loads of fun, and very funny, too, but she was also focused. Her dedication to children genuinely touched him, inspired him. Ethan cleaned up his act, got accepted at Columbia Law School, and graduated. After his very first week working for the Children's Defense Fund, he got down on one knee before Abby and proposed.

Now here they were, newly married, and trying to have children of their own. *Really* trying. That was becoming a joke between them. Not since John and Yoko had a couple spent so much time in bed together.

Ethan swallowed the last sip of Perrier-Jouët. "So what do you think?" he asked. "Do we give the DO NOT DISTURB sign a break and venture out for a little stroll on the beach? Maybe grab some lunch?"

Abby nudged even closer to him, her long, chestnut-brown hair draping across his chest. "We could stay right here and order room service again," she said. "Maybe *after* we work up a little more of an appetite."

That gave Ethan an interesting idea.

"Come with me," he said, sliding out of the canopy bed.

"Where are we going?" asked Abigail. She was smiling, intrigued.

Ethan grabbed the ice bucket, tucking it under his arm.

"You'll see," he said.

Chapter 2

ABBY WASN'T SURE what to think at first. Standing there naked with Ethan in the master bathroom, she placed a hand on her hip as if to say, *You're joking, right? Sex in a sauna?*

Ethan put just the right spin on it.

"Think of it as one of your hot yoga classes," he said. "Only better."

That pretty much sealed the deal. Abby loved her hot yoga classes back in Manhattan. Nothing made her feel better after a long day at work.

Except maybe this. Yes, this had great potential. Something they could giggle about for years, a real honeymoon memory. Or, at the very least, a tremendous calorie burner!

"After you, my darling," said Ethan, opening the sauna door with good-humored gallantry. The Governor's Club was known for having spectacular master bathrooms, complete with six-head marble showers and Japanese soaking tubs.

Ethan promptly covered the bench along the back wall with a towel. As Abby lay down, he cranked up the heat, then ladled some water on the lava rocks in the corner. The sauna sizzled with steam.

Kneeling on the cedar floor before Abby, he reached into the ice bucket. A little foreplay couldn't hurt.

Placing an ice cube between his lips, he leaned over and began slowly tracing the length of her body with his mouth. The cube just barely grazed her skin, from the angle of her neck past the curve of her breasts and all the way down to her toes, which now curled with pleasure.

"That's...*wonderful*," Abby whispered, her eyes closed.

She could feel the full force of the sauna's heat now, the sweat beginning to push through her pores. It felt exhilarating. She was wet all over.

"I want you inside me," she said.

But as she opened her eyes, Abigail suddenly sprung up from the bench. She was staring over Ethan's shoulder, mortified.

"What is it?" he asked.

"There's someone out there! Ethan, I just saw somebody."

Ethan turned to look at the door and its small glass window, barely bigger than an index card. He didn't see anything—or anyone. "Are you sure?" he asked.

Abby nodded. "I'm sure," she said. "Someone walked by. *I'm positive.*"

"Was it a man or a woman?"

"I couldn't tell."

"It was probably just the maid," said Ethan.

"But we've still got the DO NOT DISTURB sign on the door."

"I'm sure she knocked first and we didn't hear her." He smiled. "Given how long that sign's been out there she was probably wondering if we were still alive in here."

Abby calmed down a bit. Ethan was probably right. Still. "Can you go check to make sure?" she asked.

"Of course," he said. For a laugh, he picked up the ice bucket and put it in front of his crotch. "How do I look?"

"Very funny," said Abigail, cracking a smile. She handed him the towel from the bench.

"I'll be back in a jiff," he said, wrapping the towel around his waist.

He grabbed the door handle and pulled it toward him. Nothing happened.

"It's stuck. Abby, it won't open."

Chapter 3

"WHAT DO YOU mean the door won't open?"

In a split second, the smile had disappeared from Abby's face.

Ethan pulled harder on the handle, but the sauna door wouldn't budge. "It's like it's locked," he said. Only they both knew there was no lock on the door. "It must be jammed."

He pressed his face against the glass of the little window for a better view.

"Do you see anyone?" Abigail asked.

"No. No one."

Making a fist, he pounded on the door and shouted, "Hey, is anyone out there?"

There was no response. Silence. An annoying silence. An eerie silence.

"So much for it being the maid," said Abby. Then it dawned on her. "Do you think we're being robbed and they've locked us in here?"

"Maybe," said Ethan. He couldn't rule it out. Of course, as the son of a billionaire, he was less concerned about being robbed than being locked in a sauna.

"What do we do?" asked Abby. She was starting to get scared. He could see it in her eyes, and that frightened him.

"The first thing we do is turn off the heat," he answered, wiping the sweat from his forehead. He hit the Off button on the control panel. He then grabbed the ladle sitting by the lava rocks and held it up to show Abby. "This is the second thing we do."

Ethan wedged the ladle's wooden handle into the doorjamb as though it were a crowbar, leaning on it with all his weight.

"It's working!" she said.

The door shifted on its hinges, slowly beginning to move. With a little more muscle Ethan would be able to—*snap!*

The handle splintered like a matchstick, sending Ethan flying headfirst into the wall.

When he turned around, Abby said, "You're bleeding!"

There was a gash above his right eye, a trickle of red on his cheek. Then a stream. As a doctor, Abby had seen blood in almost every conceivable way and always knew what to do. But this was different. This wasn't her office or a hospital; there were no gauze pads or bandages. She had nothing. And this was *Ethan* who was bleeding.

"Hey, it's fine," he said in an effort to reassure her. "Everything's going to be okay. We'll figure it out."

She wasn't convinced. What had been hot and sexy was now just hot. Brutally hot. Every time she breathed in, she could feel the sauna's heat singeing the inside of her lungs.

"Are you sure the sauna's off?" she asked.

Actually, Ethan wasn't sure at all. If anything, the room was beginning to feel hotter. *How could that be?*

He didn't care. His ace in the hole was the pipe in the corner, the emergency shutoff valve.

Standing on the bench, he turned the valve perpendicular to the pipe. A loud hiss followed. Even louder was Abby's sigh of relief.

Not only had the heat stopped, there was actually cool air blowing in from the ceiling vent.

"There," said Ethan. "With any luck, we've triggered an alarm somewhere. Even if we didn't, we'll be okay. We've got plenty of water. Eventually, they'll find us."

But the words were barely out of his mouth when they both wrinkled their noses, sniffing the air.

"What's that smell?"

"I don't know," said Ethan. Whatever it was, there was something not right about it.

Abby coughed first, her hands desperately reaching up around her neck. Her throat was closing; she couldn't breathe.

Ethan tried to help her, but seconds later he couldn't breathe, either.

It was happening so fast. They looked at each other, eyes red and tearing, their bodies twisted in agony. It couldn't get worse than this.

But it did.

Ethan and Abby fell to their knees, gasping, when they saw a pair of eyes through the small window of the sauna door.

"Help!" Ethan barely managed, his hand outstretched. "Please, help!"

But the eyes just kept staring. Unblinking and unfeeling. Ethan and Abby finally realized what was happening. It was a murderer—a murderer who was watching them die.

Chapter 4

IF I'VE SAID it once, I've said it a thousand times. *Things aren't always as they appear.*

Take the room I was sitting in, for instance. To look at the elegant furniture, plush Persian rugs, and gilt-framed artwork adorning the walls, you would have thought I'd just walked into some designer show house out in the burbs.

Definitely not some guy's office on the Lower East Side of Manhattan.

Then there was the guy sitting across from me.

If he had been any more laid-back his chair would have tipped over. He was wearing jeans, a polo shirt, and a pair of brown Teva sandals. In a million years you'd never have guessed he was a shrink.

Up until a week ago, I seemed pretty laid-back, too. You'd never have known that I was on the verge of trashing a somewhat promising eleven-year career at the FBI. I was hiding it well. At least that's what I thought. .

But my boss, Frank Walsh, thought otherwise. Of course, that's putting it mildly. Frank basically had me in a verbal headlock, screaming at me in his raspy, two-pack-a-day voice until I cried uncle. *You have to see a shrink, John.*

So that's why I agreed to meet with the very relaxed Dr. Adam Kline in his office disguised as a living room. He specialized in treating people suffering from "deep emotional stress due to personal loss or trauma."

People like me, John O'Hara.

All I knew for sure was that if this guy didn't ultimately give me a clean bill of mental health, I would be toast at the Bureau. Kaput. Sacked. The sayonara special.

But that wasn't really the problem.

The problem was, *I didn't give a shit.*

"So, you're Dr. Grief, huh?" I said, settling

into an armchair that clearly was supposed to make me forget that I was actually "on the couch."

Dr. Kline nodded with a slight smile, as if he expected nothing less than my cracking wise right from the get-go. "And from what I hear, you're Agent Time Bomb," he shot back. "Shall we get started?"

Chapter 5

THE GUY CERTAINLY didn't waste any time.

"How long ago did your wife die, John?" Dr. Kline asked, jumping right in.

I noticed there was no pen or notepad in his lap. Nothing was being written down. He was simply listening. Actually, I kind of liked that approach.

"She was killed about two years ago."

"How did it happen?"

I looked at him, a bit confused. "You didn't read any of this in my file?"

"I read all of it. Three times," he answered. "I want to hear it from you, though."

Part of me wanted to leap out of my chair

and pop the guy with a right hook for trying to make me relive the single worst day of my life. But another part of me—the part that knew better—understood he wasn't asking me to do something that I hadn't already been doing on my own. Every day, no less. I couldn't let it go.

I couldn't let *Susan* go.

Susan and I had both been FBI special agents, although when we first met and married, I was an undercover police officer with the NYPD. I became an agent a few years later and was assigned to a completely different section from Susan's, the Counterterrorism Division. A few exceptions notwithstanding, that's really the only way the Bureau allows for married couples.

Susan gave birth to two beautiful boys, and for a while everything was great. Then everything wasn't. After eight years, we divorced. I'll spare you the reasons, especially because there wasn't one big enough to keep us apart.

Ironically, it wasn't until I worked on a case involving a black widow serial killer who nearly poisoned me to death that we both realized it. Susan and I reconciled, and along with John Jr. and Max, we were a family again. Until one afternoon roughly two years ago.

I proceeded to tell Dr. Kline how Susan was driving home from the supermarket when another car ran a stop sign and plowed into her side at over sixty miles an hour. The posted speed limit on the road was thirty. Susan died instantly, while the other driver barely had a scratch on him. What's more, the son of a bitch was drunk at the time of the accident.

A drunk *lawyer,* as it turned out.

By refusing the Breathalyzer and opting instead to have his blood drawn at a hospital, he was able to buy himself a couple of hours— enough time to allow his blood alcohol level to dip under the legal limit. He was charged with vehicular manslaughter and received the minimum sentence.

Was that justice? You tell me. He got to see his kids again while I had to sit mine down and explain that they were never going to see their mother again.

Dr. Kline remained quiet for a few seconds after I finished. His face gave nothing away. "What was she buying?" he finally asked.

"Excuse me?"

"What was Susan buying at the super-market?"

"I heard you," I said. "I just can't believe that's the first question you're asking after everything I told you. How is that important?"

"I didn't say it was."

"Butter," I blurted out. "Susan was going to bake cookies for the boys, but she didn't have any butter. Pretty ironic, don't you think?"

"How so?"

"Never mind."

"No, go ahead," said Dr. Kline. "Tell me."

"She was an FBI agent; she could've died on the job many times over," I said.

Then it was as if some switch inside me had been flipped on. Or maybe off. I couldn't control myself; the words spilled angrily out of my mouth.

"But no, it's some drunk asshole who plows into her on the way back from the supermarket!"

I was suddenly out of breath, as though I'd just run a marathon. "There. Are you satisfied?"

Dr. Kline shook his head. "No, I'm not, John. What I am is concerned," he said calmly. "Do you know why?"

Of course I did. It was why the Bureau had

suspended me. It was why my boss, Frank Walsh, insisted on my coming here to get my head examined.

Stephen McMillan, the drunk lawyer who killed Susan, was being released from prison in less than a week.

"You think I'm going to kill him, don't you?"

Kline shrugged, deflecting the question. "Let's just say people who care very much for you are worried about what you might be planning. So, tell me, John…are they worried for a good reason? Are you planning revenge?"

Chapter 6

RIVERSIDE, CONNECTICUT, IS about an hour's drive from midtown Manhattan. Channeling my inner Mario Andretti, I drove it in forty minutes flat. All I wanted to do was get home and hug my boys.

"Jeez, Dad, you trying to crush me or something?" chirped Max, who was throwing a baseball against a pitchback on our front lawn when I pulled in. For a ten-year-old, the kid could really rifle it—all fatherly bias aside, of course.

I finally unwrapped my arms from around him. "So are you all packed?" I asked.

School had been out for a week. Max and

his older brother, John Jr., were heading off to sleepaway camp the next morning for a month.

Max nodded. "Yeah. Grandma helped me get everything together. She even wrote my name in all my underwear with a Sharpie. Weird. *Whatever*."

I would've expected nothing less from Grandma Judy. "Are she and Grandpa here?"

"No. They're out shopping for dinner," said Max. "Grandpa wanted steaks for our last night all together."

When Susan died, her parents, Judy and Marshall Holt, insisted on moving up from Florida, where they'd retired. They said it would be impossible for me to raise the boys alone while I was still working at the Bureau, and they were right. Also, I think they knew that being around Max and John Jr. would help—if only a little bit—ease the pain of having lost their daughter, their only child.

They'd been nothing short of incredible since the day they arrived, and while I could never fully express my gratitude for their time, love, and sacrifice, the least I could do was treat them to a four-week Mediterranean cruise while the boys were off at camp. I was just glad I paid for it while I was still getting a paycheck from the Bureau. Not that I would've changed my mind. It's that Marshall and Judy would've never accepted the trip. That's the kind of people they are.

"Where's your brother?" I asked Max.

"Where else?" he answered with an eye roll underneath his Yankees cap. "On his computer. The geekazoid."

Max went back to striking out imaginary Red Sox batters while I headed inside the house and upstairs to John Jr.'s room. Naturally, the door was closed.

"Knock, knock," I announced, walking right in.

John Jr. was indeed sitting at his desk, in front of his computer. He immediately threw up his hands at the sight of me.

"C'mon, Dad, can't you knock for real?" he said with a groan. "Haven't you ever heard of the right to privacy?"

I chuckled. "You're thirteen, dude. Talk to me when you can shave."

He rubbed the peach fuzz on his chin, smiling. "It might be happening sooner than you think," he said.

He was right. My older boy was growing up fast. Too fast, maybe.

John Jr. was eleven when he lost his mother, a very tricky age. Unlike Max, J.J. was old enough to feel everything an adult would feel—the full pain and anguish, the overwhelming sense of loss. But he was still just a kid. That's what made it so unfair. The grieving forced him to mature in ways no kid should have to endure.

"What are you working on?" I asked.

"Updating my Facebook page," he answered. "They won't let us do it at camp."

Yes, I know. That's one of the reasons why you're going, sport. No video games, cell phones, or laptops allowed. Only fresh air and Mother Nature.

I walked behind him and shot a peek at his MacBook. He instantly flipped out, slapping his palms against the screen. "Dad, this is personal!"

I never wanted to be a parent who spied on his kid or secretly logged on to his computer to make sure he wasn't saying or doing things he wasn't supposed to. But I also knew that there was nothing "personal" about the Internet.

"Once you post something online, anyone in the world could be looking at it," I said.

"So?"

"So you need to be careful, that's all."

"I am," he said. He was looking away.

It was moments like these when I really missed Susan. She'd know just what to say and, equally important, what not to say.

"John, look at me for a second."

Slowly, he did.

"I trust you," I said. "The thing is, you have to trust me, too. I'm only trying to help you."

He nodded. "Dad, I know all about the creeps and stalkers out there. I don't give out any personal information or stuff like that."

"Good," I said. And that was that.

Or so I thought. Walking out of J.J.'s room, I had no idea, no clue at all, that I was just about to crack one of the biggest and craziest cases of my career.

And as fast as you can say "Dinner is served," it was all about to begin.

Chapter 7

"DO YOU KNOW what the Italians call dining outdoors?" asked Judy, looking at her two grandsons as if they were sitting at desks in a classroom instead of at our round patio table.

Susan's mother had been an elementary school teacher for twenty-eight years. Old habits sure die hard.

"Honey, give the boys a break," said Marshall, cutting into a full pound of New York strip. "School's out."

Judy happily ignored him. They'd been married even longer than she'd been a teacher.

"Alfresco," she continued. "It means 'in the fresh air.'" She then repeated the word slowly, as it would have been pronounced on one of those classic Berlitz language tapes. *"Al-fres-co."*

"Hey, wait a minute, I know him!" announced Marshall, shooting the boys a wink from behind his wire-rimmed glasses. "Al Fresco! He and I fought in Vietnam together. Good old Al Fresco. What a character."

Max and John Jr. cracked up. They always did at their grandfather's jokes. Even Judy cracked a smile.

As for me, I was smiling, too. I was looking around the table at a family that had been devastated by a tragedy but had somehow managed to regroup and carry on.

Gee, any thoughts of regrouping and carrying on yourself, O'Hara? Maybe get your badge back? Some semblance of a life? Yes? No?

A couple of minutes later, Judy was even doing something she hadn't done since Susan's death. She was talking about someone else's death. For a while there, the mere mention of the word would trigger her crying.

"I saw the most awful thing on the news earlier today," she said. "Ethan Breslow and the doctor he just married were murdered on their honeymoon."

Marshall shook his head. "I never thought I'd say this, but I actually feel sorry for his father."

"Wait—who's Ethan Breslow?" asked John Jr.

"He's the son of a very wealthy man," I said.

"A very, *very* wealthy man," added Marshall. "Warner Breslow is a lot like Donald Trump...only less modest."

Judy shot him a disapproving look, although she wasn't about to disagree. Warner Breslow's ego was world-renowned. It even had its own Wikipedia page.

"Have they caught the killer?" I asked.

"No," said Judy. "The news said there were no witnesses. They were in Turks and Caicos, I think."

"Turks and where?" asked Max, unaware that he'd just walked into another one of his grandma's teaching moments.

"Turks and *Caicos*," she said. "It's an island in the Caribbean—really a bunch of islands."

As she began a brief history lesson about the British West Indies, I heard the phone ring inside the house. I was about to get up when Marshall beat me to the punch. "I'll get it," he said.

Less than twenty seconds later, he returned to the table, looking utterly shocked and confused. He had his hand over the phone.

"Who is it?" I asked.

"It's Warner Breslow," he said. "He wants to speak to you."

Chapter 8

COINCIDENCE WAS NOT the word; *downright spooky* was more like it.

Marshall handed me the phone and I walked inside the house, finally sitting down in the den off the kitchen. I'd never met Warner Breslow, let alone spoken to him. Until now.

"This is O'Hara."

He introduced himself and apologized for calling me at home. I listened to every word, but what I really heard—what really struck me—was his voice. When I'd seen him on television doing interviews, he spoke every bit like the powerful and überalpha male that he was. A true world beater.

Now he just sounded beaten, and maybe vulnerable.

"I assume you've heard about my son and his wife," he said.

"Yes, I have. I'm very sorry."

There was silence on the line. I wanted to say something more, but I couldn't think of anything useful or appropriate. I didn't know this man, and I didn't know yet why he was calling.

But I had a gut feeling.

"You were recommended to me by a mutual friend," he said. "Do you think you can help me?"

"I guess that depends. What do you need? What kind of help are you looking for?"

"I can't put my faith in a bunch of palm-tree detectives," he said. "I want to hire you to conduct your own investigation separate from the police in Turks and Caicos."

"That's a little tricky," I said.

"That's exactly why I'm calling you," he retorted. "Do I need to recite your resumé?"

No, he didn't. Still.

"Mr. Breslow, I'm afraid FBI agents aren't allowed to moonlight."

"What about *suspended* FBI agents?" he asked.

I was racing through my mental Rolodex, trying to think who our mutual friend at the Bureau could be. Breslow had access to somebody.

"I suppose I could talk to my boss," I said.

"I already have."

"You know Frank Walsh?"

"He and I are old friends. Given the circumstances, both yours and mine, he's willing to make an exception in this case. You have a green light from the Bureau."

Then, before I could even take a breath, Breslow got right down to it. He might have been consumed by grief, but he was still a businessman. An extremely formidable one.

"Two hundred and fifty thousand dollars," he said.

"Excuse me?"

"For your time and services. Plus expenses, of course. You're worth it."

When I didn't respond right away, he applied some pressure. Or was it leverage?

"Correct me if I'm wrong, John, but your suspension is without pay, correct?"

"You certainly do your homework."

"What about your boys?" he asked. "Do

they do their homework? I mean, are they good students?"

"So far," I said, a bit hesitant. He was bringing my children into this. "Why are you asking about my boys?"

"Because I didn't mention the bonus. You should know what it is before you give me your answer," he said. "It's what you get if your work helps give me the only small measure of relief that I could ever have in this situation," he said. "Justice."

And then Warner Breslow told me exactly what justice was worth to him. He specified my bonus.

And I'll tell you this: the man really knew how to close a deal.

Chapter 9

THREE THOUSAND MILES away, on the seventh floor of the Eagle Mountain Psychiatric Hospital on the outskirts of Los Angeles, thirty-one-year-old Ned Sinclair lay in his bed counting the white ceiling tiles above him for maybe the one millionth time. It was a mindless routine, all in the name of self-preservation—and, well, sanity. Counting the tiles, over and over, was his only escape from this godforsaken hellhole.

Until now.

Ned heard the squeaking wheels of the drug cart heading down the gray linoleum floor of the hallway, as it always did for what the nurses sarcastically called the nightcaps—the various narcotics used to keep the psychiatric patients nice and quiet during the night, when the hospital employed a skeleton crew.

"Time for your meds," came a voice at the door. "No playing games tonight, Ned."

Ned didn't turn to look. He kept counting the ceiling tiles. *Twenty-two...twenty-three...*

For the past four years, ever since Ned arrived at Eagle Mountain, the same female nurse had pushed that drug cart on weekday nights. Her name was Roberta, and she was about as friendly and engaging as one of the hospital walls. She was built like one, too. She hardly ever spoke to her fellow workers, and certainly didn't chat up the patients. All she did was what she got paid to do: dole out drugs. Nothing more. And that was fine by Ned.

But two weeks earlier, Roberta had been fired. Sticky fingers with some of the pills, it was rumored. *It's always the quiet ones.*

Her replacement was a guy who liked to be called by his nickname, Ace. *Asshole* would've been more fitting. The aide was loud, obnoxious, ignorant, and didn't know when to shut up. Clearly, the applicant pool for the graveyard shift was as shallow as a California puddle in August.

"C'mon, Ned. I know you can hear me in that screwed-up little head of yours," said Ace, wheeling in the cart. "Say something. Talk to me, dude."

But Ned had nothing to say.

Ace didn't let up. He hated being ignored. He got enough of that in the L.A. bars, where he would hit on women with the deft touch of a wrecking ball. Glaring at Ned, he wondered, *Who the hell is this dickwad patient to give me the silent treatment?*

"You know, I did some asking around about you here," he said. "Found out you were some kind of math genius, a hotshot college professor. But something bad happened to you. What was it? You hurt somebody? Hurt yourself? Is that why you're up here on the seventh floor?"

The seventh floor at Eagle Mountain was reserved for the PAINs—staff shorthand for "patients abusive in nature." Accordingly, they were never—not ever—supposed to get hold of anything that was sharp, or could be made sharp. They weren't even allowed to shave themselves.

Ned remained silent.

"Oh, wait, wait—I remember what it was now," said Ace. "They told me you lost your shit when your sister died." He smiled wickedly. "Was she hot, Ned? I bet your sister was hot. Nora, right? I'd tap that sweet ass if she were here. But of course, she's not here, is she? Nora's dead. She's a bony ass now, that's all she is!"

The aide laughed at his own joke, sounding like the kids who used to taunt Ned for his stutter all those years ago in Albany.

That's when Ned turned to Ace for the first time.

He finally had something to say.

Chapter 10

"MAY I PLEASE have my pills?" Ned asked calmly.

Ace's puffed-out chest deflated like a bounce house after a church carnival. After all his goading, his baiting, his outright cruelty, he couldn't believe this was the best Ned could do. *Nothing.* The supposed hotshot professor had no fight in him.

"Do you know what? I think you're a pussy," scoffed Ace, reaching for the pill cup on his drug cart.

The night before, though, Ace wasn't thinking at all. He'd been asked to cover for Eduardo, who usually delivered the dinner meals to all the patients. Eduardo had called in sick. Ironically, the reason was food poisoning, perhaps caused by sampling one of the hospital's entrées.

So Ace made the rounds the previous evening, mindlessly dropping off trays to every room on each floor. Including the seventh floor. That's when he forgot that the PAINs were supposed to get a different dessert from the rest of the patients. It was a simple mistake.

Then again, sometimes the difference between life and death is as simple as the difference between an ice cream sandwich and a cherry Bomb Pop...

On a stick.

"Here you go, take it," Ace said, pill cup in his hand.

Ned reached out, but it wasn't the cup he grabbed. With a viselike grip, he latched on to Ace's wrist.

He yanked him toward the bed as if he were starting a lawn mower. In a way he was. *Let the cutting begin.*

Ned raised his other hand, viciously stabbing away with the popsicle stick, which he'd honed to razor sharpness against his cinder-block wall. He stabbed Ace's chest, his shoulder, his cheek, and his ear, then went back to his chest, stabbing over and over and over again, the blood spraying high in the air like fireworks.

Then, for the finale, Ned plunged the stick deep into the incompetent aide's bloated neck—bull's-eye!—slicing his carotid artery as if it were a piece of red licorice.

How're you holding up there, Ace?

He wasn't. Falling to the floor, Ace tried to scream for help, but all that came out was more blood. The guy who couldn't shut up suddenly couldn't say a word.

Ned stood up from the bed and watched Ace bleed out on the floor, counting how long it took for the aide to die. It was just like counting ceiling tiles, he thought. Almost soothing.

Now it was time to go.

Ned gathered his personal items, the few things the hospital allowed him to have in his possession. He was checking out. He would slip past the skeleton crew as quietly as a mouse.

Or a little boy with his daddy's gun.

But before leaving, Ned took one last look

back at Ace, lying dead on the floor. The guy would never know the real reason why Ned had killed him—he would have no clue whatsoever. It didn't matter that he was a mean son of a bitch. Ned couldn't have cared less.

Instead, it was something Ace did his very first day on the job that set in motion something terrible deep inside Ned's brain.

Just awful, hideous...

Ace had told Ned his real name.

Chapter 11

A RUSH OF hot air—*whoosh!*—hit me as I stepped off Warner Breslow's private jet at Providenciales International Airport in Turks and Caicos, where the temperature was ninety-six and climbing.

Immediately, my jeans and polo shirt felt as if they were Velcroed to my skin.

Breslow's jet, a Bombardier Global Express XRS, had a maximum occupancy of nineteen passengers plus a crew, but this flight barely carried the minimum. There was only a pilot, one flight attendant, and me. Talk about extra legroom...

I no sooner had one foot on the tarmac than

I was approached by a young man, thirtyish, wearing white linen shorts and a white linen short-sleeved shirt.

"Welcome to Turks and Caicos, Mr. O'Hara. My name's Kevin. How was your flight?"

"It was Al Gore's worst nightmare," I said, shaking the guy's hand. "Otherwise, the flight was pretty amazing." He smiled, but I was pretty sure he didn't get the joke. Carbon-footprint humor is pretty hit-or-miss.

I didn't yet know who Kevin was, but everything else up to that point had been made crystal clear. I'd already spoken with Frank Walsh at the Bureau, who confirmed that he had indeed approved my working for Breslow.

As for the nature of his and Breslow's relationship, he declined to elaborate. To know Frank was to know not to press the issue. So I didn't.

Meanwhile, Breslow had dispatched one of his expensive attorneys, who arrived the following morning at my house to give me a signed contract. It was only two pages long, and was clearly more for my benefit than his. I hadn't asked to have our agreement in writing, but Breslow insisted.

"Trust me when I say you should never take

anyone at his word," he said in a tone pregnant with meaning.

In addition to the contract, I was also given a sealed envelope. "What's in it?" I asked.

"You'll see," said the attorney, smiling. "It might just come in handy."

He was right.

My only regret of the morning, however, was not being able to join Marshall and Judy on the drive up to the Berkshires to drop Max and John Jr. off at camp. After giving the boys huge hugs before they left, I promised I'd see them in a couple of weeks for the camp's Family Day.

Max, eager to make sure I wouldn't break my vow, made me "super quadruple promise" I'd be there. "No crossies, either," he warned me as John Jr. rolled his eyes.

I already missed them both like crazy.

"Shall we get going?" asked Kevin, motioning over his shoulder to a silver limousine parked nearby. When I hesitated for a second, it dawned on him.

"Oh, I'm sorry, I assumed you knew. I'm with the Gansevoort resort," he explained. "Mr. Breslow has arranged for you to stay with us while you're here."

I nodded. The Mystery of Kevin had been solved. Happily, too. I'd seen the Gansevoort featured in the *New York Times* travel section, and it was absolutely beautiful—top-notch. Not that I was down here to enjoy it. After I dropped off my bag and grabbed a quick shower, I was heading straight over to the Governor's Club to begin my investigation.

Breslow had initially assumed I'd want to stay there—the "scene of the crime"—but I told him I'd be more comfortable somewhere nearby. By "comfortable," of course, I didn't mean the thread count of the sheets.

It would've been different if I were flashing a badge, but I wasn't Agent O'Hara down here, I was just John O'Hara. And for the time being, I didn't want the Governor's Club to know even that.

Same for the local police. Soon enough, I'd pay them a polite visit and compare notes with the detectives on the case, if they were willing. With any luck, they would be. Until then, though, I'd travel as incognito as possible.

But before I could take a step toward the limo, I saw a flashing light out of the corner of my eye. I turned to see a white sedan speeding toward us. I mean, really speeding. If it had wings, it would've taken off.

The question now was, Did it have brakes?

The car wasn't slowing down. If anything, it was getting faster as it got closer.

Finally, pulling a move straight out of the Starsky and Hutch school of driving, the car skidded to a stop right in front of us, the back wheels drifting across the hot asphalt of the tarmac.

On the side of the car it read ROYAL TURKS & CAICOS ISLANDS POLICE.

I glanced over at Kevin, who looked as if he were about to soil his linen shorts. "Mr. Breslow didn't arrange for an escort by any chance, did he?" I asked.

Kevin shook his head no.

And I just shook my head, period.

So much for incognito. Apparently, I was going to meet with the police a little sooner than I expected.

Did I mention how hot it was down here?

Welcome to Turks and Caicos, O'Hara.

Chapter 12

POLICE COMMISSIONER JOSEPH Eldridge, whose jurisdiction was every square inch of all forty islands and cays that made up Turks and Caicos, lit a cigarillo behind his spotless desk, blew out some smoke, and stared at me as if he knew something I didn't.

Undoubtedly, he did. Namely, why I'd been "escorted" from the airport straight to his office.

In addition to him, there were two other men in the room: the chairman of the tourism board and the deputy police commissioner.

I didn't get their names, but it didn't matter.

They were sitting off to the side and showed no intention of talking. This conversation was strictly between Eldridge and me.

"I didn't know what to expect from Mr. Breslow," began Eldridge. "Only that it was going to be something. Or, I should say, *some-one.*"

Clearly, Breslow's wealth and reputation preceded him. I smiled. "Well, it's always good to be someone, right?"

Eldridge leaned back in his chair, letting go with a deep laugh. He looked a little like an older Denzel Washington and sounded a lot like James Earl Jones. All in all, he seemed to be a pleasant enough guy.

Still, there was a fine line between my being welcome or unwelcome on Turks and Caicos, and I was obviously straddling it like a Flying Wallenda in boat shoes.

"So what are your intentions while you're here?" he asked.

If Eldridge was savvy enough to anticipate Breslow hiring a private investigator, and thorough enough to check the manifest of every arriving private plane until he found one owned by Breslow, I wasn't about to get cute with him. My personal circumstances aside, I was an FBI agent "on leave" from the Bureau trying to help a man who had suffered an incredible loss.

That's what I told him, adding: "I'm simply here to make sure no stone is left unturned in the investigation. No harm in that, right?"

Eldridge nodded. "Are you carrying a firearm?" he asked.

"No."

"Does the FBI know you're here?"

"Yes."

"Are you working alone?"

"That depends."

"On what?"

"Your willingness to share information with me," I said. "For starters, what has your investigation uncovered so far? Any suspects? Results of the autopsy?"

Eldridge tapped his cigarillo into a large conch shell on his desk that was doubling as an ashtray. He had a decision to make.

On the one hand, I could be a help to him and his investigation. It's not likely he had anyone with my background and experience working under him. On the other hand, we'd only just met. I could be cuckoo for Cocoa Puffs for all he really knew. *Oh, and did my boss happen to mention I was seeing a shrink, Commissioner?*

Eldridge held my stare for a moment before glancing over at the two men sitting against the wall. It was the first time he'd even acknowledged their presence.

Maybe it was the look he gave them, or maybe it was the plan all along, but the two men suddenly stood up and exited the room as if they were double-parked outside.

I now had Eldridge all to myself.

Or maybe it was the other way around.

Chapter 13

I WATCHED AS Eldridge took another puff of his cigarillo, the smoke leaving his lips in a perfect thin line.

"Agent O'Hara, when you arrived here, what did you see outside my office?" he asked.

"A horde of reporters from all over the world," I answered. "Even the Middle East."

"And how did they look?"

"Hungry," I said. "Like a pack of wolves that hadn't been fed enough for the past forty-eight hours. I've seen that look before."

He smiled. "Yes, exactly. So please don't take this personally when I tell you I can't divulge any details of the investigation. If for no other reason than I'd like to think I've learned from other people's mistakes."

Right away, I understood what he was talking about: Aruba.

So much information and misinformation had leaked in the Natalee Holloway case that the Aruban authorities ultimately came off looking like the Keystone Kops. Eldridge seemed determined not to let that happen under his command.

Still, I had a job to do here, and he knew it.

"Can I at least assume that you have your entire CID working on the case? Every inspector? Every person, down to your last constable?" I asked.

I'd already done a little homework on the setup down here. Whereas NYPD detectives were ranked by grade—first, second, and third—on Turks and Caicos there were four levels of seniority to the CID, or Criminal Investigations Division: detective inspectors, then sergeants, followed by corporals and constables.

Hell, the way I saw it, even the janitor should've been trying to catch the killer.

"Yes, you can assure Mr. Breslow that we

have everyone working on the case," said Eldridge. "Everyone including you, too, now. Can I assume you'll be heading over to the Governor's Club as soon as possible?"

I nodded. "Yes."

"I'm sure you know that the Governor's Club is a private resort, and they can press charges for trespassing, if they so desire."

I stared at Eldridge again, trying to get a read on him. I couldn't. Was he really trying to stand in my way?

"Do you think that's a possibility?" I asked. "I mean, would they really consider my being there to be trespassing?"

"It's very possible," he said. "They cater to a high-class clientele, people in the know, and are very sensitive about respecting the privacy of their guests."

It suddenly dawned on me what Eldridge was doing. He was actually trying to tell me something, only not in so many words. This was off the record. Between the lines. Code.

So long as I was smart enough to figure it out.

"Yes, I see what you mean," I said. "I'd hate to put you on the spot with something as frivolous as a trespassing charge. You'd have to arrest me, wouldn't you?"

"Yes, I'm afraid I would," he said. "Without hesitation."

I stood up and shook his hand. "Then I'll do my best to save you the trouble."

Chapter 14

I FELT A little like a kid with a secret decoder ring from a box of Cracker Jack. Quite cleverly, Eldridge had managed to tell me that he had no leads and would appreciate my help, although I'd have to help him on the sly. The management of the Governor's Club had apparently been uncooperative, and while they couldn't block his access to the staff, the guests at the resort—*people in the know*—were another story.

As for that talk about my being arrested for trespassing, that was just Eldridge advising me to check into the resort as a guest. They could get wise to me and kick me off the property, but it wouldn't be for trespassing. They couldn't press charges.

So after only an hour on Turks and Caicos, my plans were changing yet again.

"Would you like smoking or nonsmoking, Mr. O'Hara? We have both types of rooms available."

The polite and pretty brunette behind the check-in desk at the Governor's Club didn't let on, but it didn't take a rocket scientist or even a suspended FBI agent to figure out that in the wake of two guests being murdered at the resort there'd be, oh, maybe just a few cancellations. How else to explain my walking in without a reservation in June—peak honeymoon season—and getting a room?

"Nonsmoking, please," I said.

"Very good, Mr. O'Hara."

I was staying in a garden-view bungalow, the cheapest they had—or, more accurately, the least expensive. It was still seven hundred and fifty dollars a night. What a bargain! Good thing Breslow was covering all my expenses.

I cooled off with a quick shower in the room before changing into my blending-in clothes for the afternoon: a bathing suit,

T-shirt, and some SPF 30. I was now just another registered guest, heading off to the pool and ready to mingle. Discreetly, of course.

Did anyone witness anything strange before Ethan and Abigail Breslow were murdered?

Unfortunately, if anyone did, he or she wasn't hanging out at the pool. Talk about discreet: the place was just about deserted. One empty chaise lounge after another.

My next stop was the beach, a beautiful strip of white sand sloping gently down into what was called Grace Bay.

I saw some guests sunning themselves, but they were spread out, literally few and far between. Not exactly conducive to striking up a conversation.

Plan D. When all else fails, start drinking.

I sidled up to the resort's beach bar, a small hut with a half dozen empty stools and a lone bartender, who looked bored. I ordered a Turk's Head, the local beer, and considered my next move.

It turned out I didn't have to move at all.

Five minutes later, a man who looked to be in his midsixties approached the bar and ordered a rum punch. While exchanging friendly nods, I noticed that his sunburn was just beginning to turn into a tan.

In other words, he'd probably been at the resort for more than a few days.

I took a sip of my Turk's Head, turning to him. I had my opening line all planned out. "Boy, it's dead around here, isn't it?" I said.

The man suppressed a chuckle. "So to speak."

I smacked my head, as if to say, "I could've had a V8!"

"Jesus, that's right. Poor choice of words," I said. "I just got here today, but I heard all about it. Scary, huh? I guess that explains why the place is so empty."

"Yeah. A lot of people skedaddled right after it happened. I suppose I can't blame them."

The man had remnants of a Western drawl. Texas, or maybe Oklahoma. Business owner, maybe a lawyer. Not a doctor, though. Doctors usually don't wear gold Rolexes.

I smiled, pointing at him. "But you decided to stick around, huh? How's that?"

"It's like that movie," he said. He thought for a second, his forehead scrunching as he came up with the title. "*The World According to Garp*. You know, when the plane flies into the house and Robin Williams still buys it?"

"Oh, yeah, I remember," I said. "What are the odds that it's going to happen again, right?"

"Exactly."

"My name's John, by the way."

"Carter," he said, shaking my hand.

"Of course, I'm sure everyone would feel a lot better if they caught the killer. Have you heard anything?" I asked.

The bartender placed a rum punch in front of Carter, who immediately removed the slice of orange and tiny umbrella from the rim of the glass as if they threatened his manhood.

"I haven't heard boo," he said between two quick sips. "It's all been very hush-hush. Obviously, the hotel—make that the entire island—doesn't want any more publicity."

"What about before the murder?"

"How do you mean?" asked Carter.

"I don't know," I said with a shrug. *Nice and easy now, O'Hara.* "Did you notice the couple talking to anyone in particular?"

"No," he said. "I only saw them one time. They were having a late dinner at the restaurant here. Very lovey-dovey, keeping to themselves."

Swing and a miss with my new buddy Carter, I thought. But then I watched as his forehead scrunched up again. This time real tight.

"What are you thinking?" I asked.

"I just remembered something," he said.

Chapter 15

SPEAK TO ME, Carter.

"I actually did see them one other time," he said. "Now that I think about it."

Carter put down his rum punch, the glass sweating from the heat, and described how he saw Ethan and Abigail Breslow taking a sunset walk on the beach. He thought it was a day or so before they were murdered. A man walking in the opposite direction had stopped to talk to them.

"You hear the conversation?" I asked, still trying to sound casual and chatty.

"No. They were down by the water and I was right here having a cocktail with my wife.

All three of them were smiling, but I sensed that Breslow and his new bride were uncomfortable." He leaned in a bit. "And not just because the other guy was wearing one of those skimpy Speedo bathing suits."

"How could you tell they were uncomfortable?"

"Body language," he answered. "I'm good at reading people."

"You a poker player?"

"Yeah, poker and craps, that's what I play. In fact, that's why I'm so surprised I forgot about this guy they were talking to. I'd seen him before...at the casino," he said. "Shit, I should tell the police about this, shouldn't I?"

I didn't say anything. At least I thought I didn't. But Carter wasn't kidding; he was fluent in body language.

He leaned in again, this time even closer. "Wait a minute. You're a cop, aren't you?"

"Something like that," I said.

I was hoping I wouldn't have to elaborate. Maybe it was how fast I bought Carter another rum punch—"Hold the fruit, please"—but he didn't pursue it. I asked him to describe this guy he saw with the Breslows.

"Dark hair, decent-looking," he said. "Probably in his late thirties."

"Tall? Short?"

"Average height, I think. Around the same height as the Breslow boy. He looked to be in pretty good shape, too."

"Do you think he's a guest here?"

"I don't know. Like I said, the only other time I saw him was at the casino."

"Which one?" I knew there were a couple on the island.

"The Casablanca," he said. "Speedo and I were at the same craps table, only he was playing the don't pass line. He was betting a lot. Winning a lot, too."

"Did he seem to know the dealers?"

"You mean, like, maybe he was cheating?"

"No . . . like maybe he was a regular, someone who lives on the island."

"Yeah, now that you mention it, the dealers did seem to know him," he said. "That's good, right? Chances are you can find him there."

Down went my last sip of the Turk's Head beer. Pretty good for an island brew.

I thanked Carter for his time and help. As I was about to push off my stool, though, I saw his eyes go wide.

"I don't effin' believe it," he said, looking over my shoulder.

I turned. "What is it?"

"That's him . . . *the guy!* Coming in on the Jet Ski. See him? Right there."

I cupped my eyes to cut out the sun's glare. The guy certainly fit Carter's description, right down to the Speedo—or, as Susan used to call it, the banana hammock. "Are you sure it's him?" I asked.

"As sure as sugar," he said.

I took that for a yes.

Chapter 16

I WALKED QUICKLY across the white sand of Grace Bay beach, the various studies and statistics I'd read over the years about criminals returning to the scene of the crime running through my head.

Burglars? About 12 percent of the time.

Murderers? Nearly 20 percent. Kick it up to 27 percent if there was a sexual component to the killing.

I didn't want this guy to think I was making a beeline for him, so I stopped first to dip my toes in the water. From about twenty feet away, I watched as he began to pull his Jet Ski up on the sand so the waves wouldn't take it.

"Need a hand?" I asked, meandering over.

"No, thanks, I'm good," he said without even looking at me. "I'm good" was an American expression, but his accent wasn't American. Mr. Speedo was Monsieur Speedo. A Frenchman.

There were two other Jet Skis—Yamaha WaveRunners, actually—that belonged to the resort sitting side by side a little farther down the beach.

"Hey, I was thinking about going out for a spin tomorrow. What do they charge you here for renting these things?" I asked.

Speedo, however, wasn't riding a Yamaha. His was a royal-blue Kawasaki, a beat-up one at that. It may or may not have been his, but it almost certainly didn't belong to the Governor's Club.

In other words, I was playing dumb. My real question was, *Are you a guest here, Speedo?*

"I'm visiting," he said curtly. "Don't know what they charge."

"I guess I'll have to ask the guy," I said, looking at a water activities hut next to the bar. The guy sitting in front of it, taking care of zero customers, looked even more bored than the bartender. It was the same theme all around. There was nothing like a couple of murders at a high-priced resort to kill off business.

Speedo turned and walked away from me, the clichéd reputation of the French attitude toward strangers fully intact.

Wait a minute, mon frère, *I wasn't done with you yet. In fact, I was just getting started.*

He was heading toward the pathway that led back to the pool. I caught up to him about halfway there.

"I'm sorry," I said. "There was one other thing I wanted to ask you."

He couldn't have looked more incredulous when he turned to me.

Sacré bleu! *What does this stupid American tourist want now?*

"I'm kind of busy," he said.

"Me, too," I shot back. "I'm trying to solve a murder."

I was hoping to see him flinch. He didn't. Cool as could be, he simply nodded. "Yes, the Breslows," he said.

"You know about it, huh?"

"Of course. It's the talk of the island."

"Funny you should say that word. *Talk,* that

is. From what I understand, you were talking to the Breslows here on this beach about a day or two before they were murdered."

"So?"

"Did you know them?" I asked.

"No."

"What were you discussing?"

He shifted his feet. "Who exactly are you?" he asked.

"Will it change your answer if I tell you?"

Speedo eyed me for a moment and I eyed him straight back.

"Snorkeling," he said, finally.

"Snorkeling?"

"Yes. They asked me about Dead Man's Reef," he said, pointing over my shoulder.

But the second I turned to look I knew I'd made a mistake.

Chapter 17

AS SUCKER PUNCHES go it was a pretty good one. Straight to my gut, hard and fast. Kind of like how I went down.

Breathe, O'Hara! Breathe!

Fat chance. I was on my knees, hunched over in a helpless ball, my arms and legs resting on the sand.

Meanwhile, Speedo looked like the start of a one-man triathlon, dashing across the beach and heading straight for the water. Except I knew he wasn't about to start swimming. *Shit!*

I pushed myself up, took one look at him dragging his Jet Ski into the surf, and immediately started running...in the opposite direction.

The guy manning the water activities hut barely had time to blink.

"I'll be back," I said to him, swiping the set of keys off his counter. With any luck he'd simply wave and tell me, "Have fun!"

Yeah, right.

"Hey, man!" I heard over my shoulder as I sprinted back down the beach. Now we had it going on. I was chasing Speedo, and Water Activities Dude was chasing me. "Hey, hey, *you!* Stop right there!"

Then, out of the corner of my eye, I saw my southern cavalry. Carter was up from his bar stool, blazing across the beach like General Sherman through Georgia. For an older man, he sure could run.

As I dragged one of the resort's two WaveRunners into the water as fast as I could, I looked up to see Carter nearly tackle the activities guy. Jesus, what a sight. This beach had never seen such action.

While Carter was quickly trying to explain the situation, I was trying to give myself a quick refresher course on the finer points of riding a Jet Ski. It had easily been more than twenty years since I'd last been on one.

Just like riding a bike, right?

I turned the key, punched the Start button, and jammed the throttle. Then I held on for dear life. Speedo had a head start, but he hadn't lost me yet.

"Go get 'em!" I heard Carter yell.

For the love of James Bond, how do I get myself in these situations?

Chapter 18

I WAS STRADDLING the seat, bouncing up and down with the waves, catching far more air than I cared to. Every time I jumped over a whitecap, the water would splash my face, the salt stinging my eyes. The engine had hit the redline. My hands and feet were shaking to the point of numbness from all the vibration.

Hey, who's having fun yet? Definitely not me. Maybe Speedo was having a blast.

Speeding after the Frenchman, I wondered where he was leading me—or whether he had even thought that far ahead. About a hundred yards separated us, and I was desperately trying to close the gap.

It wasn't happening.

If anything, I was losing ground. But as long as I could still see him, I had a shot. He couldn't drive his vehicle forever; eventually he'd have to head to shore. I saw a footrace in my future.

Then I saw something else.

Off in the distance there was a series of rock formations jutting up from the water. They looked like little black chess pieces in a game that was about half over.

Speedo was heading right for them.

Before I knew it, he'd disappeared.

He was using his home field advantage, and suddenly I felt like I was being played. But there was no time to slow down and think things over.

I kept the throttle cranked and stayed on his tail, swerving left, right, then left again through the maze. I was drenched, exhausted, and coming way too close to these rocks. *Jet Skis don't come with air bags, do they?*

Finally, I was out in the clear again. To my amazement, I'd even made up some ground.

Speedo was only about fifty yards ahead now, and looking nervously over his shoulder at me. For the first time, I actually took one hand off the handlebars.

And waved.

I was starting to get the hang of things, using the swells to propel me even faster. Keeping up? Hell, no, I was catching up!

Then Speedo made a sharp right.

He was aiming toward shore. I looked ahead and saw a stretch of beach in front of another resort. Which way would he run?

Soon I saw that running wasn't part of his plan.

Suddenly I saw a series of red markers in the water spread out in a large circle. All around the perimeter were the heads of snorkelers, their neon-colored breathing tubes bobbing up and down. But no one was *in* the circle.

Except Speedo.

And then me.

Immediately, he started swerving again, as though we were back among those jutting rocks, only I didn't see any rocks.

Until it was too late.

Thump! Bam!

I came flying off a swell only to see the water disappear beneath me, a jagged patch of rock and coral taking its place. That explained the markers.

My knees buckled as I landed, the vehicle careening hard to the right as I tried to hold on.

I couldn't. I flew over the handlebars, somersaulting through the air, head over heels, like Charlie Brown trying to kick the football.

That's all I remember.

Chapter 19

THE GOOD NEWS was that I wasn't dead.

"Now do you want the bad news?" asked Joe Eldridge. "Because I do have some bad news."

He was standing at the foot of my bed, his expression teetering somewhere between pity and annoyance. Surely the police commissioner didn't expect to see me again so soon, let alone laid up in the Grace Bay Medical Centre with a couple of cracked ribs and a mild concussion.

"What I really want is some more painkillers," I said.

I wasn't kidding, either. My head was pounding. Hell, my whole body was pounding. It hurt just to blink.

As Eldridge explained, the bad news wasn't that Speedo got away. It was that his real name was Pierre Simone, and that he was a con man and a poker cheat.

But nothing more.

"I wouldn't let him babysit my kids," said Eldridge. "But he's no murderer. He's not violent."

"How can you be sure?" I asked.

He folded his arms. "Trust me; I know him."

In Eldridge's right hand I noticed a manila envelope, but I wasn't ready to go there yet. The "trust me" explanation needed more details. This Pierre guy nearly got me killed, after all. *So riddle me this, Mr. Commissioner...*

"Why would he take off on me?" I asked.

"There's an arrest warrant on him in the States. Some bounced checks in New York, I believe," said Eldridge. "You had an American accent and, I presume, a lot of questions for him. He panicked."

"Panicked?"

"I'm sure you know that Turks and Caicos

adheres to the extradition agreement between the United States and Great Britain."

"Not only do I know it, I'm inclined to put it to good use," I said, only to watch Eldridge smile. I stared at him. "You think I'm kidding?"

He raised his palms. "No. I'm sorry, it's not that. No one told you yet, did they?"

"Told me what?"

"You blacked out after your crash. Pierre's the one who took you onto shore to get help. I guess he felt guilty."

"Wait. So you have him in custody?"

Eldridge chuckled. "He didn't feel *that* guilty," he said. "He took off as soon as an ambulance was called. But like I said before, he's not a violent person."

I was lying there in the bed listening to Eldridge, but it was what I was seeing that proved more telling. The commissioner had the same look that he had when we first met in his office. He knew something I didn't.

Then it clicked for me.

"Shit. He's an informant for you, isn't he?" I asked.

Eldridge nodded. "Pierre's been very helpful on a few cases over the years. In return, I occasionally look the other way for him. But that's not why I'm sure he isn't a suspect," he said.

With that, he handed me the envelope he'd been holding. My entire investigation was about to change. The trip to Turks and Caicos had just paid off.

Chapter 20

"ANYTHING TO DECLARE?" asked the customs agent at Kennedy Airport.

Yeah. If I never see another Jet Ski for as long as I live it will still be too soon. How's that?

Warner Breslow's pilot had given me his phone number to use when I was ready to go home. "Just call me and I'll fly back down to pick you up," he said. He assumed I'd be in Turks and Caicos for at least a few days, if not longer. So did I.

That was before I opened the envelope from Commissioner Eldridge.

By noon the next day, I was landing in New York and driving out to the Breslow estate in the Belle Haven section of Greenwich. The double vision from my crash was gone. So, too, were the tweeting birds circling my head. As for my bruised ribs, I figured if I could just avoid sneezing, the hiccups, and comedy clubs, I'd be able to muddle through.

"Come in," said Breslow, greeting me at the front door.

Not surprisingly, Breslow's voice—as well as everything else about him—was subdued. The usual sheen from his combed-back silver hair, his trademark, was missing, as was the gleam in his eyes. Instead, those eyes were bloodshot and sporting dark circles, undoubtedly from crying and lack of sleep. His cheeks were hollow, his shoulders slouched.

But most of all, it was what I couldn't see. What was missing. *His heart.* It had been ripped out of his chest.

"This way," he said after I shook his hand.

After a left turn at the Matisse, a walk down a long hallway, and then a right at the Rothko, he led me into what he called his reading nook.

Some nook. The room, lined from floor to ceiling with books, was absolutely huge. Throw in some coffee, pastries, and loitering hipsters and it could've been a Barnes & Noble.

After we sat down in a couple of soft leather armchairs by the window, Breslow simply stared at me, waiting. It went without saying that he didn't expect me back so soon, so he didn't say it. He had to assume there was a good reason, and he was right.

"Let's talk about your enemies," I said, getting right to the heart of the matter.

Breslow nodded, the corners of his mouth curving up ever so slightly. It was probably the closest he'd come to a smile all week. "Aren't you supposed to ask first if I have any? That's what they do in the movies."

"With all due respect, if this were the movies you'd be petting a cat right now," I said. "No one accumulates the wealth you have without being a villain from time to time."

"You think my son's murder was revenge, someone trying to get even with me?" he asked.

I listened to his question, but was more focused on his tone. He was far from incredulous. I suspected the thought had already crossed his mind.

"It's a possibility," I said.

"How much of a possibility?"

I didn't hesitate. "Enough that you should probably stop recording our conversation."

He didn't ask me how I knew, nor was I about to tell him. Instead, he simply reached over and flipped a switch on the back of the lamp that sat between us.

"I take it you've read my file," he said.

Chapter 21

ACTUALLY, NO, I hadn't read his FBI file. Not yet.

But I'd read the newspapers, especially those from some months earlier, when his firm purchased the Italian drug company Allemezia Farmaceutici, under a cloud of suspicion more bizarre and mysterious than anything in a David Lynch film.

It started with a video that appeared on the website of the leading Italian newspaper, *Corriere della Sera*. In vivid color, a Chinese man wearing nothing but bunny ears and a baby's diaper could be seen hopping around a hotel suite with a couple of naked Italian prostitutes. Later in the video, after a three-way that would make Ron Jeremy blush, the guy was snorting a Great-Wall-of-China-size line of coke off the stomach of one of the girls.

Okay, just your average night in Milan, perhaps—only the man happened to be Li Yichi, the deputy general manager of Cheng Mie Pharmaceutical, the largest drug company in the world. Li was in Milan finalizing the purchase of Allemezia Farmaceutici for thirteen billion euros. It was all but a done deal.

But twenty million hits on YouTube later, it was all undone. The board of Allemezia rejected the Cheng Mie offer, citing fallout from the video.

Of course, there were many unanswered questions, not the least of which was how Li could be so careless. And what the hell was up with the bunny ears and diaper and those Italian prostitutes? *Molto* kinky, no?

The biggest question of all, though, had to do with who was behind the camera—both literally and figuratively. Had the married Chinese executive been set up? And by whom? Who stood to gain?

Warner Breslow sure did.

With Cheng Mie Pharmaceutical out of the picture, Allemezia's stock took a major nosedive, leaving the company desperate for a new suitor. That's when Breslow swooped in and bought them for a billion euros less than what Cheng Mie had offered. Talk about a discount.

But that's not why I'd remembered all this, why I went online to reread all the articles.

It was the aftermath.

One day after the news broke that Breslow had bought Allemezia, Li, star of the video, hanged himself in his office. He was discovered by his father, Li Kunlun—the chairman of Cheng Mie Pharmaceutical.

"I want you to take a look at something," I said to Breslow, opening the envelope.

It was the report from Ethan and Abigail's autopsy.

Chapter 22

"AS YOU CAN see from the toxicology section, there were traces of the nerve agent cyclosarin found in both Ethan and Abigail," I said. "Once they were trapped in that sauna, the murderer wasn't taking any chances. He poisoned them."

Breslow looked up from the autopsy report, his eyes narrowing to a squint. "In other words, that's why you're here and not there. We're not looking for someone in Turks and Caicos, are we?"

I shook my head. "Cyclosarin isn't exactly found over the counter."

"Where is it found?" he asked.

"That depends on who you talk to in the intelligence world and whether they're on the record or not. The only country that for sure has produced cyclosarin in significant quantities is Iraq. After that, high on the suspect list would be—"

"China," said Breslow, beating me to the punch. He knew where I was heading with this.

Cheng Mie Pharmaceutical was rumored to have worked closely with the Chinese government on developing chemical weapons. Li Kunlun, the chairman, had even been an officer in the Chinese armed forces.

"So he blames me for his son's suicide and kills mine in return?" asked Breslow, suspicious. "That's not really the Chinese way."

"Neither is wearing bunny ears and a diaper," I said.

Breslow conceded the point with a slight nod. "What now?" he asked. "It's not like you can question him."

"Even if I could I wouldn't yet," I said. "Not without some link connecting means and motive."

"Like Chinese passports coming into the island?"

"For starters," I said.

"Do you want me to make a call to the U.S. embassy in Beijing? Perhaps they could help."

"Who do you know there?" I asked.

"Everybody," he answered.

Gee, why was I not surprised?

Still, I'd just as soon not be the suspended FBI agent who upended relations between the U.S. and China. At least not yet.

"No. Let's not play that card until we know more," I said.

I wrapped things up, telling Breslow I'd keep him informed. Then he walked me out. As he shook my hand in the foyer, I could tell there was something on his mind, perhaps a question left unanswered.

Sure enough. "I'm curious why you didn't ask me," he said.

"Ask you what?"

"Whether or not I was the one who hired those Italian prostitutes and gave them a video recorder."

"It's none of my business," I said.

"It is if it led to my son's murder."

I stared at Breslow, wondering what he was doing. Confessing? Still sizing me up? Or was it something else?

Not that it really mattered. The reason I didn't ask him was because I already knew the answer. It was straight out of those Encyclopedia Brown mystery books I used to love to read when I was a kid. Something he'd done had tipped his hand.

You're not quite as cagey as you think, Warner Breslow.

Chapter 23

I COULDN'T REMEMBER the last time I pulled up to my house knowing that no one else would be there. Between Marshall and Judy, John Jr. and Max, there was always somebody who'd answer when I'd walk through the door and shout out, "Hello? Anyone home?"

I hadn't given much thought to being alone before they all left. Now I was by myself, and it was kind of weird. A little sad, even. A little eerie, too.

I got the mail before heading inside, flipping through it as I grabbed myself a Heineken Light from the fridge. The boys had barely had time to unpack their bags up at camp, so there was no chance of getting a letter from them. Instead, it was just a couple of bills, some junk mail, and—

What's this?

Sandwiched between the latest issue of *Sports Illustrated* and an L.L.Bean catalog was a small package, one of those padded manila envelopes. My address had been handwritten in black marker, and the envelope was sealed tight with a lot—and I mean a lot—of clear tape. We're talking the whole roll.

Whatever was inside wasn't getting out on its own.

I was looking so much at the tape that I didn't notice something right away. The postmark was from Park City, Utah, but there was no return address. Not in the upper left corner, not on the back, not anywhere.

Oh, great. Cue the paranoid thoughts...

You could forgive an FBI agent for being a little...um...spooked when it came to mysterious packages in the mail. The Unabomber, anyone? Those anthrax-infected letters sent after 9/11? In fact, since then, any mail delivered to me or any other agent at my office without a return address had to be X-rayed.

But this wasn't my office. This was my home, and I didn't exactly have an X-ray machine tucked away next to the old Black & Decker tool set down in the basement.

Here goes nothing.

After giving the package a quick shake, as though I were a kid on Christmas morning, I grabbed a pair of scissors and cut open one of the ends. So far so good. There was no suspicious powder, and it certainly wasn't a bomb.

Instead, it was a Bible.

Really? A Bible?

My first thought was that some religious charity had decided to step things up with its fund-raising.

But there was no letter attached. No solicitation. Just a holy Bible.

No, wait. Make that a *stolen* holy Bible.

Flipping it open, I saw PROPERTY OF THE FRONTIER HOTEL, PARK CITY, UT stamped on the inside cover.

Frontier Hotel? I'd never heard of it, let alone been there. I was pretty sure I didn't even know anyone from Park City. I once skied at Deer Valley years and years ago, but that was it, my only visit.

I took the last sip of beer and was about

to shrug it off and move on to more pressing matters—like grabbing a second beer, for instance—when I noticed that one of the pages was dog-eared.

I turned to it.

The next thing I knew, I was practically turning my house upside down.

Chapter 24

IT WASN'T ANYTHING I read.

It was something I couldn't read.

What had been dog-eared was a section in the Old Testament, the Song of Moses, from the book of Deuteronomy. A passage was missing—literally cut out from the middle of the page—right between Deuteronomy 32:34 and 32:36.

What was 32:35?

Maybe if I'd paid more attention in Sunday school, when I was an altar boy at Saint Augustine's Church, I'd know. But I was the kid in the back of the room, staring at the clock and counting the minutes until they served the cookies and lemonade.

So off I went. A tornado from room to room.

I knew there was a King James Bible somewhere in the house. A beautiful one, too. Leather-bound, gilt-edge paper. It had belonged to Susan. John Jr. read from it at her funeral. I still remember how brave he was, holding back the tears so he could finish his passage.

"Mom wouldn't want me to cry," he told me afterward.

That's where I looked first, his room. The bookcase next to his desk was too obvious. I mean, what thirteen-year-old kid puts something where it belongs, right? After scanning the shelves, I checked the closet. Then the small table by his bed. Then under his bed.

Max's room? I went down the hall and did the same routine, checking everywhere. I felt like one of those parents in those after-school specials, rifling through his kid's room searching for his stash of weed. Of course, Max was only ten. There wasn't even a stashed-away *Playboy* to be found.

Or a Bible.

I kept looking, determined as hell to find it. This was strange, after all. Someone was trying to tell me something, and whoever it was had gotten cute about it.

Was *cute* even the word? It depended on the message, didn't it?

I searched everywhere in the guest room, otherwise known as Marshall and Judy's room. I went back downstairs and looked in the den. Finally I remembered. *Duh!*

I'm the one who had it.

I'd put it in a box of Susan's things that I kept under our bed, the side she slept on, no less. Dr. Kline would have a field day with that one, wouldn't he?

I hightailed it into my bedroom. Pulling out the box, I put on emotional blinders. I didn't want to get caught up in the other items in it, the keepsakes. That had blubbering, crying mess written all over it.

Thankfully, the Bible was right on top. No digging necessary. I sat on the bed, turning to Deuteronomy and the Song of Moses.

Scrolling down the page with my index finger, I stopped on the missing passage, 32:35. I read it once, then twice.

To me belongeth vengeance, and recompence; their foot shall slide in due time:

for the day of their calamity is at hand,
and the things that shall come upon them
  make haste.

I read it over again a few more times, although I didn't know why. Maybe I was hoping that I was missing something, that there was a different interpretation.

There wasn't.

No matter how you sliced it, I was being threatened. Someone had it out for me.

I think I need that other beer.

Chapter 25

NED SINCLAIR SAT behind the wheel of his stolen Chevy Malibu, watching from across the street as John O'Hara returned home.

He watched O'Hara get the mail. He watched him go inside.

Soon the sun would go down, and under the cover of darkness Ned would do what he'd come to do. What he was dying to do.

Outside the open windows of the Malibu he could hear the sound of a sprinkler head on a nearby lawn as it sprayed its water in a slow but steady circle.

Click, click, click, click…

It was the same sound, over and over and over. Relentless. Monotonous.

Music to his ears. As beautiful as a Brahms concerto.

Ned's memories of being a mathematics professor at UCLA had waned to the point of being only quick, distant flashes now. What little he saw, though, was almost always the same. Equations. Equations everywhere. Those beautiful patterns of numbers filling up every inch of a blackboard, one line after another.

And always he'd be pacing before them— stalking them, really—with chalk in hand. He'd solve one equation and move on to the next, and the next, and the next.

Each one a victim of his genius.

A few minutes after nine, with no more daylight left in the sky, Ned stepped out of the car. Gently closing the door behind him, he glanced left and right to make sure he was alone, not being observed. The sidewalks were clear, there were no oncoming cars. A few porch lights glowed in the distance, but nothing more. Ned was all but invisible.

As though he wasn't even there.

Slowly, he walked across O'Hara's front lawn to the side of the house, where there was a small grass pathway between a wooden fence and some hydrangea plants.

He peeked in a bay window along the way, looking for anyone else who might be home, but he was pretty sure O'Hara was alone.

Ned had been parked in front of the house all day. He saw no one else coming or going, which was exactly what he wanted.

Everything was falling into place beautifully. Perfectly. Just as he'd imagined it all those days and nights at the hospital.

Approaching the backyard, Ned began to hear the faint sound of music. He recognized the song immediately. How could he not? His father used to listen to Sinatra all the time.

"The Best Is Yet to Come"? "Strangers in the Night"?

Ned smiled. No.

The song was "Call Me Irresponsible."

Peeking around the back, Ned got a pleasant surprise. He wouldn't have to bother getting into the house. O'Hara was sitting outside on his patio. He was drinking a beer.

Ned walked a few steps toward him, emerging from the darkness into the hazy glow of a nearby floodlight.

"Are you John O'Hara?" he asked.

He knew he was, but he wanted to make doubly sure. It was just like an equation. *Always check your work. Then check it again. There can be no mistakes here.*

O'Hara, startled, sat up quickly in his chair. He cupped a hand over his eyes for a better look at his uninvited guest. Ned Sinclair stared into those eyes.

"Yeah," O'Hara said. "Who wants to know?"

Ned pulled a gun from inside his Windbreaker, the polished metal of the grip feeling like a big and wonderful piece of chalk in his hand.

"I'm Ned," he said, taking aim at O'Hara's head. "And you're dead."

Then he pulled the trigger and killed John O'Hara.

BOOK TWO

WHAT'S IN A NAME?

Chapter 26

THE WORDS PLAYED over and over in the head of a special agent named Sarah Brubaker. "There's one more out there, and you'll never find her," the sick bastard had said. "That poor, poor little girl, she won't last much longer. She'll be dead and gone like all the others. She's probably dead already."

Agent Brubaker reached up beneath her sweat-soaked blouse. She sliced the straps of her bra with the blade of a Swiss army knife. Unhooking the front clasp, she then pulled the bra out from the bottom of her blouse. She stuffed it in her slacks along with the knife.

"What the hell are you doing?" asked Doug Trout, chief of the Tallahassee police department.

"Please get me two rubber bands," Sarah said, ignoring his question, not to mention his quick peek at the way her blouse hugged the shape of her breasts.

Yep. She knew *exactly* what she was doing.

Trout disappeared into a supply room a few feet away while Sarah gathered up her shoulder-length auburn hair. She could hear the seconds ticking away in her head.

Except for the two cops stationed at either end of the hallway, the operations department above the main terminal of the Tallahassee Regional Airport had been cleared out. It was strictly NPO. Necessary personnel only.

As for the only nonpersonnel individual on the premises, his feet and hands were cuffed to a chair and table on the other side of the closed door behind her. A small, windowless conference room. A temporary jail cell.

For the past seven months, a real bastard named Travis Kingslip had terrorized the Florida Panhandle, kidnapping, raping, and murdering five young girls within a hundred-mile radius of Tallahassee.

Assigned to the case after the fourth girl went missing, Sarah had spent every waking moment trying to figure out who he was—and hoping that somewhere along the line he'd slip up and make a mistake. He never did.

Instead, some buffoon of a thief did it for him. A druggie.

A neighbor had called the police after spotting a man climbing through the basement window of Kingslip's two-bedroom ranch house in the small town of Lamont, about thirty miles from the airport.

When officers arrived at the house, they not only caught the thief but they also caught a major break in the murder case.

Papered all over Kingslip's bedroom were close-up photos of the breasts of underage girls—homemade digital prints—taken from every conceivable angle and cropped in a way that never revealed a face. It was like trying to identify a mannequin.

At the very least, they had a child pornographer on their hands. But then Sarah arrived and noticed the kidney-bean-shaped mole in one of the pictures. It matched the description given to her by the parents of one of the missing girls.

Within an hour, Sarah and half the Tallahassee police force were storming the tarmac
at the airport in 102-degree heat. Kingslip, a
baggage handler, confessed on the spot. "All
you had to do was ask," he'd said.

Then, immediately after he was read his Mi-
randa warnings, he started to laugh. It was
the kind of twisted and demented laugh that
Sarah had heard too many times in her career
chasing serial killers.

Kingslip's laugh may have been the worst of
them all.

"There's one more out there, and you'll
never find her," he had said. "That poor, poor
little girl, she won't last much longer. She'll
be dead and gone like all the others. She's
probably dead already."

Police chief Trout reappeared with two rubber bands and a puzzled look on his face.
"Here," he said.

Sarah took the rubber bands and quickly
used them to tie her hair into two pigtails behind her ears. Trout watched her and nodded.
He got it now.

"I'm not going in there with you, am I?" he
asked.

Only he wasn't really asking. It was a

rhetorical question. He'd gotten to know Sarah a little bit since she'd arrived from Quantico—enough to be sure of one thing. Two things, actually.

Sarah Brubaker was as determined as anyone he'd ever met.

And Travis Kingslip was all hers.

Chapter 27

SARAH CLOSED THE door behind her and grabbed one of the conference room chairs. She wheeled it right up in front of Kingslip and sat down. Their knees were almost touching. She didn't want to be this close to him, but it was necessary. Actually, it could be a matter of life and death.

He was wearing a blue jumpsuit two sizes too big and reeked of cigarettes, sweat, and jet fuel. His hair fell from beneath his trucker hat like strands of black string that had been dipped in grease. His teeth looked like rotted pieces of candy corn.

Immediately, his eyes went to her chest. It

was no sneak peek; it was a full-on gawk. He didn't have to say what he wanted to do to her at that very moment. His dark, cold, soulless stare left little doubt.

So far so good, thought Sarah.

There was no time for small talk or breaking the ice. No time to gain his trust. She needed him to like her, and this was the quickest way, down and dirty. *Sorry, Ms. Steinem.*

Kingslip rattled his hands and feet. "Why don't you take these handcuffs off, honey? I promise I won't bite," he said. "C'mon, take 'em off."

"Maybe I will," said Sarah. "But you have to do something for me first."

Kingslip's words on the tarmac were echoing in Sarah's head, one line in particular. *That poor, poor little girl, she won't last much longer.*

He was hiding her somewhere, he had to be. Was she already dying? Had he hurt her? Killed her?

Sarah could hear the clock ticking louder, but she knew she couldn't race through this. She figured she had only one shot; she had to get it exactly right.

"Where is she, Travis?" she asked, her voice calm but firm. "Tell me. Just tell me the truth."

"I'll never te-ell," he came back in a singsongy voice, creepy as hell.

"Is she near where you live?"

He kept staring at her breasts. "You're pretty, do you know that?"

Sarah did know that. It had been both a blessing and a curse in her life, especially in her career. Right now, though, she needed it to be a blessing.

"Is she near where you live, Travis?" she repeated.

Every inch of his house in Lamont had already been searched. There were no secret rooms, no hidden attics or basement wells, nothing in the freezer. This wasn't Buffalo Bill from *The Silence of the Lambs*.

Kingslip didn't answer. Not that Sarah needed him to. She was watching more than listening. A flinch, a twitch, a blink from him—something would tip her about what he was thinking.

She kept going. No choice. "Is she close by?" she asked. "Somewhere near the airport?"

Bingo.

It was his eyebrow. Right on the word *air-port,* the left one curled. For a split second and by a fraction of an inch, but she saw the "tell" clear as day.

Sarah leaned in even closer to him, his stench so repugnant she wanted to vomit. "She's near the airport, isn't she, Travis? Is she within walking distance, or do I need to take a car?"

He chirped again. "I'll never te-ell."

He already had, though. It was the eyebrow again, this time on the word *car.*

But she'd already searched his car in the parking lot, and there was only one vehicle registration on file for him with the Jefferson County DMV.

Unless it wasn't his car.

"Is she in a car, Travis? Do you have her in someone's car? Whose car is she in?"

He suddenly looked like the pigeon at the poker table who couldn't figure out why everyone was calling his bluffs. *How does she know? How much does she know?*

"You'll never find her," he said, turning angry on a dime. He suddenly didn't like her so much, but that was okay. Sarah had another hunch to play.

"Why won't I find her?" she asked.

"You just won't, that's why."

"That's not a good enough reason. What makes you so sure?"

"Nothing."

"C'mon, Travis. You're a lot smarter than that."

"You're right, I am," he said with a defiant nod.

Sarah's smile disappeared. It was her turn to play a mind game on him. "No, you're not smart at all. You were dumb enough to get caught, weren't you?"

"Fuck you."

"You'd like that, wouldn't you, Travis?" She glanced down at her chest. "Do you want to take *my* picture? Get real nice and close to these?"

Kingslip began to squirm in his seat, the handcuffs around his wrists and ankles rattling the chair and table like a one-man earthquake. His sudden anger toward Sarah was colliding with his sick and perverted attraction to her.

"Fuck you!" he said again, shouting it now.

"Why can't I find her, Travis?"

"FUCK YOU!"

"Why? Tell me why!"

"BECAUSE THERE'S TOO MANY OF THEM, BITCH! THINK YOU'RE SMART! YOU AIN'T SO SMART!"

Sarah sprang up from her chair, bolting out of the room.

Her hunch was right.

Chapter 28

"FOLLOW ME! LET'S go, let's go!"

Sarah yelled it to every cop she raced past, from the hallway of the operations department down the stairs to the baggage claim area and out the double doors into the stifling heat. Not even police chief Trout knew where she was going.

But he was following just the same, weaving his way through the crowd, composed mostly of tourists, as fast as his former-Florida-State-linebacker frame would allow.

Nine, maybe ten cops had fallen in behind Sarah as they crossed the taxi and limo pickup lane outside the terminal.

Cars skidded to a halt, the drivers pounding on their horns. People nearby were either staring or scattering to get out of the way.

"Holy shit," mouthed the guy working on the Avis lot, who barely looked old enough to drive. His booth was being invaded. Leading the way was a pretty woman who, well, looked like she wasn't wearing a bra.

"The trunks!" said Sarah, flashing her badge. "Open every car trunk on the lot!"

"*What?*" the guy said. He was more stunned than anything else. "I can't do that."

Sarah pushed right past him and grabbed a large bulletin board off the wall, which held all the rental car keys. With a flip and a few shakes, they all went spilling onto the floor in front of the counter.

Trout was right in step now.

"You two, stay here!" he barked, pointing at two of his officers. "Check every trunk. The rest of you, come with me!"

Sarah had already moved on to the Hertz lot. She grabbed some keys herself and started popping trunks all around her.

"What are we looking for?" one of the attendants asked.

She didn't stick around to answer. It was the

classic "You'll know it when you see it." A girl trapped in the trunk, probably bound and gagged.

God, will she still be alive? Sarah wondered. *Please let her be alive.*

Immediately, she tried to erase the image of the girl from her mind. Never get attached to the victim, she'd been taught. Messes with your focus.

It was a hard lesson to learn, and even after seven years on the job she wasn't fully there.

Pop! Pop-pop-pop!

Right down the line, from Thrifty to Enterprise, Budget to National, the trunks began to open. Economy, midsize, premium, even the SUVs.

The cops were spread out, the staff from every rental company was racing around with key fobs in hand, their thumbs pressing furiously.

Pop! Pop-pop!

Sarah ran from car to car, looking and looking and looking. Up one row and down another. Empty...empty...empty...

"Dammit! Dammit! Dammit!"

Everyone was in on the act now, all the cops and attendants, even the renters themselves.

A businessman, sweating all the way through the jacket of his tan suit, was dashing from trunk to trunk.

It was chaos, but the good kind. All the pieces working together.

"Every car! We check every car!" yelled Sarah, moving on to the next lot, which belonged to one of the local companies, Sunshine Rentals.

That's when she saw something out of the corner of her eye.

There was one piece of this puzzle that didn't fit.

Chapter 29

HE WAS THE undertow in the tide of people working with a single purpose.

One guy, a mechanic, who was walking—make that slinking—away from all the action, glancing over his shoulder while seemingly doing his best to appear invisible. But in his bright yellow Sunshine Rentals jumpsuit, that was a tall order.

Sarah caught herself. She was about to yell out to him.

Instead, she fell in line behind him, camouflaged by the commotion around her. If this guy had more in common with Travis Kingslip than just a jumpsuit, what mattered most was where he might lead her.

"Hey!" she suddenly heard.

She turned to see police chief Trout maybe twenty yards away, looking at her with a "What's up?" expression.

Sarah raised her index finger across her lips—*Shh!*—and then pointed at the mechanic, who was heading toward the back corner of the Sunshine lot, where they repaired and washed the cars.

Trout nodded, taking an angle on the guy to Sarah's left. They were coming at him in a wide V shape.

Behind them there were still a host of cars with unopened trunks, even a couple more lots from other local rental agencies. But as Sarah took a few more steps, all her focus fell upon a white Chrysler Sebring near a short cinder-block wall. The convertible was on an angle, up in the air. A jack was under the left front tire—or, rather, under the space where the tire should've been.

The mechanic was heading straight toward it.

Sarah and Trout traded glances. This guy could've simply been trying to help make sure no car was left unchecked, but there was something about his walk—and the way he'd been looking over his shoulder. If he was trying to help anyone, thought Sarah, it might only be himself.

Careful, now. Stay close but not too close. Like a late afternoon shadow ...

The mechanic, of average height and scrawny, walked up to the white Sebring. But not to the trunk. He opened the driver's side door, reaching down while keeping his back toward Sarah. She was shielded.

Trout wasn't.

"Gun!" he suddenly yelled.

Sarah reached for hers as the mechanic spun around, the barrel of a pistol aimed directly at her chest. It was a coin toss who would fire first. Instead...

Wham!

Diving through the air, Trout threw every inch and pound of his former linebacker's body against the mechanic. He'd sprinted across the asphalt, tackling the guy with a powerful hit before he could pull the trigger.

The two fell to the pavement with a horrific, bone-crushing thud—the mechanic taking the worst of it by far. He was flattened out, his head bleeding, at least one front tooth gone.

But he never let go of his gun.

Trout's momentum flung him past the mechanic, and he somersaulted onto his back. Immediately, he rolled to his stomach, ready to fire his SIG Sauer P229 pistol.

Only he was too late. The mechanic had him dead to rights.

BLAM!

The mechanic stood motionless for a second, his finger frozen on the trigger. The only movement was the blood spurting from his neck.

Sarah fired a second shot, and finally the mechanic dropped his gun. It fell to the ground. Then he did the same.

Travis Kingslip had a partner.

Sarah walked straight past the mechanic without checking for a pulse. She knew dead when she saw it.

"Thanks," said Trout, joining her at the Sebring. "You scared me."

"No. Thank you," said Sarah.

Trout opened the driver's side door, then pressed the button on the far left of the dash to unlock the trunk.

Pop!

There she was. Just as Sarah had pictured

her before reminding herself not to make it personal. *Will I ever master that rule? Do I really want to?*

Lying on the floor of the trunk, bound and gagged, was a thirteen-year-old girl who had gone missing only that morning. The sun had practically turned the trunk into an oven. She was barely conscious, suffering from heat-stroke.

But she was alive.

She was going to be okay. Maybe because Sarah had made it personal.

Chapter 30

THE DO NOT DISTURB sign outside Sarah's hotel room in Tallahassee hung there a little late the following morning. *Let it be, let it be.*

After sleeping in, she went for a four-mile run, returned for a long shower, and then happily ate the cheesiest of cheese omelets from room service, putting back all the calories she'd burned the previous day. Bacon and toast, too. Yum.

She watched barely a minute of CNN before flipping over to VH1 Classic to check out a few videos. She couldn't remember the last time she'd done that.

Most of the songs she didn't know—or

even like—but that didn't matter. She cranked up the volume anyway, even more so when they played the old Guns N' Roses video for "November Rain." She absolutely loved that song. It reminded her of her teenage years in Roanoke, Virginia. Back then, a girl either had a crush on the lead guitarist, Slash, or thought he was gross. Sarah was definitely one of those who had a crush.

As for the plan for the rest of the day, that was simple. There was no plan.

Maybe she'd go lie out by the pool, do a little reading. Sarah loved biographies and had been carrying around a biography of the cartoonist Charles Schulz, which she never seemed to have the time to start. Now she did.

A whole twenty-four hours, she figured.

This was her mental health day, long overdue, and while the aftermath of nabbing Travis Kingslip involved a mountain of paperwork, she had no intention of tackling any of it right away. Not a chance.

Tomorrow, Agent Brubaker would return to work at Quantico. Today, Sarah Brubaker was playing hooky.

And it felt positively fantastic. All the way

up until she spread her towel on a chaise lounge by the pool, stretched out, and turned to page 1 of the Schulz biography.

That's when her cell rang.

Oh, no. Please, no...

It wasn't her personal phone. That she could've ignored. This was her satellite-encrypted work phone, property of the FBI.

On the other end was her boss, Dan Driesen, and he wasn't calling just to say hi. He'd already sent his congratulatory e-mail for the Kingslip capture. This was something else.

"Sarah. Need you back here for a briefing," he said. "Fast. Today."

In person, Driesen was relatively easygoing and patient. On certain subjects—government bureaucracy, fly fishing, or classic cars, for instance—he could even talk your ear off.

But on the phone, he was like a talking telegram.

"Three homicides submitted to ViCAP from three different states," he continued. "All pointing toward a lone serial killer on the move."

ViCAP stood for Violent Criminal Apprehension Program, the FBI's national inventory of every violent crime committed in the United States.

"Over what time period are we talking?" asked Sarah.

"Two weeks."

"That's fast."

"Superfast."

"Three murders?"

"Yep."

"Three different states?"

"So far," said Driesen.

"What's the connection?"

"The victims," he answered. "They all have the same name. O'Hara. Damndest thing I've ever heard."

Chapter 31

THE SANDWICHES WERE a dead giveaway.

Sarah had attended countless briefings conducted by Dan Driesen, and not once had he provided anything remotely edible for the occasion. No muffins or bagels, no cookies or anything else to snack on. Certainly no sandwiches, not ever. It just wasn't his style. *You want catered briefings? Go work for Martha Stewart.*

Yet there they were. Sandwiches in the center of the conference room table.

After catching the first flight back from Tallahassee, grabbing a cab straight from Reagan National to Quantico, dropping off her suitcase in her office, and making a beeline for the conference room with only seconds to spare before Driesen's four o'clock briefing, it was the first thing she noticed. A platter of sandwiches. Never had assorted cold cuts carried so much subtext.

This was not your average briefing.

More to the point, Driesen wasn't completely calling the shots. He was catering to someone else.

Sarah figured she'd know soon enough. Driesen hadn't arrived yet.

In the meantime, she accepted congratulations for her work in Tallahassee from the rest of the room—a mix of agents and analysts, heavy on the analysts. The BAU, or Behavioral Analysis Unit, was first and foremost about the gathering and interpretation of information. For every agent in the field, there were three analysts back home in Quantico.

"So what's the story?" asked Ty Agosta, the unit's criminal psychiatrist and perhaps the last man on the planet who routinely wore corduroy jackets with elbow patches. Not only did he wear them, he made them work.

"I was hoping you knew," said Sarah.

"Driesen's been locked in his office for the past hour," said Agosta. "That's all I know."

"With whom?"

He nodded toward the door. *That's who.*

Sarah turned to see Dan Driesen walking into the room with his typical long strides. Accompanying him were three men in dark suits, sporting visitor badges and the rigid posture that usually came with wearing a shoulder holster all day long.

One of them looked familiar. Sarah had seen him before, but couldn't quite place the face. Surely Driesen would introduce him, as well as his two cohorts, to the room.

Only he didn't. Instead, Driesen simply started the briefing. The three men, as if they were only on hand to observe, took seats in the row of chairs along the perimeter of the room.

After they each grabbed a sandwich, that is.

"Nevada, Arizona, and Utah," began Driesen, the room lights dimming courtesy of Stan, the audio/video technician, who worked all the feeds to the monitors at the front of the room.

The largest of the flat screens illuminated behind Driesen as he continued, the specifics of the top-line summary he'd given Sarah over the phone that morning appearing as bullet points.

Three different states.

Three dead men.

All within a two-week span.

And all with the same first and last name.

The screen wiped clean as the final bullet point shot up in large type behind Driesen.

THE JOHN O'HARA KILLER, it read.

Chapter 32

"JESUS, THERE MUST be hundreds of John O'Haras out there," said Eric Ladum, a technical analyst sitting across from Sarah. Whenever he was away from his keyboard, he was always twirling a pen just to keep his fingers busy.

"More like a thousand," responded Driesen. "Give or take."

Sarah turned to the Gang of Three sitting along the opposite wall. They hadn't said a word. They hadn't even been introduced. But Sarah now knew why they were in the room. She knew who they were.

Driesen continued, detailing the police investigations for the first two victims. Both were killed with two shots from a .38. One through the head, the other through the chest. There were no suspects or solid leads, and the bodies were all "clean," meaning there was no evidence, trace or otherwise, left behind.

"Now comes the third O'Hara," said Driesen. "A ski instructor living in Park City, Utah. He was found yesterday morning on the patio behind his house."

Then the crime-scene photos of the guy appeared on the screen. He was lying faceup—that is, with what was left of his face looking at the sky—in a pool of dried blood, the edges of which had the splattered appearance of a close-range shot. It would be a closed casket for sure.

During her first year with the unit, when the gory handiwork of serial killers flashed up on a screen during briefings, Sarah would always turn away in disgust for a second or two. It was instinct. A coping mechanism. The way her mind reacted to seeing something so unsettling and out of the norm.

Now, for better or worse, Sarah barely blinked.

"In the right pocket of a Windbreaker worn by the victim there was a paperback copy of James Joyce's *Ulysses*," said Driesen. He paused for a moment as if fishing for questions. Eric Ladum, still twirling his pen, was more than happy to bite.

"You think it was placed by the killer?" the analyst asked.

Driesen nodded. "I do."

"Was anything highlighted? A passage? Some words?" asked Ladum.

"No," said Driesen. "Every page intact. Not even a dog-ear."

"Wait, hold on a second," said Sarah, chiming in. "We're talking about a guy named O'Hara, right? *Ulysses* is practically a second Bible for the Irish."

"That's true, but this O'Hara lives in Utah and the book came from Bakersfield, California," said Driesen. "It's a library book."

"Was it checked out?" she asked.

"No such luck."

"Have we contacted the library to see—"

Driesen cut her off. "Yes, the library has one copy that's unaccounted for."

"Since when?"

"Since—"

"Congratulations!" came a voice from the side of the room, cutting them both off. It belonged to one of the Gang of Three, the one Sarah couldn't quite place. With only a single word he'd managed to convey an annoying trifecta of impatience, arrogance, and sarcasm.

As everyone turned to him, he stood up. "Not only do we have this guy on three murders, but we can also nail him on a stolen library book. Well done, people! *Just marvelous.*"

Ty Agosta leaned forward, placing his elbow patches on the table. The criminal psychiatrist figured there was no crime in asking a simple question.

"I'm sorry, who are you?" he asked.

But it was as if Agosta had never opened his mouth or been in the room, for that matter. He was flat-out ignored.

"Listen, maybe the killer is trying to tell us something or maybe he isn't," said the mystery guest. "What I need you to tell me, though, is how you plan on catching this psycho."

And just like that, two bells went off in Sarah's head.

The first was the guy's name. Jason Hawthorne. He was deputy director of the Secret Service. He wasn't there on behalf of his boss, or even his boss's boss, the secretary of Homeland Security.

The reason Jason Hawthorne and his sandwich-eating entourage were in the room was due to *everyone's* boss.

The president.

That was the second bell that went off in Sarah's head.

The president's brother-in-law was named John O'Hara.

Chapter 33

"SARAH, CAN I see you in my office?" asked Driesen as the conference room emptied after the briefing. He was in the middle of a good-bye handshake with Hawthorne, which was clearly not a mutual-admiration moment.

"Sure," Sarah answered, as if it were no big deal. But it was a very big deal.

There were two levels of briefings that took place at the BAU. Both were classified, but only one was completely unfiltered. That briefing was the one that took place in Driesen's office. Like the original Lucky Strike cigarettes, Driesen gave it to you straight.

With Hawthorne gone, Sarah followed Driesen past his secretary, Allison, and into his corner office, which looked out over a large marine training field.

"Close the door behind you," he said, heading behind his desk.

She did, then sat down in one of the two chairs facing him. He stared at her for a moment. Then, of all things, he let go with a chuckle.

Sarah did the same.

There was nothing funny about a serial killer and the fact that there were three innocent people dead, but sometimes battlefield humor was the only way to stay sane. In this case, the implied joke was about the president. Specifically, what he might have been thinking in the far—and definitely off-the-record—reaches of his mind when he was first briefed about the John O'Hara Killer.

I've got one target you can have for free, buddy. Take him, he's yours.

John O'Hara, the president's brother-in-law, was a major-league screwup. If he wasn't being caught by the TMZ cameras stumbling out of a Manhattan bar at 3:00 a.m., he was on cable television—at about the same time—starring in his own infomercial selling "authentic" presidential sheets and pillowcases. "Just like they have in the Lincoln Bedroom!"

Probably because he'd stolen them.

The guy was a Billy Carter–size embarrassment. And a late-night comedian's dream come true.

"Do you think it's somehow connected to him?" asked Sarah. "I can't imagine..."

Driesen shrugged. "It wouldn't make much sense. Then again, going around killing people with the same name doesn't exactly scream 'logical,' now, does it?"

"But of all names to choose..."

"I know. Hawthorne, as you saw, is already at DEFCON 1. He placed a detail on the brother-in-law starting last night."

"Was O'Hara told why he was getting protection?" Sarah asked. She thought she already knew the answer.

"No. That's the other tricky thing about this," said Driesen. "O'Hara's big mouth aside, this can't go public. We can't have a nationwide panic involving every poor son of a bitch out there named John O'Hara, at least not yet."

"Is that why Hawthorne was here and not Samuelson?" asked Sarah.

Driesen smiled as if to say, "Good for you." He appreciated that his young agent had grown quite adept at recognizing political implications. Cliff Samuelson, Hawthorne's boss, was director of the Secret Service.

"I didn't ask, but it's safe to assume. They need as much separation from the president as they can get," said Driesen.

"God, I can see the headline already: PRESIDENT PROTECTS BROTHER-IN-LAW O'HARA BUT NONE OF THE OTHERS."

"Needless to say, that headline can never be written."

"But at some point—"

"Yes, at some point we'll have to go public with the killings, blast it from every rooftop. But between the first and third dead O'Hara, there are over forty John O'Haras on the map that the killer didn't kill. The point being we can't pretend to think we can protect them all."

"So in the meantime?"

"That only makes your job harder," he said.

Sarah cocked her head. "*My* job?"

"You didn't think you were in here to hear

about my fly fishing plans for the weekend, did you? You leave tomorrow morning."

Sarah didn't need to ask where he was sending her. The first rule of catching serial killers? Always start with the warmest dead body.

"I hear Park City's nice this time of year," she deadpanned.

He smiled. "Listen, I realize you're just back from Florida and that your suitcase is sitting in your office. So take the night off, will you? And by that I don't mean go home and do laundry."

"Okay, no laundry," she said with a chuckle.

"I'm serious," he retorted. "Go do something fun, kick up your heels. Lord knows you probably need it."

He was right about that.

"Any suggestions?" she asked.

"No, but I'm sure you'll think of something."

Chapter 34

SARAH RANG THE doorbell to Ted's penthouse apartment for a second time, waiting in the hallway of the Piermont Residences in downtown Fairfax and wondering why he wasn't answering. She knew he was there.

Only minutes earlier, she'd called his number from her own apartment four floors below, dialing *67 first to block her name from coming up on his caller ID.

It was all pretty funny, she thought, worthy of a giggle. The last time she called a boy and hung up as soon as he answered, she was probably in junior high school, listening to Bananarama on her Sony Walkman and wearing acid-washed Guess jeans.

Now here she was listening for Ted behind his door while wearing a long navy blue raincoat. And nothing else. Not a stitch underneath.

Kick up my heels? Go and have fun? If only Driesen could see me now. On second thought, that's probably not a good idea.

If only Ted would answer the door. *C'mon, honey, I'm starting to feel a draft underneath this coat. Not to mention the fact that I'm a tad bit embarrassed.*

They'd only been dating for five months, after all. Then again, that was two months longer than her last relationship, and three months longer than the one before that.

With Ted, things seemed to be different, though. And much, much better. He was a successful D.C. attorney, "high-powered and even higher-charging," according to a profile of him in the *Washington Post*. He knew all about the long hours and the strains of a professional career. Sure, maybe he had one too many macho photos of himself hanging in the apartment—white-water rafting, skiing the back bowls of Vail—but Sarah was willing to overlook a touch of vanity. He wasn't the possessive type; he didn't need to own her. That was nice; very nice.

Of course, the fact that he was totally smokin' hot was a bonus.

Sarah pressed her ear tight against the door. She thought she could hear music coming from inside the apartment, but it didn't seem loud enough to cover up the sound of the doorbell.

Then it dawned on her. It was just a hunch, but her hunches had been pretty good of late. Turning around, Sarah reached under the fire-hose cabinet attached to the wall opposite Ted's door, her hand blindly feeling for a small magnetic box.

The definition of trust in a fledgling relationship? When he tells you where he keeps his spare key.

Maybe after tonight, she'd tell him where she kept hers.

Chapter 35

SARAH LET HERSELF into the apartment, standing still in the foyer for a moment to determine the source of the music. It was coming from Ted's bedroom, at the end of the hall.

She was hardly a jazz aficionado, but within two steps she easily recognized Gerry Mulligan's baritone saxophone. Ted was a huge fan who listened almost religiously to Mulligan's recordings, especially the live ones. Carnegie Hall, Glasgow, the Village Vanguard.

"Mully's a *god*," he was fond of telling her, usually over their second bottle of Bordeaux, which they shared while hanging out on the couch.

After she'd taken a few more steps down the hallway, Sarah could hear something else. It was running water. Just as she'd thought.

Sure enough, when she reached Ted's bedroom she could see that the door to his bathroom was closed. He was taking a shower. There was even a little steam slipping out through the bottom of the door.

She smiled. *Perfect.* She couldn't wait to see the look on his face.

The only decision left was when to lose the raincoat.

Sarah quietly opened the bathroom door, then tiptoed in her bare feet across the tile, the steam billowing all around her, thick as a San Francisco fog. Ted liked his showers *hot.*

Later, she was sure, he'd crack a goofy joke about her making this one even hotter.

Here goes nothing. I can't believe I'm doing this.

The raincoat dropped to the floor as Sarah opened the fogged-up shower door. She even threw her arms out as if to say, "Ta-da! Here I am!"

Surprise, honey!

Ted was surprised, all right. Incredibly so.

Of course, so was the other woman in the shower with him.

Chapter 36

IT ACTUALLY TOOK a few seconds for it all to sink in for Sarah—a few long, torturous, and utterly humiliating seconds that seemed to last an eternity.

This is really happening, isn't it? And I'm standing here buck naked to boot.

"Sarah, wait!" said Ted.

But she wasn't about to wait. Who would? Sarah scooped up her raincoat, hastily gathering it to her chest before running out of the bathroom. As if the situation couldn't get worse, she slipped on the wet tile, nearly falling, twisting an ankle.

"Damn you, Ted!"

Ted's bedroom was a blur as she hobbled through it, but even so she still caught the clues she'd somehow overlooked. The indentations on not one but two pillows on top of the unmade bed. The two wineglasses on the table next to it. *Was it a Bordeaux, you prick?* How did she not see any of it?

She already knew why. Because she'd trusted him.

There was a part of her that wanted to turn back, to have it out with Ted right there in front of the "other woman," whoever the hell she was.

But that part of her stood no chance against the unbearable pain she was feeling. In those few seconds standing almost paralyzed in front of the shower, she'd surrendered to her instincts, and those instincts had told her to run. *Flee! Scram! Get outta there!* She couldn't help it.

And that stung Sarah even more.

At work she always managed to garner the courage, the moxie, the *balls* to stand her ground no matter what the situation. But here—not wearing her badge, not wearing anything—she could only run. She felt helpless, ridiculous, and ashamed.

"Sarah, stop! Please!" Ted called out. He was behind her now, racing to catch up while tying a towel around his waist. He was dripping wet.

Sarah stopped in the foyer. She didn't want this playing out beyond his apartment and possibly in front of a neighbor. Besides, she still had only the raincoat pressed against her body.

"Turn around," she said.

Ted blinked, confused. "What?"

She glanced down at herself. He wasn't about to see her naked, not now. Not ever again.

He got it. "Oh."

Sarah put on the raincoat while Ted faced the other way. "I just want to explain," he said over his shoulder.

"*Explain?* What's there to explain? You made a big mistake and I made an even bigger one by thinking you were different from every other player in D.C."

He turned back around. "I'm not a player, Sarah. What are you even doing here? You should've told me you were coming home."

"Why? So you could keep lying to me?"

"I never actually lied."

"This isn't a courtroom, Ted. You're not a lawyer right now."

"I could say the same for you."

"What does that mean?" she asked.

"It means you never stop being who you are."

"Is that what this is about? My job? You should've told me if you had a problem with my being an agent."

"I didn't think I did," he said.

"So the girl in the shower, what does she do?"

He didn't want to answer, but Sarah stared at him until he finally did.

"She works in my office," he said.

"Is she another attorney?" But Sarah knew she wasn't.

"She's a paralegal," he said sheepishly.

"You mean she works for you. You *oversee* her."

"So you're a shrink now, too, huh? Fine!" he said with a huff. "Next you're going to tell me that I'm threatened by you."

"Are you?"

"You know what? I came out here to apologize, but fuck it, I'm not sorry."

"I can see that. I get it, Ted. Trust me, I do."

"I'm a guy, Sarah. A guy doesn't like having a girlfriend who—" He stopped.

"What? What were you going to say?" she asked. "Apparently, I can take it."

"How do you think it makes me feel to know that my FBI-trained girlfriend can kick my ass?" he blurted out.

Sarah shook her head. "First of all, it's *ex*-girlfriend, if that's what I was to you. And second, as for how it feels...I don't know," she said. "But maybe it feels something like this."

She balled her fist and decked him with a roundhouse punch so hard that he crashed back against the wall, knocking a framed photo of him on his Harley-Davidson to the floor, the glass shattering into pieces.

Calmly, and without another word, Sarah turned and started to walk out of the apartment. Her work here was done.

But then Sarah couldn't resist. She turned back to Ted, who was still sitting on the floor, holding his jaw.

"So? How *does* it feel to have your ass kicked by a girl? I'm not even that big, Ted."

Chapter 37

MAYBE IT WAS just a coincidence or maybe it was karma, but the song streaming through Sarah's iPod headphones the next afternoon as the plane began its descent into Salt Lake City was Sheryl Crow's "A Change Would Do You Good."

She could only hope. Fingers crossed. Toes, too. But you know what else? She hated the way it had ended with Ted. She just *hated* it. It was embarrassing, just awful. And sad, too. She thought that she'd loved him.

The drive from the airport out to Park City was a good start. With nothing but wide-open road in front of her and soaring mountains on the horizon, it was like a forty-minute deep breath. Convertibles never looked good on expense reports, so Sarah made the most of the sunroof on her rented Chevy Camaro 2SS.

Sometimes it just feels damn good to stick a hand up toward the sky at sixty-five miles an hour and feel the cool air whip past your fingertips.

Sooner than she thought possible, she was in Park City at the police department.

"Agent Brubaker, I'm Steven Hummel. Good to meet you," said the local chief of police.

He greeted her personally at the front entrance of the station instead of sending out his secretary or some assistant. That was always a good sign. A good rapport usually followed.

Sure enough, Chief Hummel was the down-to-earth sort, which made sense for a town that could have doubled as the western field office of L.L.Bean. Park City was a hiker's paradise in the summer and—the two-week invasion by soulless Hollywood types for the Sundance Film Festival every January notwithstanding—a skier's paradise in winter.

Hummel may have been buttoned up in his uniform, but as she looked at his tan, weathered face and tousled salt-and-pepper hair, Sarah could easily picture his off-duty look. Jeans, a plaid shirt, and probably a cold, locally brewed beer in his hand.

"Come," he said. "Let's head back to my office. We're ready for you."

Halfway there they were intercepted by a gum-chewing young buck of an officer who "just happened" to be in their path. Clearly, he was angling for an introduction.

"Agent Brubaker, this is Detective Nate Penzick," said Hummel, obliging.

Penzick stuck out his chest. His hand followed. "Welcome to Park City," he said.

Except there was nothing about his tone that made Sarah feel welcome. Right away she knew Penzick was the homicide detective assigned to the O'Hara case.

This happened occasionally when she would show up in a town or city—an officer, or maybe two, who didn't want to be told how to do his job by some federal agent. Not that Sarah ever had any intention of doing that. Still, for the Detective Penzicks of the world, the preconceived notion stuck like glue. All FBI agents think they're hot shit.

"Thanks," said Sarah with a smile, ignoring Penzick's tone as well as the G.I.-Joe-meets-kung-fu handshake he was giving her. "It's nice to meet you."

Kill 'em with kindness, she always believed. Although on this particular afternoon, after the night she'd had, it took a little extra willpower not to grab this guy by his starched lapels and explain that wannabe macho guys weren't exactly on her Christmas card list right now. *So cool it with the attitude, dude, okay?*

Penzick squinted. "The chief has been pretty tight-lipped as to why you're here, but I'm guessing it has to do with the O'Hara murder," he said.

"That's right," said Sarah. There was no point lying to the guy.

Penzick was chomping so hard on his gum you could hear his jawbone cracking. If Chief Hummel was as laid-back as a Sunday afternoon, this guy was Monday morning rush hour.

"So what's up with the secrecy?" he asked. "I mean, we all play for the same team, don't we?"

Sarah glanced at a frowning Hummel, who was immediately regretting the introduction.

"No, seriously, what's the deal?" pressed Penzick. "What's the government hiding this time?"

Hummel finally stepped in. "I'm afraid you'll have to forgive Nate here," he said. "He hasn't been the same since *The X-Files* went off the air."

Oh, snap.

"Very funny, Chief," said Penzick. But he got the hint. *Shut it down, cowboy.* He turned to Sarah, adopting the most polite tone he could fake. "I look forward to working with you, Agent Brubaker."

"Don't worry, Nate," said Hummel, glancing at his watch. "I'd be surprised if Agent Brubaker is still in Park City an hour from now."

Sarah turned to him. This was news to her, straight from the left field bleachers. *Huh? I just got here. Where do you think I'm going?*

Hummel didn't let on, at least not in front of his young detective. "As I suggested before," he said, "let's go to my office."

Chapter 38

THE WAY HUMMEL acted after closing the door to his office, Sarah was thinking that maybe his comment about her leaving town within the hour was meant to be some kind of joke. Either that or the guy suffered from a serious case of short-term memory loss. She was definitely confused—but curious.

Hummel offered no explanation. Instead, he walked directly to a drawer behind his desk, opened it, and removed two disposable latex gloves and an evidence bag containing the paperback copy of *Ulysses*.

"I suppose you want to see this first," he said.

Sarah put on the gloves and flipped through the book. Indeed, it was exactly as advertised— a library copy with nothing highlighted, no notes added, and, as Driesen had stated, "not even a dog-ear."

Hummel leaned back in the chair behind his desk, clasping his hands behind his head. "I remember having to read it in college," he said. "Hell, I barely understood the CliffsNotes."

"I know what you mean," said Sarah. "It's not exactly a beach read, is it?"

"I'm pretty sure of one thing, though."

"What's that?"

"It didn't belong to the victim."

"Okay. How do you know?"

"Because I knew John O'Hara," he said. "How does the saying go? Guys wanted to be him, girls wanted to be with him? He was a helluva good guy. But one thing he wasn't was—" Hummel paused, searching for the right, or maybe most respectful, way of putting it. "Let's just say the only thing I ever saw John read was a menu."

"There's always a first time."

"Not with a nine-hundred-page book steeped in Irish dialect that reads like a pretzel, classic or no classic," he said. "John was no James Joyce fan. Hell, he wasn't even a Stephen King fan."

Sarah nodded. Fair point.

Like Hummel, she'd read *Ulysses* in college as well. That was more than a decade ago. Before the flight out that morning, she'd downloaded it on her Kindle and started to read it again after takeoff. Somewhere over Kansas she waved the white flag and surrendered to her iPod.

Why couldn't the killer have left behind the latest Patricia Cornwell novel instead?

"Assuming the killer did leave the book behind, do you have any thoughts on what it might mean?" asked Hummel.

"Not yet. Do you?"

He smiled. "Funny you should ask. Actually, I think I do."

Chapter 39

HUMMEL HADN'T FORGOTTEN about the comment he made outside his office. He was just setting the table before explaining it.

"Every city in the country contributes their crime reports to ViCAP," he began. "Most every town, too. But not every town, right?"

"Right," said Sarah. "Usually because they have nothing to contribute, their crime rates being so low or nonexistent. Which is a good thing."

"So even if, let's say, a murder were to take place in one of these small towns, it might not even occur to the police there to report it to ViCAP. At least not right away."

"I'm sure that's happened," she said. "Probably more than a few times."

"I was thinking the same thing," said Hummel. "Of course, how would you know for sure? The only way would be to monitor every town all the time."

"Which was the reason behind ViCAP in the first place, so no one would have to. Still, like you said, some crimes are going to fall through the cracks."

"Unless you knew exactly where to look," he said, pointing at the copy of *Ulysses*.

Sarah didn't follow. "What do you mean?"

"Ever been to Bloom, Wisconsin?"

Now she followed. Leopold Bloom was the main character in the book. "And there's a John O'Hara living there? In Bloom?"

"Yes, but maybe the location isn't based on a character," he said. "For instance, what about Joyce, Washington?"

"That's a real town?"

"Yes, and there are actually *two* John O'Haras living there."

Sarah bobbed her head back and forth, thinking this through. "The killer, now at victim number three in his third different town, decides to throw us a bone and tip his hand where he's going to kill next."

"Or where he already has," said Hummel. "These are small towns."

"Unlike, say... Dublin, Ohio."

Hummel pointed at her as though he were the host of a game show and she'd gotten the right answer.

"Exactly," he said. "Decent-size city; they report everything to ViCAP. Still, there are three John O'Haras listed there, so I called anyway."

"Wait—you've already made calls?"

"Yep."

"You didn't use—"

Hummel raised his palms, amused. "Don't worry. I didn't ask if there were any dead John O'Haras. Just any murders within the past twenty-four hours."

"Were there?"

"No. Not in Dublin, not in Joyce, not in Bloom."

Sarah looked at Hummel, deflated. His theory got an A for imagination but an F for outcome. *Why is he telling me all this? There's got to be a reason. A good one, I hope.*

"Are there other towns?" she asked. She

knew Bloom's wife in the novel was named Molly. "Is there a Molly, Nebraska, for instance? A Molly, Wyoming?"

"No, but there is a Bloomfield, New Mexico," he said.

Sarah frowned. "That's kind of a stretch, don't you think?"

"Yeah, it was a lark, all right. But there's one John O'Hara living there, so I called anyway and spoke to Cooper Millwood, the chief of police. Turns out they haven't had a murder in that town for seventeen years. But then he said it was funny that I called."

"Funny?"

"Not the ha-ha kind," said Hummel. "Chief Millwood told me that he'd just spoken with his cousin, who's the sheriff over in Candle Lake, a nearby town. They haven't had a murder there for over twenty-one years. Just this morning, though? They got a report of a missing person."

Sarah straightened up in her chair. "You're kidding me."

"What are the odds, right? Candle Lake resident John O'Hara hasn't been seen for over twenty-four hours."

Hummel was right. Sarah was only passing

through. The first rule of catching a serial killer? Always go where the warmest body is.

Good-bye, Park City. Hello, Candle Lake.

All courtesy of the second rule of catching a serial killer.

If at all possible, get lucky.

Chapter 40

GATE B20, TUCKED into the corner of the Delta terminal at Kennedy Airport, was stuffed to the gills with would-be tourists, all of them waiting—and waiting and waiting— to board their flight to Rome, which had been delayed at first for two hours and then again for an additional hour that Sunday afternoon.

Tempers were running a bit high.

Meanwhile, batteries were running low. No wonder every outlet at the free charging station in the corner was spaghetti-jammed with cords for a slew of phones and MP3 players.

Some kilowatt-slurping fool had even brought his own power strip to provide some additional outlets for five iPads, one for each member of his family.

Perhaps the only two passengers not the least bit bothered by the delay were newlyweds Scott and Annabelle Pierce, who were camped out all lovey-dovey at one of the small tables in front of the Starbucks located a stone's throw from the gate.

The two caffeine junkies had actually first met at a Starbucks. It was the one on East 57th Street between Lexington and Park Avenues in Manhattan—not to be confused with the Starbucks diagonally across the street, on the north side.

Annabelle had picked up what she thought was her grande chai latte with double foam only to realize that she had mistakenly grabbed Scott's grande nonfat cappuccino, served extra hot.

"I'll try yours if you try mine," Scott said.

Annabelle smiled, even blushed a little. "Deal."

It was love at first sip, and within minutes they had exchanged phone numbers. Almost two years later to the day, they exchanged wedding vows.

Now here they were, young and blissfully

in love, about to start their honeymoon in Rome. *Who cares if the flight's delayed? What's a few more hours?*

"Let's look at them again!" gushed Annabelle, still glowing from the ceremony and reception, held at the New York Botanical Garden. "Start from the beginning."

They'd received a gazillion gifts, many of them ridiculously expensive, thanks to the friends of their well-to-do parents, but so far the very best gift of all had been a small digital camera. A used one, no less.

Oh, but how it was used.

Scott's best man, Phil Burnham—Phil B. for short—had christened a new Canon PowerShot by taking pictures with it throughout the wedding. After the reception he slapped a bow on the camera and gave it to Scott and Annabelle as they got into their limo. Pretty darn clever.

Timely, too. While the official wedding photographer was still weeks and weeks away from delivering her fancy black-and-white shots in a customized silk-covered album, Scott and Annabelle, huddled behind the Canon camera's three-inch screen, were already able to relive their big day over and over.

That is, until everything suddenly went flying. Their table, their boarding passes, their two coffees. Everything, crash and *splat* all over the ground.

"Oh, my God!" said the clumsy stranger who had tripped over a carry-on bag that was leaning against a nearby chair. "I'm so sorry!"

"Don't worry about it," said Scott, picking up the table. Annabelle, meanwhile, was checking to see if anything had spilled on her white capri pants.

"Oh, and look, I've knocked over your coffees," said the stranger. "Please, let me buy you new ones."

"Really, it's okay, don't worry about it," said Scott, who looked a little like Colin Hanks, the son of Tom Hanks.

"No, I insist. It's the least I could do."

Scott and Annabelle exchanged glances, as if asking each other, "How do you want to play this?" One of the neatest things about them as a couple, according to their friends, was that they could have entire conversations without saying a word.

Scott raised an eyebrow. Annabelle pursed her lips. They both nodded in agreement.

"Okay, if you insist," Scott politely told the stranger. "Thank you."

"No; thank *you*. Just tell me what you were drinking."

Scott obliged, completely unaware that he and his beautiful new bride were about to learn one of the most valuable lessons in life.

Never let a serial killer buy you coffee.

Chapter 41

"OKAY, HERE WE go, good as new...one grande chai latte with double foam and one grande nonfat cappuccino, extra hot," said the stranger, who had quickly and oh so smoothly morphed from clumsy to kind in the eyes of Scott and Annabelle. "But I have to ask—how do you drink it when it's so hot?"

"I guess I have a high threshold for pain," said Scott jokingly as the stranger handed him his new cappuccino. As if to prove his own assertion, he promptly took a sip and smiled.

Oh, the irony.

The stranger smiled back—wide, real wide—before turning to Annabelle. "How about yours? Is there enough foam for you?"

"Let's see," she said, lifting the lid of her chai latte and putting the cup to her lips. She quickly gave it a thumbs-up. "Plenty of foam."

"Are you sure, honey?" Scott deadpanned.

Annabelle was sporting a cute little foam mustache. She looked like a model for the "Got Milk?" ad campaign.

"Excuse me for a second," Scott told the stranger. He promptly leaned over and kissed the mustache off Annabelle's upper lip. She blushed, he laughed.

The stranger nodded knowingly, pointing at them. "I thought so. You two are newlyweds, aren't you? I had a feeling. Am I right?"

"Spot-on," said Scott. "We were married last night."

"And with any luck we'll leave for our honeymoon before our first anniversary," said Annabelle with a wry smile.

"Are you on this flight?" Scott asked the stranger. "You going to Rome?"

"Yes," the stranger lied. "If it ever actually—"

"Wait," said Annabelle, craning her neck to

peek at the gate area. "I don't believe it! I think we're finally boarding."

Sure enough, Delta flight 6589 to Rome was finally going to take off.

"I guess I'll see you two on board," said the stranger. "First I've got to buy some gum for my ears. They pop like crazy when I fly."

"I know what you mean. Mine, too," said Scott. "Hey, thanks again for the coffee."

"My pleasure." *Really. All mine.*

Scott and Annabelle grabbed their carry-on bags, then walked with their coffees to the back of the line to board the plane. After a few more sips, they turned to each other. Scott squinted. Annabelle scrunched her nose. They both stuck out their tongues.

"I know," said Scott, looking down at his nonfat cappuccino, extra hot. "Yours tastes a little funny, too, right?"

"It didn't at first. Maybe I couldn't tell with the extra foam. But now..."

"Let's just toss 'em."

"We can't." Annabelle glanced over her shoulder. She was always keen on manners and etiquette, a Junior League version of Letitia Baldrige. "Not here."

Scott understood. He turned to see the stranger standing outside the Hudson News stand, unwrapping a piece of gum.

"We'll get rid of them on the plane," he whispered.

"Good idea," Annabelle whispered back.

"This is the final boarding call for flight 6589 to Rome," came the announcement from the front of the gate.

Annabelle looped her arm around Scott's. "What should we do first when we get there?" she asked.

"You mean after we christen the bed?"

She poked him playfully in the ribs. "Yes, *after* that."

"I don't know; maybe we could go christen the Colosseum."

Annabelle was about to poke him again when she suddenly screamed. Scott was hunched over, vomit spewing from his mouth. It was like a scene from *The Exorcist*. Only the vomit wasn't pea-soup green, it was bright red. He was throwing up his own blood, buckets of it.

"Honey, what's—"

But that's as far as Annabelle got before she collapsed to the ground, the knees of her white capris landing—*splat!*—in her own spew of vomit.

Helplessly, they looked at each other. They didn't speak. They couldn't speak. They were dying. So fast, too. Unbelievably so.

Gasping his final breath, Scott turned back and locked eyes with the stranger, who was crumpling up the foil wrapper from a stick of Juicy Fruit.

How's that high threshold of pain working out for you now, buddy?

The stranger smiled—wide, real wide—and waved good-bye to the newlyweds of flight 6589.

Sogni d'oro! Arrivederci!

Chapter 42

"WELL, LOOK WHO it is," said Dr. Kline as I stepped into his office in midtown Manhattan. "You're alive."

Not that he ever thought I was dead. Why would I be dead? This was his way of needling me for missing our previous session, not unlike the way my old high school football coach would announce, "Nice of you to join us, Mr. O'Hara!" if I was even a second or two late to practice.

The difference being that Kline wasn't about to bark, "Now drop and give me twenty!" as a follow-up. At least I hoped that wouldn't be the next thing out of his mouth.

"You spoke to Frank Walsh, right?" I asked, taking a seat across from him on "the couch."

My boss at the Bureau was now doubling as my mother. I felt like a kid in kindergarten with a note pinned to his jacket. *Dear Dr. Kline: Please excuse little Johnny from his last psychiatric appointment because he was trying to catch a bad guy in Turks and Caicos.*

"Yes. Walsh filled me in on your involvement with Warner Breslow," said Kline. "Then he told me to forget everything he told me."

Typical Frank Walsh.

"The FBI isn't officially involved in the case," I explained. "That's why he said that."

"I understand, and no worries. This room is even better than Vegas. What happens here *legally* has to stay here."

"With one notable exception," I said.

Kline smiled. "You're right, absolutely right. Unless *you* tell me you plan to kill somebody."

This guy was the master of all segues.

"I'll make it easy for you," I said. "Frank was right. From the moment I took up the Breslow cause I haven't thought once about Stephen McMillan. Not once. Honest."

"That's good," he said.

It was good. It didn't mean I didn't still want to kill the bastard for what he did to my family. It only meant that I wasn't thinking all day and night about how I'd do it.

Baby steps, O'Hara. Baby steps.

I noticed that, in contrast to our first session, Kline now had a notepad in his lap. He was jotting something down.

"Am I allowed to ask what you're writing?"

"Sure," he answered. "I was making a note to myself about something you just said, a certain word, actually."

"Which one?"

"You referred to your involvement with the murder of Ethan Breslow and his new bride as a *cause*. I find that interesting."

I wasn't even aware I'd said it. "Is that some sort of Freudian slip?"

Kline chuckled. "Freud was a drunk and serial womanizer with mommy issues."

Yeah, but how do you really feel about him, Doc?

"Okay, we'll leave Sigmund out of it," I said. "Still, what is it about my saying *cause*?"

"It points to your motivation," he explained. "Why you do what you do for a living, and the role your profession plays in your personal life."

Cue the skepticism. "All that from a single word?"

"Causes are personal, John. If you make every case personal, what's going to happen when something truly *is* personal, like dealing with the man responsible for your wife's death?"

"I end up here with you, that's what happens," I said, folding my arms. "I get where you're going with this, but maybe that's what makes me good at what I do. That I take it very personally."

He leaned forward, staring straight into my eyes. "But you're no good to anyone if you're out of a job. Or worse, behind bars."

Hmm.

I hate people who say "touché" when conceding a point, but if there was ever a moment when it was appropriate, this was it. Kline wasn't really telling me anything that I didn't already know deep down. He was just bringing it to the surface in a way that I never could or was willing to.

Suddenly, I wasn't looking at Kline. I may have been staring right back at him, but it was my boys I was seeing instead. How much they truly needed me.

And how selfish I'd been.

Hadn't they already been through enough? Was I that blind? That stupid?

I'd been so fixated on wanting revenge for their mother's death that I'd neglected to celebrate her life—*our* life—with our sons. What a huge, giant, colossal mistake.

"Doc, do you mind if we cut this session short today?" I asked.

I expected him to be surprised, maybe even a little ticked off. After missing our last session, here I was trying to duck out early on this one. I'd barely sat down.

Instead, Kline simply smiled. He knew progress when he saw it. "Go do what you have to do," he said.

Chapter 43

EDWARD BARLISS, DIRECTOR of Camp Wilderlocke, looked at me as if I were from Mars. No, worse. He looked at me as if I were the parent from hell.

After a three-hour drive straight from Manhattan, I'd walked unannounced into his small, pine-scented office on the camp's fifty-acre complex in Great Barrington, Massachusetts. Did I mention the unannounced part?

"Mr. O'Hara, what are you doing here?" he asked.

"I'm here to see my kids."

"Family visiting day isn't until next week, though."

I was well aware of this. I was also well aware that I was breaking the rules at Camp Wilderlocke, and that Edward Barliss and his fellow "Wilderlockians" took their rules very seriously. In addition to not being permitted to use electronic gadgets—a ban I wholly supported—the kids weren't allowed to call home until they were ten days into their four-week session. That was a rule I begrudgingly supported.

"I know it's not visiting day, and I'm sorry," I said. "But this couldn't wait. I need to see them."

"Is it some kind of family emergency? Has someone died?" he asked.

"No, no one has died."

"But it is an emergency?"

"Yes, you could say that."

"Is it health-related?"

He stared at me, waiting for my answer. I stared right back at him, a vision in a red plaid shirt and hiking shorts, wondering how long this little game of twenty questions was going to continue. To glance around his tidy office—the neatly stacked files, the pushpins all aligned perfectly on the bulletin board—was to know immediately that Barliss was a man who prided himself on being organized, on top of things. As an uninvited guest, I was about as welcome as a bedbug in one of his cabins.

Wait until you hear the rest, buddy. Brace yourself, okay?

If he didn't like my being there to see Max and John Jr., he really wasn't going to like what I had planned for them.

Screw beating around the bush. I blurted it out.

"You want to do what?" he asked. It was complete disbelief. As though I'd just told a kid there was no Santa Claus, Easter bunny, or tooth fairy while eating a piece of his Halloween candy.

"Think of it as a brief field trip," I explained. "I promise to have them back in a couple of hours."

"Mr. O'Hara, I'm afraid—"

I cut him off. I had to. Barliss was exactly what you wanted from someone you've entrusted your kids to . . . up to a point. But ultimately he was camp director, not camp dictator, and I hadn't driven all this way just so I could turn around and go home. Desperate times, desperate measures. It was time to rearrange his pushpins.

"*Afraid?* Don't be afraid, Ed," I said. "The fact that I just came from the shrink my boss at the FBI is making me see because he's afraid I'm going to go completely postal on someone should in no way make you feel ill at ease. And even if it did, rest assured I've been stripped of my firearm—at least the one the Bureau knows about. Now can you have someone round up my boys?"

The poor guy. Slowly, he reached for one of those short-range walkie-talkie things and radioed a couple of counselors with the message that they should find Max and John Jr. All the while he kept one eye trained on me, watching for any sudden moves.

Two minutes later, the boys walked through the door. They were tan and sweaty in their shorts and T-shirts, scrapes on their knees, smudges of dirt on their necks and elbows. They looked and smelled exactly like...well...camp.

Max's face lit up; he was excited to see me. J.J.? Not so much. He had the same first question as Director Barliss.

"Dad, what are you doing here?"

"I need to take you guys somewhere, a place you need to see."

"Right now?"

"Yes, right now. It won't take too long, I promise. I'll have you both back by dinner."

J.J. looked at me as only a thirteen-year-old boy who's embarrassed to share your DNA can.

"Are you crazy?" he asked.

"No," I said. "I'm your father. Now let's go."

Chapter 44

TEN MINUTES INTO the ride, the boys finally waved the white flag and gave up asking where I was taking them. I must have sounded like a broken record. "I'll explain when we get there," I kept saying.

Twenty minutes later, we finally got there.

"A hotel? You're taking us to a hotel?" John Jr. whined as he looked at the sign in front of the Poets Inn in the town of Lenox, Massachusetts.

"First of all, it's not a hotel. It's an inn," I explained calmly, nodding at the majestic white Victorian, complete with a turret and wraparound porch. "Second of all, yes, this is where I'm taking you."

"I thought you said we'd be back at camp for dinner," said Max through a frown. "Tonight's pepperoni pizza night, my favorite."

"Don't worry, we're not spending the night." I put the car in Park, turning to the backseat. They looked like a couple of lumps sitting there. Mopey times two. "Just trust me, guys, okay? Can you do that? *Please?*"

They followed me inside, feet dragging, and I told them to wait by the entrance while I had a word with the owner, Milton, who was behind the front desk. When I'd called ahead before leaving Manhattan, I'd had only two questions for him: "Is the Robert Frost Room taken?" and "Do you mind if I borrow it for a few minutes?"

"It's available," said Milton to the first question, followed by "Be my guest" to the second. Talk about hospitality. Indeed, Milton was as nice now as when I first met him...fifteen years ago.

"Let's go, guys," I said to the boys after being handed the key. Yes, an actual key. No magnetic-strip card or annoying beeping red light after your first seven tries here.

We climbed the three flights up to the top

floor and the Robert Frost Room. The rugs in the hallways were worn, the paint was peeling a bit along the moldings, but the feeling was far more cozy than worn. Just as I remembered it.

"Have you been here before, Dad?" asked Max, sounding a bit winded from taking two steps at a time to keep pace with his older brother and me.

"Yes," I said as I unlocked the door and we walked in. "Once."

John Jr. immediately glanced around at the four-poster and velvet curtains, a far cry from his camp cabin. "So why are we *back*?" he groaned.

"Because I owe you boys something," I said. "And it starts here."

Chapter 45

WE STOOD IN the middle of the room, half-way between the bed and the oversize fireplace, with its cherrywood mantel. Max and John Jr. were side by side, staring at me. In that very instant I could remember each of them as babies cradled in Susan's arms.

I drew a deep breath and exhaled.

"When your mom died I stopped talking about her to you guys," I began. "I told myself it would just make you miss her more. But that was a mistake. If anything, I was the one scared of missing her more. What I realize now is that even with her gone she's still your mother, and she always will be. Nothing can ever change that. So for me not to talk about her, to not share with you boys the stories and memories I have of our relationship, is to deprive you of something very important. And I don't want to do that, not anymore. That's why we're here."

Max looked at me, puzzled. I knew this was a lot for a ten-year-old, but he wouldn't always be ten. "I don't get it, Dad," he said.

John Jr. gave him a push on the shoulder. "He's saying he stayed here with Mom."

I smiled, the memories now rushing over me. "Fifteen years ago, with a foot of snow falling outside, your mother and I sat before that fireplace and drank a bottle of Champagne," I said. "Then I did the smartest thing I'd ever done in my life. I proposed to her."

"*Really?* Right here in this room?" asked Max.

"Yep, really," I said. "In fact, I can prove it." I stepped over to the closet, next to a chest of drawers, and opened the door. "Come here, guys."

They walked over and looked. There were only a handful of empty hangers. "It's empty," said John Jr.

"That's what you think." I scooped up Max,

lifting him above my shoulders. "Do you see the very last plank there in the ceiling?" I asked. "Push on it."

Max stretched his arm toward the last plank, along the back wall of the closet. "Hey, wow," he said as it gave way to the push of his small fingers.

"Now reach all the way to your left," I said.

He felt around for a moment. "There's nothing there," he said, giving up too quickly. "What am I looking for?"

"Keep searching," I said. "It's small, but I'm sure it's still there."

The words were barely out of my mouth before he hit paydirt.

"Got it!" he practically shouted, so excited.

I lowered Max to the floor. He turned, opening his palm. The layer of dust notwithstanding, it was exactly as I'd left it fifteen years ago. The cork from the bottle of Champagne that Susan and I shared that night.

John Jr. leaned in to take a closer look. He didn't say a word.

"Can you guys read it?" I asked.

Max placed the cork between his thumb and forefinger, spinning it slightly until he could see the date. JANUARY 14, 1998, I'd written in black felt-tip marker. Followed by SHE SAID YES!

Then Max saw what Susan had written. "Is that Mom's handwriting?" he asked.

I nodded.

"Hi, kids!" he read aloud. His jaw dropped; he couldn't believe it.

"It was her idea that one day we'd bring our children back here," I said. "She thought it would be cool to show you this."

I looked over at John Jr., who still hadn't said a word. Now he couldn't. He was too busy pretending it wasn't a tear that had just fallen from his right eye. He wiped it away so fast that only I saw it, not his little brother.

Without a word, I reached out and gave him a hug. I squeezed hard. He squeezed back even harder. That was a first.

"So, like, what do we do with this, Dad?" asked Max. "Can we keep it?"

I hadn't thought that far ahead. "Sure," I said. "You guys hold on to it, okay?"

"Or maybe we can put it back," said John Jr. softly. "You know, where it's always been."

I turned to Max, who wasn't so sure. He was biting his lower lip.

"Your brother might have a good idea,

buddy," I said. "There's something comforting about knowing the cork will always be here. It's like a great memory you can keep forever."

I watched as Max's face suddenly lit up. Now it was my turn to cry.

"Yeah," he said. "Kind of like Mom, right?"

Chapter 46

TRUE TO MY word, I got Max and his brother back to camp in time for pepperoni pizza night. I should've grabbed a slice for myself. Less than halfway home, I was starving. Who knew all this catharsis stuff would give me such an appetite?

Salvation came soon enough with a place off the Taconic State Parkway called the Heavenly Diner. A handmade sign in the window read SINNERS WELCOME, TOO! Nice touch.

I passed on one of their blue vinyl booths for a seat at the counter and promptly ordered the Lipitor Special: a bacon cheeseburger, fries, and a chocolate milk shake, extra thick.

"Coming right up," said the seasoned waitress, whose blond wig needed a little tug to the left, to put it politely.

She shuffled off and I reached for my cell to check my e-mail. Nothing pressing. Unless, that is, you count that dead uncle I apparently have in Nigeria who left me thirty-five million dollars.

I was about to slip the phone back into my pocket when it rang in my hands. The caller ID didn't come up with a name, but I recognized the number. It was police commissioner Eldridge down in Turks and Caicos.

"Hey, Joe," I said.

We were now on a first-name basis with each other. In fact, he even threw out a "Johnny-o" at me the last time we spoke. That's when I asked if he could find out how many Chinese passports had entered his country over the past couple of weeks.

The results were in.

"Seven," said Eldridge.

A billion Chinese people in the world and only seven had traveled to Turks and Caicos. Oddly enough, that sounded about right.

"Anyone jump out at you?" I asked.

"What is it your Sarah Palin says up there? *You betcha.*"

There were three Chinese couples—six people total—who arrived on three separate days, he explained. In each case, the hotel they listed on the customs declaration was the hotel at which they stayed. He'd checked it out.

"Not that the killer had to be staying at the same resort as Ethan and Abigail Breslow," he acknowledged. "But guess who was?"

That's right. Contestant number seven.

"Who is he?" I asked.

"His name is Huang Li," he said. "He checked into the Governor's Club two days before the murders."

"When did he check out?"

"Two days after."

"Do we know anything else?" I asked.

"Not really. A pool guy remembered seeing him, but that's it so far. I'm having to conduct these interviews off campus, if you know what I mean."

"I'll look into the guy from here, see what I can dig up."

"Let's hope it's more than I can find," he

said. "Of course, with all this I'm assuming that where the Breslows were honeymooning was public knowledge, right?"

I didn't answer. In fact, I barely heard him. He might as well have been the adult in a *Peanuts* cartoon.

"John?" he asked. "You there?"

I was there, all right. But from the corner of my eye, I suddenly saw something that made me realize there was somewhere else I needed to be.

"Joe, I've got to call you back," I said.

"Is everything all right?"

"I'm not sure."

Chapter 47

THE PATHOLOGIST DIDN'T even bother to look up from his lunch. "You're a friend of Larry's, right?" he asked me.

Truth be told, I didn't know Larry from Adam or the man in the moon, but I did know the woman with the Joint Terrorism Task Force who worked with Larry at the New York Port Authority, whose brother at the NYPD forensics lab was a friend of the guy in the Queens medical examiner's office sitting before me at his desk with a diet peach Snapple in one hand and a half-eaten ham sandwich on rye in the other.

Call it six degrees of O'Hara needs a favor.

All starting with two words I saw on the television perched above the counter at the Heavenly Diner.

A CNN reporter was standing outside Kennedy Airport. The sound was muted, but the headline in big white type above the news crawl was screaming, at least to me. NEWLY-WEDS DEAD.

As soon as I hung up with Joe, I immediately began calling in favors from my days with the NYPD. I needed details. I needed access.

Maybe these honeymooners dying so soon on the heels of the Breslows was nothing more than a coincidence, but as I learned the gruesome details of what happened at that Delta terminal, it was easy to think otherwise.

The hard part would be getting confirmation. Fast.

The totally uninterested pathologist—officially the deputy chief medical examiner—finally looked up at me in his cramped office in Queens. His name was Dr. Dimitri Papenziekas, and he was a Greek with a Noo Yawk attitude. "Hey, I'm not freakin' Superman," he informed me.

Yeah, and I'm not the Green Hornet. So now that we have that settled...

"How fast?" I asked. "That's all I need to know."

How fast could he complete a test to determine if cyclosarin was present in the airport couple's bodies?

"Tomorrow afternoon," he said.

"How about tonight?"

How about you go screw yourself? said his expression. And that was *screw* spelled with an *f*, by the way.

"Okay, okay...make it tomorrow morning," I said as if I were the one doing him the favor.

Dimitri took a bite of the ham sandwich, his head bobbing in thought as he chewed.

"Fine, tomorrow morning," he said. Then he wagged his finger. "Just don't be one of those guys who call me in a few hours to see how it's going. That's when I really take my time."

"Yeah, I hate those guys," I said. "Those guys are dicks."

Christ, good thing he said that. I would've called him for sure. *That would've gone over well, huh, O'Hara? Like a fart in a crowded elevator.*

No, the next morning was okay. I didn't need to press him. Besides, more important than the "when" was the "who," as in, Who else would know he was doing me this favor? No one, I hoped.

"So this is just between the two of us, right?" I asked, wanting to make sure.

"That's what Tiger Woods said," he shot back.

He laughed while I wondered if that was actually a yes or a no. Finally, he assured me that I had nothing to worry about. No one would know.

"Thanks," I said.

"Don't sweat it. Any friend of Larry's is a friend of mine," he said. Then, of all things, Dimitri winked. "And if you actually ever meet Larry, you can tell him I said so."

Chapter 48

HURRY UP AND WAIT.

That was pretty much the feeling I had as I returned home to Riverside for an overnight holding pattern, my next move at the mercy of a ham-sandwich-eating Greek pathologist who didn't like to be rushed.

In the meantime, I still owed Warner Breslow an update. After dialing his office, I was told by his secretary that he was out. "But let me patch you into his cell," she quickly added.

Clearly, I was on the guy's short list.

"What've you got?" he asked right off the bat. There was no polite chitchat upfront. Hell, there wasn't even a hello.

My update covered everything I knew on what I said was "our Chinese angle," including the fact that I was waiting on a full background check on the one Chinese passport holder who'd stayed at the Governor's Club.

What I didn't say a word about, though, was my trip to the Queens medical examiner's office and the possible connection—or lack thereof—between Ethan and Abigail's murder and the death of those honeymooners out at the airport. Until I got my answer back on the cyclosarin question, there was no point getting into it.

"Are you sure you don't want me to call my friends at our embassy in Beijing?" Breslow asked. "You know, maybe expedite that background check?"

The impatience in his tone wasn't so much with me as it was with the general concept of waiting, something billionaires never seemed to be very good at. My only play was to make clear what exactly he was waiting on.

"With all due respect to your friends at the embassy," I said, "the kind of background check we're talking about doesn't exactly come through official channels."

That wasn't me at my most subtle, but

sometimes less isn't more. More is more. Especially with a guy like Breslow.

"Fair enough," he said. "Call me as soon as you know anything else."

"Will do."

I hung up the phone, grabbed a beer from the fridge, and quickly flipped through the mail that I'd brought in. There was no second coming of a Bible or any other mysterious package.

In fact, bills and catalogs notwithstanding, the only actual "mail" was a postcard from Marshall and Judy, who were on their Mediterranean cruise. On the front was a picture of Malta. On the back, in Judy's handwriting, was a brief essay on the history of Malta. Of course. The only thing not Malta-related was her postscript. "Don't forget to water my garden!"

Oops.

Beer in hand, I went out back and turned on the sprinkler, not a minute too soon. Judy's garden was in dire shape. Droopy petunias and begonias everywhere.

After waiting a minute to make sure the sprinkler was reaching them all, I took a seat on a nearby chaise. Stretching my legs out, it occurred to me that this was the first time in days that I actually had a moment to relax. I drew a deep breath, closing my eyes. Maybe it wasn't such a horrible thing, having a little time to kill.

Suddenly I opened my eyes.

"John O'Hara?" came a voice behind me.

Chapter 49

THE BAD FEELING engulfed me well before I turned my head. When I saw who it was, the feeling only got worse.

"What the hell are you doing here?" I asked.

It was far from a Christian welcome, but I couldn't help it. Hit your thumb with a hammer and you're going to scream. Step barefoot on a piece of glass and you're going to bleed. See the lawyer for the guy who killed your wife standing uninvited in your backyard?

You're going to be pissed off.

"I tried ringing the doorbell," said Harold Cornish. "I think it might be broken."

"I'll put it on my to-do list," I said.

Harold Cornish, perpetually tan and perfectly coiffed, stood before me wearing a three-piece suit and a tie with a Windsor knot. It was late June, hovering in the mideighties, and there wasn't even a suggestion of sweat anywhere on him. Amazing. He was as cool out of the courtroom as he was in it.

I hated the guy.

And that's what *really* pissed me off. Because deep down I knew that I was being completely irrational.

I didn't hate Cornish for representing McMillan. Due process; I get it. Even the biggest pricks in the world deserve a lawyer.

No, I hated Cornish because he was a *good* lawyer. Facing a maximum sentence of ten years or even more, McMillan basically got the minimum. Three years. All because of Cornish.

"You certainly don't owe me any favors, but I want to ask you something," he said. "You're aware that my client will be released from prison in a couple of days, right?"

I nodded. Nothing more. I wasn't about to let on that McMillan's release had preoccupied me to the point of near self-destruction.

"So this is what I'd like to ask you," continued Cornish. "McMillan very much wants to apologize to you." He immediately raised his palms. "Now, before you react, please let me finish."

"Did I react?" I asked calmly.

"No, you didn't, and I appreciate that," he said. "I know my client apologized to you and your family in court, but after doing his time he wants to apologize again, in person. Privately. Would you consider that?"

I immediately thought of Dr. Kline and all the great strides I was making with him. I could even hear his voice inside my head, telling me to keep my cool, stay under control. No more Agent Time Bomb.

But I couldn't help it. Cornish had lit the fuse and there was no stopping me. I got up, walked straight over to him, and stood facing him toe to toe. Then, at the top of my lungs, I gave him my answer.

"TELL YOUR FUCKING CLIENT TO GO TO HELL!"

Cornish blinked slowly, took one step back, and nodded. "I understand," he said.

Whether he really did or not, I didn't know and I didn't care. He turned and left without saying another word.

I waited until he disappeared around the corner, heading toward the front of the house. There was still half a beer left in my hand, and I polished it off with one long swig.

Then, without thinking, I added something else to my to-do list: clean up the broken glass from the patio.

Smash!

I heaved the bottle against the house so hard my shoulder nearly popped out of its socket.

Apparently, I hadn't made the great strides that I'd thought.

In fact, I still had a long, long way to go.

BOOK THREE

"OH, THE PLACES YOU'LL GO"

Chapter 50

"YOU MUST BE Agent Brubaker," said the officer greeting Sarah outside the sheriff's office in Candle Lake, New Mexico.

"Yes." *And you must still be in high school,* Sarah thought as she shook the young man's hand. *Seriously, I have food in my refrigerator that's older than you.*

"Sheriff Insley asked that I bring you out to the lake as soon as you arrived," he said. "He's there now. You ready to go?"

"Is that where you're looking for John O'Hara?"

"Yeah. O'Hara's wife thought he'd gone either drinkin' or fishin', and there was no one who saw him at any of the bars in town."

Drinkin' or fishin'? Sarah eyed the officer for a moment, wondering if he had any idea how funny that sounded, in a town-of-Mayberry sort of way. He didn't.

"I'm sorry, I didn't get your name," she said.

"Peter," he answered. "Peter Knoll."

Sarah climbed into his Chevy Tahoe police interceptor, which was parked along the curb. Before she'd even buckled up, Knoll had flipped on the cherry and peeled out with sirens blaring. *Boys and their toys...*

"What else can you tell me about John O'Hara?" she asked once they hit the outskirts of town. "Besides the fact that he likes to drink and fish."

Knoll thought for a few seconds, his fingers tapping on the steering wheel. "He's a retired plumber, I know that. Two children, only they're hardly children anymore. Grown up and moved away, both of them."

Sarah tucked her hair behind her ears. The windows were open, and the wind whipped through the Tahoe. God's air-conditioning.

"Do you know if he was into books at all? Did he read a lot?" she asked.

"Not that I'm aware of. I've never been inside his home."

"How long has he been missing?"

"We got the call from his wife early this morning. Officially, it hasn't been a full twenty-four hours since she last saw him, but we weren't about to nitpick," he said. "I've got an uncle who always says that nitpicking is for nitwits."

"Smart uncle," said Sarah.

The houses started to thin out over the next few miles, until she saw nothing but trees and the occasional piece of roadkill. Knoll hung a left at an unmarked road, which quickly turned to dirt and gravel.

"The main entrance is still another minute or two up the road, but this is the shortcut to the teardrops," he said.

"The what?"

"That's the part of the lake with the best fishing. Only the locals know about it. If O'Hara's out here, that's where he'd be," he said. "Sheriff Insley has another officer with him doing a search."

"Is it a big area?"

"Yeah, with lots of little nooks," he said. "Most of them are shaped like teardrops, that's why the name."

The road narrowed to little more than a

sliver through the woods. Then they finally came upon a small clearing that served as a parking lot, where two patrol cars sat side by side. Knoll pulled up next to them, cutting the engine.

"Let me radio ahead to Sheriff Insley, let him know you're here," he said. But before he did he couldn't help himself. "Why *are* you here? If you don't mind me asking."

"To help you find John O'Hara," she answered. It certainly wasn't a lie.

She was spared any follow-up questions by the sound of approaching voices. There was no need to radio Sheriff Insley. He was heading right for them.

Sarah stepped out and got a quick introduction to Insley and the other officer with him—Brandon Vicks—who looked no older than Knoll. Add their two ages and they still couldn't join AARP.

"What's the latest on our missing person?" she asked.

Insley removed his sheriff's hat, scratching a forehead that featured an endless constellation of freckles.

"John O'Hara isn't missing anymore," he said in a deep drawl. "And it ain't pretty."

Chapter 51

SHERIFF DICK INSLEY had the look, the voice, the mannerisms—indeed, the whole aura—of a seasoned veteran, but twenty-one years between murders in his town was a long time. Sarah could practically see the wheels spinning in his head as he headed toward his patrol car to retrieve an evidence kit.

Sarah accompanied him, calmly convincing him that the first thing he needed to do was to show her the body.

The walk back down to the lake was along a steep and winding downhill path, with a few makeshift rope railings along the way. The results of Sarah's morning wardrobe decision were officially in. The jeans were a good call. The cross-trainers on her feet were a *really* good call.

"Almost there," said Insley, leading the way.

Sarah had this strange custom—more of a quirk, actually. Whenever she came upon a crime scene involving a dead body, her mind would immediately conjure up a newspaper headline about the killing—how it might read in the local paper. She couldn't help it; her mind just did it. It was a reflex. A *weird* reflex, she always thought. That probably explained why she'd never told anyone about it.

After another hundred yards, the pathway ended at the water's edge, where there was one of the curved inlets—a teardrop—that Officer Knoll had described. Because the inlet was bookended by thick brush, the rest of the lake was barely visible. John O'Hara had his own private fishing hole. He was all alone.

Until he wasn't.

His large body was laid out on the ground, arms outstretched, legs apart. He looked as if he were making a snow angel. But there was no snow: instead, all that was beneath him was blood. Lots and lots of it. One shot to the chest and one point-blank to the head.

He was basically a carbon copy of the photos Sarah had seen during her initial briefing back at Quantico.

The John O'Hara Killer was consistent, all right. Perversely dependable. Same name for each victim, same execution-style killing.

"Jesus, how am I going to tell Marsha?" muttered Insley under his breath, as if he were just realizing there was one more task on his postmurder must-do list. Breaking the news to O'Hara's wife.

Sarah blinked, her mind spitting out a potential headline in the *Candle Lake Gazette*, or whatever the local paper was called.

SAD SCENE AT THE TEARDROPS.

Chapter 52

ACROSS THE LAKE, an orange glow began to seep through the tall pines. The sun was setting, and there were things that needed to be done in the remaining daylight. Isolating the killer's footprints, for starters.

But as Sarah slipped on a pair of latex gloves, her immediate focus was O'Hara's body. A copy of *Ulysses* had brought her here, a little parting gift from the killer. Would there be another?

"Has anyone touched the victim in any way?" she asked Insley and his young entourage. It wasn't so much a question, though, as it was a plea. *Please tell me no one was foolish enough to disturb a crime scene.*

"No," said Insley. "We didn't even check for a wallet."

Translation: Candle Lake, New Mexico, was a small town. Closely knit. Neighborly. They didn't need to ID John O'Hara, because they all knew him.

Carefully, Sarah began reaching into every pocket the victim had. She wasn't about to undress him—a more thorough search could be done at the morgue—but she couldn't help thinking that whatever it was she was looking for wouldn't be too hard to find.

The killer wanted her to find it, right? Something that didn't belong? It was a game, like that old bit from *Sesame Street*. "One of these things is not like the others."

She kept searching, the shadows growing longer all around her.

The more she searched, though, the more she realized that this John O'Hara either traveled extremely light or had been picked clean.

Check the wallet for ID? There was no wallet.

Or anything else, for that matter. No pocket

change, no cell phone, no chewing gum or ChapStick. There were also no car keys, which explained why O'Hara's car, or whatever it was that got him to the lake, wasn't parked up at the clearing.

Meanwhile, Sheriff Insley looked on in silence. He knew enough not to pepper Sarah with questions. If the FBI was involved, they had their reasons. If he didn't need to know what they were, they sure as shit weren't going to tell him.

The two young officers were another story. Especially Knoll. He simply was too green, too wet behind the ears, to know better.

"What are you looking for?" he asked Sarah.

Again, she didn't have to lie. "I'm not sure," she answered, standing up. "But I'm pretty sure it's here somewhere."

Sarah stepped back from John O'Hara's corpse. She stepped back from everything. Suddenly, she realized the problem. She was so focused on what was in front of her that she couldn't see the whole picture. Not what was there. But what was missing.

"Wait . . . where's his fishing rod?" she asked Insley.

The sheriff glanced left and right, his expression saying it all. *Good question.*

"The killer probably took it," said Knoll. "Just like he took John's wallet and car."

"Maybe," said Sarah. "But the wallet and car serve a purpose. Why the fishing rod?"

"And what about his tackle box and fish bucket? John for sure would've had those, too, but they're not here, either," said the other officer. What was his name again? Sarah had already forgotten.

"Good point," she said, stealing a peek at the nameplate on his uniform. VICKS, it read. *Like the cough medicine.*

"For all we know, the killer took the gear because he likes to fish, too," said Knoll. "In fact, he could be fishing right now in another county, trying to catch his dinner."

Sarah nodded. Knoll was being facetious to make a point she'd often heard when it comes to killers. You can't always expect them to act logically. If they're crazy enough to kill someone, they don't think like the rest of us.

Still.

"Or maybe the gear is somewhere we haven't looked yet," she said.

"Sure," said Vicks, agreeing with her. He

glanced down at O'Hara. "Maybe John went looking for another inlet—right here—and that's when the killer got him."

"Which direction were you guys searching?" asked Sarah.

"Clockwise around the lake, north to south," said Insley. "We've covered midnight through...oh, about ten o'clock."

"Yeah, ten o'clock," Vicks echoed.

In other words, most of the lake. But not all of it.

Like a synchronized swim team, they all turned to their left. Sarah gripped her hips with her hands and shrugged. "Let's go see the news at eleven," she said.

Chapter 53

THEY PUSHED THROUGH the brush along the lake's edge, Insley leading the way. There was a certain music to the sound of the twigs snapping beneath their feet. Random, but still a rhythm. Like the first kernels of popcorn popping in a microwave.

With each step, the strange feeling Sarah was having grew stronger. It wasn't really Insley leading the way. It was the killer. If he hadn't outright orchestrated this little conga line along the lake, he at least knew it would happen. A sure thing. Like...well, clockwork.

"There!" said Insley, first through the brush.

Sarah didn't have to look hard to see what

he was pointing at. It was all right in front of her, everything that had been missing, smack in the middle of this next teardrop: a fishing rod lying on the ground next to a tackle box and bucket. Sort of creepy.

No, she thought. *Definitely* creepy.

"Okay, so we found the gear. Now what?" asked Knoll.

Boy, does this guy ask a lot of questions. And not the right ones, either.

Sarah simply ignored him. There was nothing to search for in the rod and bucket, but the dark green tackle box with its closed lid was just calling out to her. Beckoning. No doubt about it.

She walked straight to it, dropping to her knees. With the latex gloves still on, she flipped up the latch. It opened easily. Of course it did.

"Christ, that's a lot of lures," said Vicks, looking down over Sarah's shoulder.

That was an understatement. The box was not one of those neatly organized jobs with separate compartments and multiple layers of sliding hinged drawers. It was simply one big catchall for seemingly every lure this John O'Hara had ever owned.

"Not that any of them were doing him much good," said Knoll, looking into the empty fish bucket. "Talk about having no luck at the lake."

Insley snickered while Sarah began sifting through the box, the endless hooks repeatedly grabbing at her latex gloves. Frustrated, she finally just flipped the box over, the lures spilling everywhere.

Staring at them all was like reading a Dr. Seuss book. There were long ones, short ones, fat ones, and skinny ones. Some were shiny silver, others were bright colors. There was even one with—

Wait: red light...Hold it right there.

Sarah's eyes locked on something in the middle of the pile, a piece of folded white paper.

The lures were mostly old and rusty; some were even encrusted with the dried remains of worms. But this paper was new. Clean. White.

"What is it?" asked Insley. "Don't hold us in suspense."

Sarah unfolded the paper, her mind wishing for the impossible—like the killer's name, address, and telephone number. Maybe even his Twitter handle and the best times to find him unarmed. *Gee, wouldn't that be a great ending for this case?*

"It's a receipt," said Sarah, turning it right side up to read it. "From the Movie Hut?"

"That's that vending machine," said Vicks. "You know, the one they have at Brewer's supermarket? You rent DVDs from it for, like, a buck a night."

"Oh, yeah," said Insley. "I've seen it. Never used it. Looks too complicated."

"Hell, I've even kicked it," said Knoll. "The thing ate my dollar one night."

"What were you trying to rent?" asked Vicks.

"*Speed Racer,* I think."

"Trust me, the machine was doing you a favor."

The two chuckled. Even Insley cracked a slight smile. That is, he smiled until he noticed Sarah still staring at the receipt. "So what is it?" he asked her again. "What are you thinking?"

"Today's the twenty-fourth, right?" she asked.

Insley nodded. "Yep. My daughter's birthday, actually. Why?"

"Because this receipt is from *today*."

He bent down to take a look. "That's a little weird, isn't it? If that's the right word."

"Yeah, I think that's the right word," she said. "Now look again. There's something even weirder."

Chapter 54

DEFINITELY *WEIRDER*.

Sarah had polished off her southwest-style burger and sweet-potato shoestring fries and was below the label on her second bottle of Bud. She was thinking about this killer she was closing in on.

To her left and right, the rest of the packed bar at Canteena's was living up to its reputation as Candle Lake's epicenter of nightlife. This according to Sheriff Insley, who had recommended the joint. And make no mistake: with its low ceiling, fifteen-watt lighting, and sawdust-covered floor, Canteena's was definitely a "joint."

Had Sarah been eavesdropping, she would've heard the shocked chatter from the locals around her about the murder of John O'Hara. *What was Sheriff Insley saying? Are there any suspects? Do we have a murderer among us?*

But Sarah wasn't eavesdropping. The only thing she could hear was her own thoughts, loud and echoing in her head, and all centered around one single question: What was the killer trying to tell her with this latest clue?

Printed on the receipt from the Movie Hut was the title of the movie. It was *You've Got Mail*, the Tom Hanks and Meg Ryan romantic comedy. A chick flick. In other words, not exactly the DVD that a drinkin' and fishin' kind of guy like John O'Hara would be renting.

Still, there was always the chance he was renting it for his wife, Marsha. Or so Sarah thought—right up until she and Insley made the drive across town to O'Hara's white shingle ranch-style home to break the horrible news.

Turned out the O'Haras didn't even own a DVD player.

The receipt was a clue, all right. Of that

much Sarah was certain. As to what it actually meant, she had no idea.

Keep thinking, Brubaker. Keep your focus. The answer's out there somewhere...this bastard just likes his mind games.

In the meantime, she had a date with Brewer's supermarket in the morning to see if there was a security camera aimed at the so-called Movie Hut. Maybe the killer was caught on tape. Of course, she was hardly holding her breath. That seemed too sloppy for this guy, whoever he was.

Sarah fell back into her thoughts, replaying the afternoon's events in her head. Had she missed something, overlooked anything?

Nothing sprang to mind. Instead, she kept coming back to that moment when Insley told Marsha O'Hara that her husband was never coming home. The poor woman collapsed to the floor in her living room, crushed by the weight of her sudden loss. Death trumps us all, as the saying goes.

Sarah also couldn't shake what Insley had told her on the drive back from the O'Haras', that the couple had been married for forty-two years. Sitting in the front seat of Insley's cruiser, she felt guilty to be thinking about herself at that moment. But the thought was inescapable. It was the first thing that came to her.

Forty-two years? I can barely stay in a relationship for forty-two days.

Suddenly Sarah heard a voice to her left, someone talking to her. It was a man's voice. A really attractive man, actually. Sometimes you can just tell those things before you even look.

"Wow, I really just did that, didn't I?" he asked.

Chapter 55

SARAH TURNED TO face him. He sort of reminded her of Matthew McConaughey—a little younger, without the Texas accent, and maybe without the need to always be taking off his shirt. At least so far.

He was holding a beer. *Her* beer. Had he grabbed it by mistake? His own bottle of Bud was close by.

"Don't worry about it," said Sarah. "I was practically done with it."

On a dime, he broke into a smile—a great smile, she noticed—and started to laugh. "I'm just kidding. I knew it was your beer."

Sarah joined in. "You had me there for a second," she said.

"I'm sorry. I have an offbeat sense of humor. Please, let me buy you another one."

"Really, that's okay," Sarah said. "It's totally not necessary."

"But I'm afraid it is, if only so I don't disappoint my mother," he said.

Sarah looked around. "Is your mother here?" she asked, half joking.

"No. But she'd be mortified if she knew her son wasn't able to make amends. She was a stickler for manners."

He flashed that amazing smile of his again.

"Well, I suppose we don't want to disappoint your mother," said Sarah.

"That's the spirit," he said. He turned and got the attention of the bartender, ordering another Budweiser. Then he put out his hand. "My name's Jared, by the way. Jared Sullivan."

"Nice to meet you. I'm Sarah."

Sarah then did something she'd never done in all her years with the FBI.

She shook hands with a serial killer.

Chapter 56

"LET ME TAKE a guess," said Jared, his index finger tapping the air. "New York, right?"

"Wrong," said Sarah. "Not a New Yorker. Not even close."

"But you're definitely not from around here. I mean, I'm almost positive of that."

"I was going to say the same about you," she said. "You did get the East Coast part right. Fairfax, Virginia."

Jared nodded. "I'm Chicago, born and raised."

"Cubs or Sox?" asked Sarah.

"I'm a North Side boy," he said. "Wrigley all the way."

"So when you're not cursing the plight of the Cubbies, what do you do there in Chicago?"

"Fill out expense reports, for the most part. I'm a sales rep for Wilson Sporting Goods. That's where they're based. The Southwest is my region, though, so I'm rarely home."

"I know the feeling," she said. "I own one houseplant and it's suing me for negligence."

Jared laughed. "You're very funny. Cool."

The bartender returned with Sarah's beer, sliding a cocktail napkin underneath it with a well-practiced flick of his wrist.

Sarah was about to take a sip when Jared raised his bottle. "Here's to life on the road," he said.

"To life on the road," she echoed. "And maybe one day, the possibility of parole."

Jared laughed again as they clinked bottles. "She's pretty *and* she has a sense of humor. Talk about a double threat."

"Uh-oh," said Sarah, shooting him a sideways stare.

"What? What is it?"

"While your mother was a stickler for manners, my mother was always warning me about strangers bearing compliments."

"That's why I introduced myself. We're not strangers anymore," he said. "As for the compliment, you don't strike me as the blushing type."

"What type do I strike you as?" she asked.

He thought a lot before answering. "Independent. Self-reliant. And yet not without a vulnerable side."

"Gee, are you sure about that?"

"Think so. I like to go with my gut."

"Me, too."

"What does yours tell you?" he asked.

"That if I play my cards right, there might be a free tennis racket in my future," she said.

"That's a possibility."

"Too bad I don't play tennis."

"What a shame," he said. "Lucky for you, Wilson makes other very fine equipment."

Sarah tapped her head. "That's right, how could I forget? That movie, what was it called again? The one with the volleyball named Wilson?"

"Oh, yeah," he said. Nothing more, though.

"It's on the tip of my tongue," she continued. "Jeez, what was the name of that movie?"

"I know; I hate it when I get a mental block like that," said Jared. "Drives me crazy."

Sarah took a long sip, digesting more than the beer. Finally she shrugged. "Oh, well. I'm sure it will come to me later."

"I hope I'm there when it does."

"We'll see about that," she said, easing off the bar stool. "In the meantime, why don't you order us a couple of shots while I go to the ladies' room? Bourbon okay by you?"

Jared hit her with his biggest smile yet. "You certainly are a live one," he said.

She smiled back, tucking her hair behind her ears. *That's right, handsome. Keep thinking I'm the fish.*

Chapter 57

SARAH WALKED THE long, narrow hallway in the back of Canteena's and turned the corner, heading toward the ladies' room. Two steps from the door she stopped and pulled out her cell.

Eric Ladum picked up on the second ring. As usual, he was still in his office at Quantico. The late night cleaning staff called him El Noctámbulo. The night owl.

"Are you in front of your keyboard?" she asked.

"Aren't I always?"

"I need the current employee list for Wilson Sporting Goods in Chicago cross-checked with the DMV."

"Chicago DMV or the entire state?"

"All of Illinois," she said.

"Who's the lucky guy?"

"Jared Sullivan."

"Jared Sullivan with Wilson Sporting Goods," Eric repeated over the sound of his fingers typing away. "Can he get me a free tennis racket?"

Sarah laughed to herself. "That's even funnier than you know," she said. "How much time do you need?"

"How much you got?" he asked.

"Two minutes, tops. I told him I was going to the bathroom."

"So *that's* why women take so long."

"Yeah, now you guys know what we're really doing. Running background checks on you," she said. "Call me back, okay?"

She hung up and stepped over to the corner of the hallway leading back to the bar. She peeked around the edge, catching a quick glimpse of Jared right where she'd left him. *That's a good boy. Have you ordered those shots yet?*

Sarah knew damn well the name of the movie with the volleyball called Wilson. *Cast Away.* Another Tom Hanks film, no less.

Question was, how did a guy who worked for Wilson Sporting Goods not know it? That was like the mayor of Philadelphia not being able to name that boxing movie starring Sylvester Stallone.

If anything, if you worked for the company, you'd probably be sick of talking about *Cast Away* and that damn volleyball.

Sarah took another peek around the corner, only to have her view blocked by a burly older man with a gray beard coming down the hallway.

She quickly pulled back, watching as he waddled by her on the way to the men's room. He smelled of tequila and Old Spice cologne, heavy on both.

There was another thing bugging Sarah, something else about Jared. He asked where she was from but not what she did for a living—even after discussing his own job. Maybe it was an oversight.

Or maybe it was because he already knew the answer to the question.

Sarah's cell, set to vibrate, shook in her hand. Eric was calling back already. *What a guy.*

"So much for our free tennis rackets," he

said. "No Jared Sullivan with Wilson Sporting Goods."

"What about for the city?"

"Two Jared Sullivans in Chicago, five for the state. The two in Chicago are forty-six and fifty-eight."

"Too old," said Sarah. "Anyone in their late twenties?"

"One from Peoria; he's twenty-nine. He's also tall, six foot four. What's your guy?"

"Sitting down, unfortunately." She peeked around the corner again to see if she could better size him up. "Oh, shit!"

"What?"

"I'll call you back!"

Got to run. Literally.

Chapter 58

SARAH JAMMED THE phone in her pocket and nearly slammed into the tequila-and-Old-Spice fat man, who was coming out of the men's room. He mumbled something at her—"Watch it!" maybe—or maybe it was just a belch.

Either way, it was distant noise. Sarah was sprinting, a blur, and already halfway down the hallway to the bar, the same bar that was now without Jared Sullivan, or whoever he was.

For a few frantic seconds, she stopped in front of the empty seats where they'd been sitting. The only remnants of their being there were the two bottles of Bud. His was finished, hers was half full. Or more like half empty.

Sarah spun around, her eyes searching every corner of Canteena's. But he was nowhere. At least not inside.

Damn! Damn! Dammit!

Lickety-split, she headed for the front entrance, the sawdust on the floor kicking up everywhere in her wake. Pushing through the heavy wooden slab of a door, she practically sprang outside, the hot night air immediately slamming against her face.

To her left were two women smoking. They looked like mother and daughter.

"Did you see a guy walk out a minute ago?" Sarah asked, half out of breath. "Good-looking? Sort of like Matthew McConaughey?"

"We just stepped out here, honey," said the older woman, holding up her cigarette to show it had just been lit.

"But if he really looks like Matthew McConaughey, I'll help you look for him," said the younger one with a chuckle.

Sarah forced a smile, if only not to be a bitch, but her eyes had already moved on to the parking lot that wrapped around the building. It was three-quarters pickup trucks and 100 percent jam-packed, not a space to be had.

Off she ran, clockwise. Just as she and the officers had gone around the lake.

There was a chance he was parked in the back, maybe even still heading toward his car.

She ran through the lot, circling the building. She circled it again. She was in the back, standing near a couple of overstuffed Dumpsters, the only light coming from the mostly full moon overhead.

It was the sound she heard first.

The roar of an engine behind her, so loud it was as if she were standing in the middle of a runway at Dulles International Airport. The second she spun around, she was blinded by a pair of headlights. The lights were getting bigger. Very quickly, too. The car was heading straight at her.

No time for overthinking this. She dove. Part leap. Part cartwheel. Straight between the two Dumpsters to her right, the asphalt practically knocking the wind out of her as she landed.

Make and model! License plate! Get something!

But by the time she could look up and focus, his car was turning the corner, gone. It was so dark out that she couldn't even tell what color the car was. She got nothing.

No, wait—not quite. She still had her own car.

Sarah pushed herself up, sprinting in the direction of her rental car. She could still catch him, she thought. *Hell, yeah, let's see what this Camaro can do!*

"Shit!" she screamed the second she laid eyes on it.

Jared Sullivan knew who she was, all right. He knew what car she was driving, too.

Sarah stopped at the right rear tire, flat to the rim. Ditto for the left rear one. "Shit!" she yelled again. "Shit! Shit! Shit!"

The bastard had slashed all four tires, and as if to rub it in he left his folding knife resting on the hood of the car.

Only it wasn't his knife.

Sarah picked it up with the bottom of her shirt, then took out her phone for some light. There were initials inscribed on the ivory handle. J.O.

John O'Hara.

It was his fishing knife. And it was no longer missing. Sarah had found another piece of the puzzle.

Chapter 59

SARAH CALLED DAN Driesen the next morning to brief him. She didn't want to make the call, but she had to. It was like going to the dentist. To have a tooth pulled. Without Novocain.

"Hell, Sarah, you're supposed to be chasing *him*, not the other way around," he said in a tone that was bordering on ticked off but nonetheless contained a hint of genuine concern. "He could've killed you."

"That's just it. He *could've* killed me, but he didn't," she said, standing by the window of her third-floor room at the Embassy Suites. Nothing but cacti and highway as far as the eye could see. "He was probably hiding at the lake and saw me with the local police. From that moment on he could've killed me at any time, and he chose not to."

"So now you're saying he didn't try to run you over with his car?"

"Think about it. If he really wanted to, why did he flip on his headlights?"

"Is that supposed to make me feel better? He knows who you are, and that's not good."

"Maybe I can turn it to my advantage. I'm thinking about that possibility now."

"Really?" Driesen asked, incredulous. "How?"

"I haven't figured that part out yet, but I will. Before he changes his mind and comes back to get me."

"In the meantime, you have no idea where he is or where he's heading. Unless, of course, you're going to tell me you've cracked those clues he's been leaving behind."

"Hey, I got here from *Ulysses*, didn't I?"

"Yes, courtesy of a lucky break, don't you think? Any thoughts on where *You've Got Mail* is going to put him next?" he asked sarcastically. "Should we be trying to find a John O'Hara who works for the post office?"

The really crazy thing was, Sarah had already considered that.

She hated to admit it, but Driesen's point was valid. The John O'Hara Killer still had the upper hand on her. And, yes, maybe even more so now.

"There's still a lot I can do out here, though," she said. "I haven't even begun to work the town. Maybe he interacted with other people."

"Maybe. But I don't want you having to look over your shoulder all the time. Whatever game you think he might be playing, who's to say it doesn't end with you getting killed?"

"So that's that?"

"For now, at least. You're coming home," he said. "Besides, there's someone back here who's requested a briefing from you."

"Who?"

Driesen chuckled. She could practically see his sly smile through the phone.

"Who is it?" she repeated.

"You'll see," he said. "Come home, Sarah. That's an order, by the way."

Chapter 60

"YOU COULD'VE GIVEN me a heads-up," Sarah whispered out of the corner of her mouth. "Seriously."

Dan, sitting in the chair right next to hers, folded his long legs under the seat. It was bright and early the next morning in D.C., barely 7:00 a.m. "Nah, that would've just made you nervous," he whispered back.

"Like I'm not nervous now? I am very nervous. And I don't ever get nervous."

As if on cue, the door next to them opened. An older woman with a mother-hen aura walked out, giving them a slight nod. She was clutching a clipboard against her chest.

"The president will see you now," she said.

Sarah stood up, took a deep breath, and straightened some imaginary wrinkles out of her white blouse. A couple of panicked thoughts flashed through her head. *Did I forget to put on deodorant? How do you talk—intelligently—to the president?*

"After you," said Dan, his arm outstretched. "He wants to see you, not me."

So many times, Sarah had watched this scene play out when she used to tune in to *The West Wing* on television. But those were all actors. Make-believe.

This was the real deal. With only one step into the Oval Office, she could feel her heartbeat going into overdrive.

Is it too late to call in sick today? Not funny, Sarah. None of this is funny.

Clayton Montgomery, the most powerful man in the free world—and not too shabby a figure everywhere else—was a Blue Dog Democrat from Connecticut who'd been an All-American lacrosse player at Duke. Although that adopted southern pedigree helped him a bit on Super Tuesday, he never would've captured the general election without his wife.

Rose Montgomery—née Rose O'Hara— was a former Miss Florida and beloved TV news anchor at WPLG in Miami for five years before meeting Clayton. In other words, before the election she not only had better name recognition in Florida than her husband but also had better name recognition than his Republican challenger.

Oh, and she was also fluent in Spanish and could supposedly play "Hava Nagila" on the clarinet.

Montgomery won the presidency by twenty-eight electoral votes. The total number of electoral votes he won by taking Florida? Twenty-nine.

"Everyone, I want you to meet FBI agent Sarah Brubaker," said President Montgomery, who was sitting at the Resolute desk signing a flurry of documents. His jawline was even stronger in person than it was on TV. He hadn't even glanced up at her yet. "Two nights ago, she had drinks with a serial killer who tried to run her over afterward in the parking lot. Isn't that correct, Agent Brubaker?"

"Uh, yes, I guess it is, Mr. President," she said.

President Montgomery finally looked up and stared right at Sarah for the longest five seconds of her life.

Then he cracked a smile. Just as he did whenever he scored a point against his opponent during the debates. Just as he did when he posed for his campaign poster.

"And I thought I'd had some bad first dates," he said. "Take a load off your feet, Sarah."

Chapter 61

THE BRIEFING ITSELF was actually the easy part. The president listened intently while throwing in the occasional nod. Not once did he interrupt her. Sarah was clear, concise, and in full command of the facts. Not fazed at all. *Go figure*, she thought. *Maybe this man is just easy to talk to, a good listener.*

Then came the Q and A.

Sitting in an armchair that was clearly "his chair," the president was joined by his chief of staff, Conrad Gilmartin, and his press secretary, Amanda Kyle, who actually—and ironically—looked a bit like C.J. from *The West Wing*. Given the practiced way in which they both took their seats on the couch to the president's left, these were clearly "their seats."

That left the opposite couch. Driesen sat on one end; Jason Hawthorne, the deputy director of the Secret Service, sat on the other. Squeezed in between them with all the comfort of the middle seat on an airplane was Sarah.

Just one big cozy gathering.

The president cleared his throat, firing his first question at Sarah. "Do you have any reason to believe that my brother-in-law would be a target of this killer?"

"Do you mean, sir, more of a target than anyone else named John O'Hara?" she asked.

"Yes, that's what I mean."

"The short answer is I don't know yet."

The president shook his head slowly. The room suddenly didn't feel so cozy to Sarah.

"I can get that answer from anyone, Agent Brubaker," he said. "Are you just anyone?"

Ouch.

Driesen was about to throw her a life preserver and intercede when Montgomery motioned with his hand for him to hold off. The gesture was subtle yet unmistakable.

The president stared at Sarah, waiting. She knew this time there was no smile and punch line in the offing.

Keep it together, Brubaker! Better yet, tell him what you really think.

"You're right, Mr. President. Let me try that again," she said finally. "The killer's motivation has absolutely nothing to do with your brother-in-law. That's what I believe."

The rest of the room, save for Driesen, did everything they could not to blurt out their objections. *That's ridiculous! How could you be so sure at this point?*

But they didn't want to step all over their boss. They bit their tongues.

As for the president, he simply leaned back in his armchair, intrigued.

"Go on," he said. "Convince me."

Chapter 62

THE ROOM WAS so quiet Sarah thought she could actually hear herself blink.

"Mr. President, I'd like you to consider what would attract the killer to a specific John O'Hara out there, whether it be your brother-in-law or someone else," she began. "Maybe they were classmates, maybe they had business dealings—in theory, it could be anything. Whatever the connection, though, the killer's reaction to knowing this John O'Hara would have to be so strong, so violent, that it manifested itself as a need to kill basically *anyone* named John O'Hara."

"Are you saying that's not possible?" asked the president.

"No. Quite the opposite, sir. It's very possible," she said. "I'm convinced the killer has a specific John O'Hara in mind."

"But just not my brother-in-law."

"Exactly."

"Why not? Lord knows he's probably got some enemies out there."

"I'm sure he does," Sarah said, a little too casually. The second the words left her mouth she wanted to take them back. "I'm sorry, I meant no disrespect to him."

President Montgomery let go with a slight chuckle. "That's quite all right. If Letterman and Leno can rank on him, so can you," he said. "I do it myself." He looked across the room. "We all do."

"What I meant," she continued, "is that on the surface it would make sense that the killings had something to do with your brother-in-law, given his . . . well, let's just say his notoriety. But that idea changed for me."

"Once you met the killer."

"Yes," said Sarah. "I realized that this guy could've killed me if he wanted to. Rather easily, too. But he didn't. Why? And why would he reveal himself to me in that manner?"

The president's couch consiglieri couldn't restrain themselves any longer. They needed in on the conversation.

"Because it's a game to him, right? He's playing with you," said Gilmartin, the chief of staff.

"Yes, but it goes deeper than that," said Sarah. "He wants me to be scared, to live in fear, and I can't do that once I'm dead. Neither can the real John O'Hara."

Amanda Kyle, the press secretary, looked like she'd just solved the puzzle on *Wheel of Fortune*. "So that's why he kills a bunch of John O'Haras, because he wants *the real one* to live in fear."

"That's what I believe," said Sarah. "It's also why I think the John O'Haras who are no longer alive—the well-known author, for instance—are irrelevant. These aren't tribute killings. There are no shades of John Hinckley here."

"But this hasn't gone public," said Hawthorne, the deputy director of the Secret Service. "Whoever the 'real' John O'Hara is, he doesn't know anything."

"I'm afraid he's about to," said the president. "The whole country is."

"We could still wait, sir," said Hawthorne. "God knows how many John O'Haras are out there, not to mention all their family members. Think of the panic."

"Up until this morning I was," said the president. "But if another John O'Hara turns up dead and it gets out we were aware of the threat and didn't warn anyone, we'll all be eating from a big bowl of shit stew."

Sarah looked around the room. There was clearly something final about the president cursing, because that was the end of the discussion. Period.

"Shall I start preparing a statement, sir?" asked Kyle, already jotting some notes on the yellow legal pad in her lap.

"Yes," he said. "But I'm still missing something." He turned to Sarah. "I still don't know why my brother-in-law couldn't be, as you say, the real John O'Hara."

"If I may, I'll pose it to you this way," she said. "If you were to tell your brother-in-law that he'd somehow managed to inspire a serial killer, no less one who was bent on killing not just him but anyone named John O'Hara, what would be his first reaction?"

The president rolled his eyes. He got it.

"Funny, the word *fear* doesn't come to mind, does it?" he said. "It would be the biggest thing he'd ever done in his life. He'd be over the moon. Everyone knows that about him."

Sarah nodded. "Including our serial killer."

No one else said anything. No one needed to. Except the president.

"Nice work, Agent Brubaker. I like the way you think."

"Thank you, sir."

"Actually, you should be thanking your boss, Dan, here," he said. "He's the one who insisted on bringing you here this morning."

Sarah turned to Driesen, who'd barely said a word the entire time. She couldn't believe it. He'd told her the president liked being briefed from the "front lines," that he had specifically requested her being there.

In other words, he'd lied to her.

And she couldn't thank him enough.

Chapter 63

HALF KIDDING, DAN warned her about it on the ride back from the White House. "Look out for the letdown," he said.

"The what?" asked Sarah.

"The letdown," he repeated. "Just wait."

She didn't have to wait long. Within a minute of landing behind her desk at Quantico, she felt it. She'd been flying high, mixing it up in the Oval Office with the commander in chief. POTUS. The prez. And now what? She was back to, well, being herself. Just another FBI agent.

Hanging over Montgomery's shoulder, she'd noticed, was the original of Norman Rockwell's *Working on the Statue of Liberty*. Sitting atop the credenza was Frederic Remington's iconic sculpture *The Bronco Buster*. Both were courtesy of the greatest interior designer of them all: the Smithsonian.

Sarah sighed. Here she was, all alone now in her tiny office decorated by the weekly circular from Staples. The only thing hanging on her wall was a scuffed-up dry-erase board, and the closest thing she had to a sculpture was a little magnetic porcupine on her desk that held her paper clips.

In other words, the letdown.

There was something else, too. In front of Sarah, practically taunting her, was the case file on the John O'Hara Killer. On the outside it looked like every other file in her office—an overstuffed manila folder. But on the inside...

There was no escaping the fact that this case felt different, a little more personal. She'd met him face-to-face, shook his hand. Stared him straight in the eyes. They were slate gray. And they were still looking at her, daring her.

Sarah opened the file. For the umpteenth time, she pored over the various police reports and available autopsies. She reread her notes. She logged on to her computer, searching again for anything and everything she could find on *Ulysses* and *You've Got Mail*.

Next, she worked the phone. She spoke with the manager of Brewer's supermarket back in Candle Lake. There was no security camera near the Movie Hut. In fact, there were no security cameras at all in the market. "Shoplifting isn't much of an issue around here," the manager explained.

She called Canteena's and spoke with the bartender who had served "Jared" his first beer, the one he had before he conveniently drank from hers.

"Any chance he paid for it with a credit card?" she asked.

She knew that chance fell on the far side of slim to none, but she didn't care. Sometimes the only way to catch a break is to chase down the long shots.

Speaking of which...*isn't there someone who was supposed to call me back?*

Sarah grabbed her phone log and the list of people for whom she'd previously left messages. A sheriff in Winnemucca, Nevada. A detective in Flagstaff, Arizona. The head librarian from the Kern County Library in Bakersfield, California. Everyone had gotten back to her.

Except one.

In the past year, there'd been a total of sixteen escapes from all domestic prisons and mental institutions, this according to the FBI crime database. Of those sixteen escapees, only two remained at large. One was an inmate from state prison in Montgomery, Alabama; the other a patient at Eagle Mountain Psychiatric Hospital in Los Angeles.

The photo accompanying the Alabama inmate's file ruled him out as the killer. Not unless the "Jared Sullivan" Sarah had met had somehow managed, among other things, to lose two hundred pounds, not to mention the two tattoos of daggers on either side of his face.

The psychiatric patient from L.A., though, was another story. Or, more accurately, no story at all. Sarah had requested a copy of the police report made after his escape, but it hadn't reached her desk yet. Other than that, the Bureau didn't have anything on him, which wasn't too big of a surprise. Most states, California in particular, had a litany of rules and regulations regarding patient privacy.

The best way to cut through them? A good old-fashioned phone call.

Assuming you could get someone to call you back.

Sarah had left two messages for Lee McConnell, chief administrator at Eagle Mountain. Of course, this guy would probably sooner get a root canal than have to discuss a patient who escaped on his watch.

"Round three," mumbled Sarah as she started dialing.

She couldn't be sure, but the woman who answered seemed to be different from the one she'd spoken to the previous two times. A temp, maybe? That would certainly explain her announcing chipperly that "Mr. McConnell just walked in; let me patch you through." What followed was easily ten seconds of dead air, during which McConnell was probably busy chewing out the poor woman for not checking with him first. Finally, he picked up.

"Agent Brubaker? Lee McConnell," he said. "Talk about timing. I was just about to call you back."

Yeah, right. And I was just about to elope with Johnny Depp.

Sarah riffled through her notes, checking for the name she'd scribbled down. McConnell's patient. Or former patient, as it were.

She found it.

"So what can you tell me about Ned Sinclair?" she asked.

Chapter 64

THERE WAS A hitch in McConnell's voice. Not a stutter or stammer but, weirdly, something more like a swallow, a sort of dyspeptic reflex, as if the pastrami-on-rye sandwich he had for lunch was repeating on him. The result was that he randomly accentuated words for no reason.

Talk about a Monty Python skit, she thought. Paging John Cleese...

"Ned Sinclair, huh? What...*would*...you like to know about him?" he asked.

Sarah suppressed a laugh and asked her first question, a no-brainer. "What's his race? Is he white, black, Hispanic?"

If Ned Sinclair wasn't white, this was going to be a very short conversation.

"He's white," said McConnell. "I'm afraid I don't have his file...*in*...front of me, so I can't give you height and weight, or even exactly how old he is."

"Can you ballpark his age?"

"I'd say thirtyish, maybe a bit older. I didn't have much interaction with him; in fact, no one here...*really*...did. Ned Sinclair barely spoke."

The age, thirtyish, was a possible match, but the part about his not speaking couldn't be any more different from the guy back at Canteena's. Jared Sullivan was definitely a talker, a very smooth talker.

"What else can you tell me about him?" she asked.

"The guy you'd probably want to speak with is the admitting psychiatrist. Ned was his patient for some time, but I don't know his name offhand," he said. "Let me actually...*grab*...the file. Hold on a second, okay?"

Before Sarah could even respond, she was listening to a trombone-heavy Muzak version of the Beatles' "The Long and Winding

Road." Not an appropriate song title when you've been put on hold.

If only to kill a few seconds, she quickly checked her e-mails. Make that singular. There was only one new message since she last checked after leaving the Oval Office. *An invitation to the next state dinner? A seat at the president's table?*

Sarah smiled. A girl could always dream…

She looked at the sender's name. *Who?* She didn't recognize it at first. Then it came to her.

Mark Campbell. From her call log.

He was the sheriff from Winnemucca, Nevada, the town where the first John O'Hara victim lived.

Sarah's eyes slid over to the subject heading and immediately lit up.

FOUND SOMETHING, it read.

Chapter 65

SARAH QUICKLY CLICKED on the e-mail, the promise of "found something" edging her closer to the screen. The message couldn't load fast enough.

Meanwhile, she was still on hold with McConnell. *Where did he go for Ned Sinclair's file? Cleveland?*

She'd originally spoken to Sheriff Campbell in Winnemucca before heading out to Park City. The thinking was simple. If the John O'Hara Killer had indeed left behind that copy of *Ulysses*, perhaps he'd also left something behind with his first victim. A clue that hadn't been found yet.

She wanted Campbell to reexamine the crime scene, every last inch of it, paying particular attention to the victim himself.

"Check all the clothing again," she'd told him. "Socks, underwear...everything."

Sarah knew she was being a pain in the ass, but it had to be done, simple as that. *Sometimes the only way to catch a break is to chase down the long shots.*

Campbell's e-mail popped open at the exact moment McConnell got back on the line. Figured.

"Sorry about that," said McConnell. "Couldn't find it at first, but I've got it now."

Curiously, he didn't seem to be emphasizing random words in his sentences anymore, or maybe that was because Sarah was barely listening to him. Her ears had given way to her eyes as she began reading Campbell's message.

"You were right," it began.

Campbell described how his men had overlooked the cuffed hems that the first John O'Hara victim had on his khaki slacks. Peeling them back, the sheriff found a small, crumpled piece of paper, a note that was jammed into the fold of the right cuff, as if it were a prayer stuffed into the Western Wall. On it were two handwritten lines.

Sleep now little children who hear the
* monster roar.*
Make me a witness of what he has in store.

Sarah's first thought was that it came from an old children's book, albeit one she didn't know. She read the lines again. Maybe it was from a poem. Or maybe it wasn't from anything—except the killer's own mind.

She brought up Google while McConnell continued talking. He was reciting the highlights from Ned Sinclair's file in bullet-point fashion. "Mathematics PhD...professor at UCLA...fired nearly four years ago..."

Sarah typed in the lines from the e-mail.

McConnell droned on. "Diagnosed with obsessive-compulsive disorder...unnatural fixation with sibling...Nora, his sister..."

"Damn!" Sarah muttered under her breath as she looked at her screen.

The search results—there were thousands of them. She forgot to put the lines in quotation marks. Quickly, she added them, and—bingo—thousands of results turned into one.

It was a website for a certain musical group. The name said it all.

Sarah suddenly jumped up from her chair, practically lunging for her shoulder bag, which was on the floor behind her. The DVD of *You've Got Mail* was in the side pocket. She flipped it over to the back, scanning the credits. She'd read the name, knew it well, but wanted to make sure.

Back at her desk she rifled through her notes on *Ulysses*. She was positive she'd written it down, the woman James Joyce married.

"What did you say Ned's sister's name was again?" she asked McConnell, interrupting him.

His dyspeptic swallow and punching of random words had returned. But there was nothing random about this one word. It was dead-on.

"His sister's name was . . . Nora," he said.

Chapter 66

THE CALLER ID on my cell said QUEENS MED. EXAM.

I put down my glass of OJ, muted the small television in my kitchen, and answered "Hello?" before the second ring.

"Agent O'Hara, this is Dr. Papenziekas," he said.

The deputy medical examiner was getting back to me in the morning, as promised. Bright and early, too.

"What's your verdict on our airport couple?" I asked. "You have anything good for me?"

"You were right," he said.

"Cyclosarin?"

"Lots of it."

"Are you sure?"

I'd expected the doctor with the Noo Yawk attitude to fire back with a smartass retort like, "Hey, numbnuts, feel free to get a second opinion if you want!" But the ground had shifted a bit. I was no longer just some random guy with a crazy hunch. I was clearly on to something.

So the attitude was gone. Sidelined. "Yes, I'm sure it's cyclosarin," he said. "I take it you've had some experience with poisoning?"

"Yes," I answered. *Firsthand, no less. Let's just say I'm very careful who cooks for me nowadays.*

"Of course, this isn't just any poison," he said, his voice trailing off.

He was hinting around now, trying to see what, if anything, I might tell him. I could practically read his mind, what he was thinking. *A busy New York airport. A deadly substance unleashed by terrorists.*

But I wasn't about to elaborate, if for no other reason than I still didn't know what to make of all this. Two dead newlywed couples, both victims of an exotic poison. It wasn't officially a pattern, but—call me Einstein—it was certainly more than a coincidence.

"When are you due to deliver the autopsy report?" I asked.

"Tomorrow," he said. "Unless, of course, there's a reason I shouldn't be delivering it."

I had to hand it to the guy; he wasn't giving up easily. He was basically offering to delay the report in exchange for my telling him how I knew he should look for cyclosarin.

The fact that he had TMZ on the TV in his office when I was there made complete sense now. Dr. Papenziekas liked to be in the know. Of course, I couldn't really blame him; he spent his days dissecting dead people. Anything to liven things up, right?

"That's okay," I said. "You can release that autopsy report when—"

"Jesus Christ!" he blurted out.

"What's wrong?"

"Are you anywhere near a television?"

Clearly, he had one front and center.

"Yeah, why?" I asked.

"Turn to CNN, because…um…well…"

He was stumbling over his words, as if trying to figure out how to explain it. "It's…um…"
I pushed him. "What? What is it?"
Finally, he spit it out.
"It's *you!*" he said.

Chapter 67

I GRABBED THE remote, immediately flipping over to CNN. Even before my thumb could hit the Mute button again to get the sound back, I was...well, speechless.

It was me, all right. That is, it was my name—in big, bold letters near the top of the screen. But the real kicker was the two words following it. I wanted to rub my eyes and check the focus. *What the hell is going on?*

JOHN O'HARA SERIAL KILLER

The sound returned as the studio anchor was throwing it over to a correspondent outside the

White House. At the same time, I could hear another sound—my name, no less—as I realized I still had Dr. Papenziekas on the phone.

Not for long.

"Agent O'Hara, are you there?" he was asking. "Agent O'Hara?"

"I'm here, I'm here."

"What's going on?"

"I'm about to find out," I said. "Thanks for the heads-up."

And, like that, I hung up. Abrupt, yeah, but I'd just read my name on the same line with the words *serial killer* on the TV. Hell, I wasn't even sure yet what that meant, only that it couldn't be good.

I focused back on the correspondent outside the White House, some guy with helmet hair and horse teeth, just in time to hear him mention the "press secretary's earlier statement." Jump cut: we were inside the White House briefing room.

Finally, the details came. I sat there listening to Amanda Kyle, the president's press secretary, explain that "for reasons yet unknown" someone was going around killing guys named John O'Hara. Four so far in four different states.

She stressed there was no indication that the killer's motive had anything to do with the president's brother-in-law, but the cynic in me thought otherwise. Of course, I wouldn't be the only one. She was simply anticipating the onslaught when she opened the floor for questions. It came.

The room erupted into a Darwinian shouting match until the loudest and most persistent voice prevailed.

"Has security been increased for the president's brother-in-law?"

Amanda Kyle wasn't the press secretary for nothing. She knew exactly where she wanted to take the conversation.

"John O'Hara, the president's brother-in-law, has been afforded Secret Service protection since before the inauguration," she began before pivoting. "But why I'm here today—why the president thought it was so important we make this threat public—is because we obviously can't afford to give that same protection to everyone in this country named John O'Hara. The last thing we want is to cause a panic, but at the same time we have a responsibility, a duty, to let people know."

The room erupted again, but there might

as well have been a "mission accomplished" banner hanging behind her. One that was actually true this time. She'd cleverly deflected the spotlight away from the president's brother-in-law.

Next question.

"Where have the killings taken place so far?"

Kyle calmly checked off the towns and cities. Winnemucca...Park City... Flagstaff...Candle Lake.

Wait a minute, I thought. Park City?

I bolted off the stool in the kitchen, heading straight for the den. That's where I'd left it, the Bible that had arrived in the mail. Sender unknown.

I opened the cover, staring again at the stamp in red ink as I walked back into the kitchen. PROPERTY OF THE FRONTIER HOTEL, PARK CITY, UT.

I put the Bible down on the granite countertop, flipping to the page where the passage had been cut out—Deuteronomy 32:35, the Song of Moses. I had it marked with a yellow sticky note on which I'd written the missing words.

To me belongeth vengeance, and recompence;
their foot shall slide in due time:
for the day of their calamity is at hand,
and the things that shall come upon them
  make haste.

I'd barely finished reading the last line when I heard a voice over my shoulder. Someone was in my house, right in my kitchen. Someone I was sure I didn't know this time.

"Are you John O'Hara?" the stranger asked.

Chapter 68

I FROZE, MY body holding perfectly still for a few seconds. Those seconds felt like a lifetime. Or was it that I felt like my lifetime only had a few seconds left?

If I had been anywhere away from home, I would already have been doing the world's fastest deep knee bend to reach for my shin holster.

But that baby, and, more important, the 9mm Beretta it was holding, was sitting somewhere in my bedroom upstairs, along with my wallet, pocket change, and a half-eaten roll of Pep O Mint Life Savers.

Now what?

It was the next best thing. Lunging to my right, I grabbed the closest handle from the block of Wüsthof knives next to the stove and spun around with my arm cocked, ready to throw.

Again, I froze.

Good thing, too. Otherwise she probably wouldn't have done the same—and she was the one with the gun.

"FBI!" she shouted, collapsing into the crouch position they teach you your first year. Smaller target, more vital organs shielded. Only when she saw that she had the upper hand did she reach for her badge. Even from twenty feet away I knew it was legit.

"Jesus Christ, you scared the shit out of me!" I said, lowering the knife. I exhaled so heavily I could've blown up a Macy's Thanksgiving Day parade balloon.

Her exhale was just as big. A Rocky to my Bullwinkle. "My God, I could've shot you!" she said, lowering her gun.

"That's what I was afraid of."

I nodded at the TV. The CNN anchor was back on the screen, as were the same four words: "John O'Hara serial killer."

The second she saw it she rolled her eyes. They were green, I couldn't help noticing, and about as attractive as the rest of her. Interesting, though. With her hair pulled back and minimal makeup, I could tell she was trying her best not to advertise her looks. Just the opposite, actually.

"I'm John O'Hara," I said, acknowledging what we both saw on the screen. "And you are?"

"Special Agent Brubaker," she said. "Sarah." She holstered her Glock 23. "You thought I was—"

"About to make me the fifth victim, yeah," I said. "Wait, how did you get—"

We were officially finishing each other's sentences. "I rang the doorbell but no one answered. I came around back, the patio door was open...you didn't hear the doorbell?"

"No one can—it's broken," I said. "Gee, maybe I should get that fixed, huh?"

She started to laugh, but it wasn't on account of my sarcasm.

"What?" I asked. "What's so funny?"

"Oh, nothing," she said, looking at the counter in front of me.

I glanced down to see the badass blade that I was ready to throw at her like some ninja warrior. Yeah, real badass. *Way to go, O'Hara.* It was a three-inch paring knife.

I shrugged. "Not too impressive, huh?"

"Don't worry, I've seen smaller," she said. "Besides, it's not the size but how you use it, right?"

She was funny, too. "Do women actually believe that?" I asked.

"No, not really."

"Ouch," I said. "So you really are here to hurt me."

"Ah, there it is," she said, pointing.

"What's that?"

"False modesty. Self-deprecating humor. Your file says you're an expert at it."

"Really? What else does it say?" I asked.

"Tons of really interesting stuff, at least the parts I'm cleared to read," she said. "In fact, that's why I'm here."

"To discuss my file?"

"No. To help you."

"The Bureau already has me seeing a shrink."

"I know. But he can't do for you what I can," she said.

"Oh, yeah? What's that?"

"Keep you alive."

I stopped and stared into those green eyes of hers. "Okay. I think we've just hit on a common interest we have."

Chapter 69

THE NEWS REPORT? The fact she was now here in my house? It would've been flat-out redundant to ask what division she was with at the Bureau.

Still, "I'm assuming the BAU isn't making house calls to everyone named John O'Hara in this country, are they?" I asked.

"No," she said. "It's just you, I'm afraid."

More afraid than I should be?

We sat down at the kitchen table, and I watched as she reached for her shoulder bag and pulled out items as though it were the first day of school. Notepad. Pen. Folder. There was one thing I knew she wouldn't have on her, however.

"My file…DNR?" I asked.

"DNC, too," she answered. "You're quite famous."

"Infamous is more like it."

"Self-deprecating, see?"

When your file is marked both "do not remove" *and* "do not copy," chances are you've managed to FTU a few times over the years.

Fuck things up.

"So you've obviously seen the news report," she began. "There's a guy out there killing John O'Haras and only John O'Haras."

"Except the news report didn't say anything about the killer's gender, and you just did. A guy. You know who he is?"

"Not only that, I've met him. Had a beer with him, in fact. Long story."

"How romantic. Have I met him, too?"

"I don't know," she said. "I'm sure of one thing, though. He really—and I mean *really*—must not like you."

"Why's that?" I asked.

"Something to do with his sister's death."

My mind immediately kicked into overdrive as every case I ever worked flashed before me like a slide show on steroids. There were a few possibilities, but something in my gut was pointing to a single name. Hell, I'd just been reminded of her only minutes before, with Dr. Papenziekas.

Talk about something in my gut. She was pure poison, up and down, all around. It still hurt just saying her name.

"Nora?" I asked. "He's the brother of Nora Sinclair?"

Chapter 70

AGENT BRUBAKER STARED across the table at me. I'd just mentioned Nora, and in return, she hadn't said anything. Not yes, not no, not boo. There was no nod or even a touch to the tip of her nose. Nothing.

Instead, she simply folded her arms, tan and fit as they were.

"Do you happen to know the name of James Joyce's wife?" she asked.

Strange time for a pop quiz on world lit. "No," I said. "I don't."

"Nora. Her name was Nora Joyce," she said. "Do you know who directed the movie *You've Got Mail?*"

That one I did know. What can I say? A Netflix subscription gets you watching a lot of movies you normally wouldn't have time to see. Plus we had a pattern going here.

"Nora Ephron," I said.

Agent Brubaker seemed a bit surprised by my movie trivia prowess, but kept going. "And have you ever heard of the Nora Whittaker Band?"

I shook my head. "No."

"Me, neither. They're a small group out of Philly. No major hits, but they do write some interesting lyrics," she said. "More important, do you know who *has* heard of them?"

"I give up."

"Ned Sinclair."

"Nora's—"

"Brother, right. He's been leaving me clues with every victim, although I highly doubt he thought I'd get here before he did," she said. "I just got lucky."

"Sounds like we both did."

Agent Brubaker went on to detail Ned's escape from the psychiatric hospital and the chief administrator happening to mention Nora's name. Somehow Ned knew of my involvement with her.

Of course, he wasn't the only one.

Once Sarah had Nora's name, connecting her to the FBI was as easy as a criminal database search. After a few internal calls Sarah was sitting in front of Frank Walsh's desk. I could just picture his face. *As if you didn't have enough problems, huh, O'Hara? You're the target of a serial killer?*

"Like I said, Ned Sinclair probably blames you for Nora's death. The fact that on his way to get you he's murdering innocent guys with your name only underscores his anger," she said.

"So what does that make me, the *guilty* John O'Hara?"

Sarah looked at me incredulously. "Nora Sinclair was killing her lovers for money and it was your job to prove it. Instead, you gave new meaning to being an undercover agent and ended up in bed with her. Would you like me to continue?"

No, thank you. That's quite all right. Point taken.

"I'm not the one who killed Nora, though," I said.

"Yeah, but does Ned know that? All he could know is that the killer was never caught."

"Fine—so let him come after me. I'll be waiting."

"With a bigger knife?"

"Very funny," I said. "Better yet, you can go catch him. You said the two of you had a first date, right?"

"Which is why I got pulled from the case. Or at least off his trail. Instead, I'm on orders to take you off the map."

"Is that what they're calling it down at Quantico these days?" I asked. "Up here we still say 'off the grid.' Either way, I'm not doing it."

"We put you someplace safe for a stretch—what's the problem?"

"I'm working on a case, that's what. Didn't Walsh tell you?"

"I'm sure Warner Breslow will understand."

Now it was my turn to shoot her the incredulous look.

"Okay, so maybe he won't understand," she said. "He'll just have to accept it."

I got up, grabbing the Bible off the counter. Without a word I placed it down in front of her, watching as she flipped to the page with the missing verse. After she read my sticky note, she intuitively flipped back to the inside cover to see if it was stamped. I was impressed with that.

Meanwhile, she looked like a kid on Christmas morning. I'd given her the gift of fresh evidence. There was nothing better than that for an agent.

"Let me ask you a question," I said. "Does it bother you that you're no longer out there chasing Ned Sinclair?"

"Of course it does. Totally. It makes me crazy, actually."

"And instead of that job, your job now is getting me out of this house, right?"

"Right. That makes me crazy, too."

"So what would you say if I told you maybe there was a way to do both?"

Sarah thought for a few seconds, those green eyes of hers narrowing to a squint. She was wary. But she was also intrigued.

"I'd say, keep talking, John O'Hara. Maybe we have a couple of things in common."

BOOK FOUR

THE VOWS WE MAKE, THE VOWS WE'RE GIVEN...

Chapter 71

I REALLY SHOULD'VE called ahead. What was I thinking?

Actually, I knew exactly what I was thinking. Olivia Sinclair was up in Langdale, New York, and I didn't want to risk being told over the phone, "Now's not a good time."

And okay, yes: a small part of me was showing off a bit for the woman sitting shotgun next to me.

"Anytime you want to tell me where we're going, fire away," said Sarah more than once as we were driving north along I-684.

"We'll be there soon enough," I said.

Part guilt, part curiosity, and a slight sense

of responsibility had me checking up on Olivia Sinclair since her daughter, Nora, was murdered. Once a year, sometimes twice a year, I'd call the head nurse, Emily Barrows, to see how her most intriguing patient was doing. In a way, that sort of added to the irony of Ned Sinclair wanting to kill me.

"Pine Woods Psychiatric Facility?" asked a puzzled Sarah as we drove by the sign on the way into the parking lot.

I turned to her as I pulled into a space, cutting the engine. "Pop quiz: What do all serial killers have in common?"

Sarah looked at me blankly.

"They all have a mother," I said.

Her face lit up. Exactly as I'd thought.

From the moment I'd met Special Agent Sarah Brubaker I could tell how laser-focused she was on Ned Sinclair, presumably even more so since she'd been ordered off his trail. That just made her hungrier for a break in the case. Call it human nature. Also call it the reason she was willing to drive with me for more than an hour without knowing where she was going.

It wasn't just your rapier wit and charm, O'Hara.

I led Sarah up to the eighth floor nurses' station, where, sure enough, Emily Barrows was on duty. The last time she and I spoke was the previous summer, but it had been about five years or so since we'd seen each other face-to-face. She looked more tired than I remembered, a bit more run-down.

Time is especially hard on those whose workday is defined as a "shift."

After introducing Sarah, I apologized to Emily for showing up unannounced. "I was hoping, though, that we could speak with Olivia. She's still down at the end of the hall, right?"

Emily paused, unsure at first how to respond.

"I know, I know," I said. "I'm probably supposed to go through your chief administrator for that request, but we're sort of pressed for time, and—"

"No, it's not that," said Emily. She paused again. "Olivia's no longer here."

"Oh, I see. You mean she was released?"

As I said, I really should've called ahead.

"No," said Emily. "I mean she's dead."

Chapter 72

"HOW?" I ASKED. "When did it happen?"

"Two months ago," answered Emily. "Pancreatic cancer. It took her very fast."

She was about to say something else, but stopped.

"What is it?" I asked. "You were going to say..."

"Nothing, really. I was just remembering what Olivia told me after she was first diagnosed. She said the cancer was from the grief—you know, from her daughter's death. She holds herself responsible."

"She loved Nora very much," I said. I couldn't resist the segue. "Do you remember her ever mentioning that she also had a son?"

Emily thought for a few seconds before shaking her head. "I don't believe so."

I looked over at Sarah, who surely had thoughts of decking me right there in the hallway for taking her on a wild goose chase. To her credit, though, she seemed determined to make the most of it. Or, at the very least, to exhaust every angle.

"Her son's name is Ned," said Sarah. "Maybe that helps."

It didn't. "You have to keep in mind, Olivia barely talked at all for years," said Emily. "It wasn't until after Nora's death that she actually spoke more than a few sentences to me. But it's not like we struck up a friendship."

Sarah listened and nodded, but I could tell she was already a few questions ahead in her mind. "Did Olivia pass away here?" she asked.

"No. Toward the end she was transferred to a hospice. That's where she died."

"What about her personal effects? Did they go with her to the hospice?"

Emily hesitated. It was as if she was trying to figure out how to answer without lying. I'd seen that hesitation countless times in the course of interrogations. Clearly, so had Sarah. We traded glances.

"Is there something you need to tell us?" asked Sarah.

It was a simple question, but through her tone and inflection my "bad cop" partner had managed to insinuate that Emily's world would come crashing down like a house of cards were she not to level with us. Pretty damn intimidating, actually.

Dick Cheney could keep his waterboarding kit. I had Sarah Brubaker.

Emily nervously looked left and right to make sure no one else was within earshot. "Wait here," she said. "I'll be right back. Please. Just give me a minute."

She disappeared into the room behind the nurses' station. No more than ten seconds later, she returned with something wrapped in a plastic shopping bag.

"Olivia kept it hidden at the bottom of a box in her closet," said Emily. "I know it was wrong of me, but after everything I learned about her daughter, Nora...well, I just couldn't help myself."

And with that, she handed the bag to Sarah.

Chapter 73

I DROVE. SARAH READ.

"Hey!" I must have called out a half dozen times when Sarah's voice would trail off. She was so engrossed she didn't realize she'd stopped reading aloud.

The date of the first entry was August 9, 1990, right as Olivia began her prison sentence for murdering her husband. Only she wasn't the one who killed him. It was Ned. She took the fall for her seven-year-old son. Or so she claimed.

Would she lie to her own diary?

There was no denying the unsettling, slightly disconcerting nature of what Sarah and I were doing—and, yes, what nurse Emily Barrows had done before us. This was the ultimate invasion of privacy, and the fact that Olivia was dead hardly mitigated that fact.

Still.

If there was one iota of information in this little brown leather-bound book that could help us catch Ned Sinclair before he killed again, then that justified our actions. It didn't get more Machiavellian than that.

And, oddly, having met Olivia Sinclair, I had the feeling she'd completely understand.

"Jesus Christ," muttered Sarah, interrupting herself midsentence.

I glanced over at her from behind the wheel. She looked disgusted. "What is it?" I asked.

"Nora was molested by her father," she said. "Repeatedly."

The rest was like the last few pieces of a jigsaw puzzle. It all fit together easily.

Ned had known about the incest, taking matters into his own little hands. The fact that Olivia knew nothing about what her husband had been doing—until it was too late—surely accelerated her decision to take

the fall for Ned. It was her last act of mother-
hood.

Sarah continued to read. In gut-wrenching
detail, Olivia described the guilt she felt, the
pain of learning that her children would be
sent off to an orphanage.

It only got worse. A year later, she learned
that Ned and Nora had been separated, sent
to two different state-run foster care facilities.

Sarah suddenly closed the book, snapping
it shut.

"What are you doing?" I asked.

"Taking a break. I can't read any more right
now," she said. "What a terrible story."

For someone so intent on bringing down
Ned Sinclair, that was saying a lot. Not that
I could blame her. Olivia's diary described a
nightmare come to life—for all the Sinclairs.

No matter where you stood on nature versus nurture, it was all but impossible to think
that this hadn't permanently scarred both
Ned and Nora.

I glanced over at Sarah, who was holding
Olivia's diary like I hold the refrigerator door
when I'm trying to lose a few pounds. Sure
enough, she opened it again.

"That was a quick break," I said.

"Can't help it," she said. "I need to get through this, to read everything. Probably a couple of times."

I understood. She was *really* intent on bringing down Ned Sinclair. She had total focus on her goal. So much so that everything else seemed inconsequential. For example, where the hell were we heading? South, yes, but certainly not to my house. At least not on Sarah's watch.

I kept driving while she kept reading, both of us unsure of what lay ahead. Then, about ten miles and twenty pages later, everything changed.

"Holy shit," muttered Sarah, her head still buried in the diary.

"What is it?" I asked.

As I turned to look, she held up the page she was reading. I saw it immediately.

The key to everything.

Chapter 74

SARAH SHOOK HER head for practically the entire flight out to Los Angeles. After a while, I had to laugh.

"What's so funny?" she asked.

"You," I said. "You're like my mother when I was a kid. I'd come home from school boasting that I got ninety-eight percent on my math test, and the first thing she'd say was, 'Who got the other two percent?'"

Sarah had been savvy enough to do a title search for any property that Ned Sinclair might still own. But now she was beating herself up because—*the other two percent*—it didn't occur to her to also check for property owned by other members of the Sinclair family. Especially Nora. Just because she'd been dead for years didn't mean she still couldn't own a home.

Sure enough.

It was a two-bedroom split-level in Westwood near the UCLA campus, where Ned had been an associate professor. Nora had bought it for her brother and, according to the diary, for Olivia as well.

Here's the key, Mother, for the day when you get released.

That's what Nora had told her during one of her visits to Pine Woods. The key was a token of optimism, something to keep Olivia's spirits up. Nora wanted her mother to think that one day she might actually be set free.

Deep down they probably both knew it would never happen.

So it was only Ned who lived in the house. That is, he lived there until he was committed to Eagle Mountain Psychiatric Hospital.

But what had Sarah and me flying across the country was that the place was never sold. It still belonged to Nora's estate.

Welcome to a very special episode of House Hunters.

"That's it over there," said Sarah about thirty minutes after we were on the ground in Los Angeles. She was pointing from the backseat of the cab we took from LAX. "The number's on the mailbox. Two seventy-two."

We pulled up, paid the driver, got out, and stared at Ned Sinclair's last known residence. I expected it to be run-down and creepy, with overgrown grass and weeds. Instead, it was in great shape, well maintained and impeccably manicured.

That somehow made it *really* creepy.

"Nora's estate probably provided for a care-taker on the assumption that Ned would one day be released," said Sarah.

"Maybe," I said.

She looked at me. "Why? You don't think—"

"That he's in there? Nah. He's been killing in only one direction: east," I said. "Lousy odds that he'd be commuting back and forth."

The better odds were that Ned had made a stop at the house after springing himself from Eagle Mountain, only twenty miles away. Pack a suitcase? A shower and a shave? Grab a little travel cash?

The real question, though, was whether he'd managed to leave something behind—some clue, anything, that could help us track him down.

"I'll let you do the honors," I said as we approached the front door of the cedar-shake house with white trim.

Sarah removed the key from her pocket. It was still a little sticky from all the tape Olivia had used to adhere it to her diary.

"Tell me again there's no chance he's in there," she said.

"Okay, there's no chance he's in there."

We both laughed. Ha-ha. Then we both quickly took out our guns.

Just in case we were both wrong.

Chapter 75

KNOCK, KNOCK. WHO'S THERE?

Nobody.

After a quick sweep of the entire house, there was no Ned to be found. Sarah and I were back in the small ceramic-tiled foyer, where we began.

"You take the upstairs, I've got downstairs," she said.

Now it was all about finding clues, something that would point us in the right direction. A Ned decoder. Where was he heading next?

Had this been a movie, it would've been so simple. We'd walk into a room and discover with mouths agape that every inch of every wall was covered with pictures of me, each one with a giant X over my face. Then we'd stumble upon some marked-up road map that gave us the exact location of where Ned was planning to kill again.

But as close as we actually were to Hollywood, this was no movie.

There was no shrine to me, no obvious clue ready and waiting for us. In fact, there wasn't much of anything. Talk about minimalist. Nora Sinclair, the interior designer with a killer eye, may have bought the place for Ned, but she clearly didn't decorate it.

No one did.

In the two bedrooms upstairs, the only pieces of furniture were the beds themselves. There were no dressers, no nightstands, not even a lamp.

That left only the closets. Two of them, to be exact. So much for the first one in the guest bedroom, though. It was empty.

Finally, in the closet in the master bedroom, I found the only sign that someone had actually ever lived in the house. Ned's clothes. At least I assumed they were his.

Hanging very neatly on some wooden

hangers, which looked to be purposefully aligned at exactly two inches apart, were some pants, shirts, and a few sport coats. Checking the pockets, though, was a swing and a miss. They were all empty.

I'd normally feel a little weird about going through someone's personal belongings— Olivia's diary notwithstanding. But there really wasn't anything that seemed "personal" here.

Until I turned around and saw it.

There was something tucked underneath the bed. I thought maybe it was a suitcase at first, but dropping to my knees for a better look, I could see that it was a wooden storage chest. An old one at that.

Pulling it out, I lifted the scuffed brass latch, the hinges rusted and squeaky. *What have you got for me, Ned?*

Disappointment, that's what.

It was toys. The chest was stuffed to the brim with children's toys.

I stared at them all, frustrated. Then suddenly I realized something. They were all the same.

Not exactly the same, but a version of the same thing. Big, small, broken, or in perfect condition. Everything in the chest was a toy version of a very specific car. A one-of-a-kind car, actually—a blast from the past.

The DeLorean.

Huh.

Chapter 76

I DIDN'T WANT to overthink it, especially because I couldn't see any way in which Ned's interest or even obsession with this one car would get us any closer to him. Sometimes a box of toys is just a box of toys.

Still, I had to go through them all. You never know.

One by one I began pulling them out. I wasn't sure what I was looking for. With any luck, I'd know it when I found it.

But all I was finding was one DeLorean after another, whether it was wooden, plastic, or metal.

Until I reached the bottom.

There, lying facedown, was a small picture frame. Even before I picked it up and turned it over, I knew whose picture I was about to see.

Nora Sinclair.

I wiped away some dust on the glass and stared. She looked every bit as stunning as I remembered. The high cheekbones and full lips. The radiant eyes and sun-kissed skin.

Yep: by far the most beautiful serial killer I'd ever slept with.

"How's it going?" Sarah yelled up. "Anything?"

Freud would've had a field day with the way I suddenly fumbled with the frame, as if I'd been caught doing something I shouldn't have been doing.

"Not yet," I yelled down, putting the frame back on the bottom of the chest.

Almost immediately, though, I picked it up again.

It wasn't Nora's picture I was staring at now. It was the back of the frame, where it opened.

I'm not exactly sure why I did what I did next. Was it my once reading about a guy who discovered a copy of the Declaration of Independence behind a painting he bought at a yard sale? Was it the way my grandmother used to add new photos of me to her frames while leaving the old ones behind them?

All I knew was that *something* made me open the back of that frame.

Chapter 77

ALL OF A SUDDEN, Sarah was calling out again, only her call wasn't aimed at me.

"Don't move!" I heard her yell.

I immediately reached for my shin holster and raced out of the room, flying down the stairs. Landing with a thud in the foyer, I saw him from behind, his hands up. *Sinclair? Really? No, it couldn't be!*

Instinctively, he turned around at the sound of me, his eyes popping wide with terror as he realized his predicament. Sarah was in front of him; I was at his back.

"Who are you?" demanded Sarah.

He turned to face her. Every nervous word

tripped over his tongue. "I'm...uh, I'm...my name is Dr. Bruce Drummond. I'm...um, a psychiatrist."

"Why are you here?" she asked—no, demanded.

"The news," he said. "When I...uh...got home from work, I saw it on the news."

Sarah and I both lowered our guns at the same time. Just like that, we'd already filled in the blanks.

"You treated Ned Sinclair?" she asked.

"Yes, for a year," he answered, breathing for the first time. "Are you the police? I hope you're the police."

"FBI," she said, flashing her badge. "I'm Agent Sarah Brubaker and that's my partner, John."

Cleverly, she avoided saying my last name. That would've surely confused the already shaky psychiatrist. As it was, he had more pressing concerns.

"Can I put my hands down now?" he asked.

"Sure," said Sarah. "In fact, you can do a heck of a lot more than that. You can help us."

We walked into Ned's living room, where the theme of "sparsely furnished" had been carried even further. There was one couch, one armchair. That was it. The idea of a coffee table had apparently been deemed superfluous.

Not that we were offering Dr. Bruce Drummond any coffee. No drinks or hors d'oeuvres, either. Ixnay on the cocktail weenies, too—all we wanted to do was pump him for information.

"To start with, why are you here?" asked Sarah. "Have you been in contact with Ned?"

"Not for a couple of years," he explained. "On the off chance that he was here, though, I was hoping to get him to surrender. The door was open when I arrived."

"You didn't think of first going to the police?" I asked.

Drummond folded his legs. "Ned never would have surrendered to the police," he said matter-of-factly. He was calmer now, more composed; his scholarly aura began to assert itself.

Sarah clearly picked up on this and softened her tone. Smart cookie: she wanted to make Drummond feel appreciated for what he'd been trying to do. That was the best way to get him to open up about Ned.

"It's understandable you would care about

his well-being," she said. "How long ago were you his psychiatrist?"

"He became my patient about five years ago, right after his sister was killed. The chair of the math department at UCLA, a friend of mine, had suggested that Ned see me."

"For grief counseling?" I asked. I certainly had a little experience in that area.

"Yes, he was very close with his sister," said Drummond. Then he tacked on something under his breath, almost by accident. "Too close."

If there was ever a line that begged for a follow-up question, that was it. "What does that mean?" I asked.

Drummond hesitated. "Have you seen Ned's personnel file from the university? Do you know why he left?"

"Yes," said Sarah. "It said he was fired based on consistently poor student feedback."

"That figures," said Drummond. "It would've been a PR nightmare otherwise."

"What would have?" I asked.

"The truth," he said.

Chapter 78

I'LL GIVE THE doctor this: he certainly had our full attention.

Drummond leaned forward in the armchair, clasping his hands. "Ned was caught in his office on campus masturbating to a picture of a young woman," he explained.

Sarah barely batted an eyelash. "One of his students?" she asked.

"Worse, if you can imagine," he said. "It was a picture of Nora."

Okay, that's a different story. We just took a right turn onto Weird Avenue. And depending on what picture it was, I might have to go wash my hands.

Drummond continued, "It's called a psychosexual fixation disorder. It's rare among siblings, but it does happen."

"And you continued to counsel him after the incident?" Sarah asked.

"Yes. At least I tried to," he said. "The fact that Nora was dead, though, made it more difficult. Not only was he fixated on her but, as you might imagine, he also became obsessed with the question of who killed her. He claimed he knew who it was."

"Did he actually give you a name?" I asked.

"No, and that was the worst part," he said. "He kept insisting that he was going to take care of it himself."

"It?" repeated Sarah. "Like he was planning to kill the guy?"

"That's the impression I got," he said. "Of course, without a name it wasn't exactly a *Tarasoff* situation."

"Still, you thought he was a threat to *somebody*," said Sarah. "So you had him admitted to Eagle Mountain, right?"

"Almost a year to the day after he became my patient, yes."

I raised my hand. *"Tarasoff?"*

"The court case," said Sarah. *"Tarasoff versus*

Regents of the University of California. The rul-
ing obliges a therapist to breach confidentiality
with his patient if he knows a third party is in
danger."

I shot her a sideways look. "Show-off."

She smiled before turning again to Drummond. "Here's what I don't get, though," she
said. "Ned goes to Eagle Mountain and stays
there for over three years without incident.
Then one day, out of the blue, he decides
to escape. He violently murders a nurse and
goes on a killing spree, all the victims having
the same name."

"Obviously he blames someone named
John O'Hara for his sister's death," said
Drummond. "I mean, he *really* blames him."

"Yes," said Sarah. "But why act on it now?
Why did he wait?"

"Think of his fixation disorder as a cancer,"
he said. "Ned was in remission. He was on
medication, and whatever urges he had, they
were under control. In check."

"So that's my question. What happened to
change that?" she asked.

"I had the same question," said Drummond. "That's why before I came here I
paid a visit to Eagle Mountain. It turns out

a new nurse had been assigned to Ned's floor."

"What did she have to do with anything?" I asked.

"You mean what did *he* have to do with anything," he said. "He was a male nurse."

"Is that the one Ned killed?" asked Sarah.

"Yes. His nickname was Ace."

I shrugged. "So?"

Drummond leaned back in the armchair. "So now ask me what his real name was."

Chapter 79

SCORES OF MILES of driving, thousands of miles in the air, multiple time zones, and all within twenty-four hours, thanks to a red-eye flight from LAX that we just made with only seconds to spare.

Sarah and I were back in New York and in my car, pulling out of the short-term parking lot at Kennedy Airport.

"Do you smell that?" I asked, fidgeting with the vent. "What's that smell?"

Sarah laughed. "I think it's us."

I sniffed down at my shirt, then recoiled. "Wow—maybe it's just me. Sorry about that."

"It's *us*, John. Now we have something else in common. We stink to high heaven."

Showers were in our near future, that much we knew. The agreement before we landed was that we'd drive to my house in Riverside and clean up. The fact that Sarah's rental car was there made the decision a no-brainer.

The disagreement, however, was about what would happen next.

For the umpteenth time I argued that we should camp out at my house and simply wait for Ned Sinclair to show up.

"It's not too late to change your mind," I said as we pulled onto the Van Wyck Express-way, heading toward Connecticut.

And for the umpteenth time she shut me down.

"It's not my call," she said. "And speaking of calls, if I don't make one soon to my boss, I'm going to be in big trouble. Seriously."

I was pretty familiar with Dan Driesen, her boss, albeit only by reputation—a stellar rep-utation, I might add.

Quick, name a serial killer active within the last ten years who's still at large.

Enough said.

"What are you going to tell him?" I asked.

"That it took a while to track you down, but I finally found you," she said.

"Then what happens?"

"Like I said, you go somewhere safe. And that won't be your house in Connecticut."

"The Bureau Hotel, huh?"

"Now with free HBO," she said jokingly.

"Very funny. Well, kind of funny. No, actually, not funny at all."

The Bureau Hotel was what agents called the various safe houses across the country that the FBI used. They were mainly for trial witnesses who needed protection, but sometimes, as in my case, an agent was forced to check in.

"Seriously, though, you should decide what you want to do about your boys," she said.

"I already have," I said. "If someone's trying to kill me, I hardly want them at my side, no matter where I'm being stashed."

"Should they still be at camp, though?"

"Yes—but they're about to get two new counselors, if you know what I mean."

She did. "I'll make the arrangements from your house," she said.

I thought for a moment about Director Barliss and his perfectly aligned pushpins up at Camp Wilderlocke. I tried to imagine someone telling him that he was about to have two young FBI agents joining his staff for a bit. Other than that, though, there wasn't much to smile about.

If only to take my mind off everything, I turned on the radio to get the traffic report for the approaching Whitestone Bridge. The station was 1010 WINS—"All news, all the time."

Amazingly, my timing couldn't have been any better.

If I didn't kill us first, that is.

"Look out!" yelled Sarah.

I whipped my head up from the radio to see the back of a Poland Spring delivery truck filling up my entire windshield. Had I been a nanosecond later on the brakes, we would've rear-ended it for sure. Boom, smash, air bag city.

And all I could say to her, pointing at the radio, was, "Did you hear that?"

Chapter 80

I CRANKED UP the volume, all the way to eleven. It was a news story about the murder of a young couple.

Killed on their honeymoon.

First came Ethan and Abigail Breslow, then Scott and Annabelle Pierce. So much for co-incidences.

Two's company; three's a serial killer.

My head was spinning. Sarah and I both officially had one now. A his-and-hers set, like washcloths—that is, if washcloths went around murdering people.

"Reporting from Long Island is Bianca Turner with more on this story..."

Parker and Samantha Keller were avid sailors, leaving Southampton two Sundays ago aboard their forty-two-foot schooner, heading for Saint Barts. On their way back they'd spent a night docked in Bermuda, meeting up with friends and shopping for additional supplies. An hour out of port the following morning, the boat apparently suffered some type of explosion, killing them both.

"At this time, the Coast Guard has no comment on the nature of the explosion or what might have caused it."

"Try *who* might have caused it," I said, only to be shushed by Sarah, who wanted to hear the rest.

"Friends said Parker and Samantha Keller had delayed their honeymoon until after their law school graduations. They were married this past April in Sag Harbor, New York."

Sarah suddenly screamed so loud I nearly rear-ended another truck. "Oh, my God, that's the couple!"

"What couple?"

"I read about them in the *Times*," she said. "I can't believe it! They were the Vows couple."

She'd lost me after "I can't believe it." I looked at her blankly.

"The Vows couple," she repeated. "Every week in the wedding section they highlight one couple and tell an in-depth story of how they first met and stuff like that. You've never seen it?"

I wanted to explain that until they started printing the sports section in the middle of the wedding section, the odds were pretty slim that I was ever going to come across any "Vows couple."

Instead, I simply shook my head. "No. I've never seen it," I said.

By then, though, Sarah wasn't even looking at me. She had her head buried in her Black-Berry.

"What are you doing?" I asked.

"Checking something," she answered. "A hunch."

With one eye on the road, my other eye was watching her thumbs jab away at the phone. She was typing something. Furiously.

Then she stopped. She was staring at the screen, waiting.

Waiting some more.

"C'mon...c'mon," she muttered impatiently.

Finally, she slapped the dashboard. "I knew it!"

There was something in her voice, a sense that whatever plan we had was all about to change.

"I'm not even going to get my shower, am I?" I asked.

"Not quite yet," she said, looking over her shoulder. She was checking out the traffic heading in the other direction.

"Okay, lay it on me. Where are you taking us?"

"Manhattan," she answered. "We need to get off at the next exit and turn around."

I glanced over at Sarah, smiling at the way her hunch—whatever it might be—was like a shot of pure adrenaline. Not just to her, but to the both of us.

I grabbed the wheel at twelve o'clock, then spun it like a top as we jumped the median into the southbound lanes. Then I straightened out the wheel and hit the gas like I was stomping out a fire.

"So where in Manhattan would you like to go?" I asked calmly.

Chapter 81

WITH BARELY ONE foot in the door, you couldn't just hear the hum of the New York Times building. You could feel it.

Sarah and I walked quickly through the cavernous lobby, looking at the hundreds of small screens hanging from wires that were showcasing snippets of the news, the type flipping and scrolling in a seemingly synchronized dance.

After stepping off the elevator on the twenty-second floor, Sarah gave her name to a fresh-faced young woman wearing tortoise-shell glasses and a white cardigan. It was a pretty safe bet that she was the only receptionist in Manhattan who was reading Proust behind her desk.

"Ms. LaSalle is expecting you," she said. "One moment."

She buzzed the editor's office, and within seconds we were following another fresh-faced young woman through a busy hallway, its walls lined with photographs of some of the paper's more than one hundred Pulitzer Prize winners.

"By the way, I'm Ms. LaSalle's personal assistant," she announced over her shoulder.

The tone was confident, but it was also a false front. Her walking-on-eggshells body language as we approached the corner office left little doubt that she was thoroughly intimidated by her boss.

It was easy to see why.

Emily LaSalle, editor of the *New York Times* wedding section and doyenne of Manhattan high society, was an unsettling one-two punch of prim and proper. Her hair, her makeup, her outfit—complete with a double strand of white pearls—seemed composed. In control.

That is, she seemed in control right up until her personal assistant closed the door and left us alone. That's when Ms. Prim and Proper basically turned into a puddle.

"I feel so responsible," she said, tears suddenly streaming down her high cheekbones. "I chose those couples."

That was silly, of course. It was hardly her fault. Still, I could understand her being distraught. A serial killer was knocking off people on their honeymoons, people who had just one thing in common—they had all been featured in the Vows column.

"You can't blame yourself," said Sarah, sounding like her best friend. "What you can do, though, is help us."

"How?" she asked.

"The past two weekends featured the Pierce and Breslow couples. But the Kellers, the latest ones, actually appeared nearly two months ago," I said.

"Yes, I remember," said LaSalle. "They were delaying their honeymoon. Law school graduation, right?"

"Exactly," said Sarah. "That means there's a five-week gap between victims. We counted."

"Or, to put it another way, five weeks of other Vows couples who are still alive," I said.

"Why do you think they've been spared?" asked LaSalle.

"I don't know. But first, we actually have to make sure that's the case," I explained. "At least one of those couples could still be on their honeymoon."

"Oh, God," said LaSalle, the reality sinking in.

There was only one thing worse than three dead Vows couples.

Four dead Vows couples.

Chapter 82

"I'VE NEVER SEEN anything so beautiful," said Melissa Cosmer, approaching the top of Makahiku Falls in Maui's Haleakalā National Park.

"Me, neither," said her husband, Charlie Cosmer.

Only he wasn't looking at the majestic two-hundred-foot waterfall. He was admiring his new bride of barely a week. He'd never felt so lucky, and in love, in his entire life. Melissa was his sun, moon, and stars all in one.

A gift from the heavens, he called her when

they were interviewed for the Vows column in the *Times*.

Charlie's only regret was that his parents, who had died in a plane crash five years earlier, never got to meet her. A real keeper, his dad would've called her. Charlie was sure of it.

"C'mon," said Melissa, smiling like a devil. "Let's see how close we can get to the edge."

She took Charlie's hand, and the two wove through the thick banyan trees and high grass drenched with mist. Maui's weather was always spectacular, but on this day nature had really outdone herself. The sky appeared to be an almost neon blue.

Their tour group, and the official path to the waterfall—which they'd taken a slight detour from—was maybe a hundred yards away. It wasn't a bad tour, the newlyweds thought; it was just a little crowded. Too many fanny-pack tourists. All they wanted was a little alone time amid so much beauty.

"Careful," said Charlie as the ground began to slope downward toward the edge.

But they were so close to the roar of the water now that they couldn't hear each other.

"What?" asked Melissa, craning her neck toward him.

Never mind, he thought. He'd just hold on tight to her hand. Better yet, he'd hold on tight to all of her.

With a playful tug, Charlie pulled Melissa into his arms, gazing deep into her eyes for a second before kissing her soft lips. As she kissed him back, the thought seemed to hit them both at the same time.

What a spectacular place to make love.

Slowly, the two made their way down to the grass, never once letting go of each other. So in love, so full of passion.

So caught up in the moment that they didn't see the man standing behind them.

Chapter 83

COME OUT, COME OUT, wherever you are...

Faruth Passan had all the information he needed about young Charlie and Melissa Cosmer, including a photograph of them. It came straight from the wedding section of the *New York Times*, a candid shot of the smiling couple on the dance floor during their reception at the St. Regis hotel.

VOWS, said the headline above them.

I know you're out there, Charlie and Melissa. Where are you hiding?

Faruth kept to the trail previously used by the tour group that the happy honeymooners had ditched. With each step his eyes moved like the second hand of a watch, scanning in a circle, covering every inch of the terrain around him.

They called it Haleakalā National Park, but it was really more like a jungle in most places. The trees, the arching branches, the incredibly lush and green leaves—it was so dense it was almost dizzying.

It was loud, too.

The chirps, squawks, and calls from the more than forty species of birds in the park were relentless, but they were nothing compared to the wall of sound created by the various waterfalls along the route.

As Faruth approached one of the largest, Makahiku, he was already well aware that there was no offshoot from the trail that led to the very top of it.

Of course, that didn't mean an adventurous young couple wouldn't give it a shot.

Pushing his way through the banyan trees, Faruth almost gave up and turned around. He was so close to the falls, but that was all he could see.

Wait just a second. Hold on.

Amid the tall grass near the very edge there

was something moving. With a few more steps forward he saw what it was. Make that *who* it was.

Talk about an element of surprise.

Faruth smiled. How could he not? *These two don't have the slightest clue that someone wants to kill them.*

Oh, well…

The smile left Faruth's face as he took a deep breath, his hands hanging at his waist. His fingertips were mere inches from the knife strapped to his belt.

It was time to break the news to Charlie and Melissa.

Their honeymoon was over.

Chapter 84

"YOU'RE NOT GOING to believe this," said Sarah, hanging up the phone in our makeshift FBI command post, which was really a spare conference room in the New York Times building.

I couldn't get a read from her face. "Were they found?" I asked.

She broke into a laugh. "Oh, they were found, all right," she said. "In fact, that was the park ranger himself who did the honors. Turned out the two had ditched the tour group their hotel had arranged for them."

"So where were they?"

She told me. Including what they were doing when the ranger found them. "Can you imagine?"

I smiled. "I'll do my best."

That got me one of those half-amused, half-disapproving looks that women have been perfecting since the Stone Age. "Would it help if I dimmed the lights?" she cracked.

"It might."

"Maybe put on some Barry White?"

"Now we're talking. I think I have the picture now."

No one could blame us for kidding around a bit. And as my father used to say with his hand wrapped around a Ballantine Ale, "Screw 'em if they tried."

After a ridiculous number of phone calls and a considerable amount of maneuvering, we'd finally managed to account for all the remaining Vows couples through local police. They were safe and sound. For some reason the killer had spared them. Now, why was that?

As for Charlie and Melissa Cosmer, they were currently packing up their suitcases at the Ritz-Carlton, Kapalua, in Maui and heading home with an FBI escort, courtesy of the Honolulu office. Needless to say, they weren't too pleased. But better to cut short their honeymoon than their lives.

Sarah reached for her cell. "I've got to call Dan back," she said. "He's waiting to hear where we stand."

Of course, Sarah's first call to Dan Driesen hours earlier had been to let him know that the John O'Hara Killer wasn't, as she put it, "the only game in town." He had company. The Honeymoon Murderer, we were calling him.

Unfortunately, coming up with the name was the only thing that was easy. Coming up with anything else—his motive, why he chose some Vows couples and not others, and how he knew where they were honeymooning—was proving a little more difficult.

Trying to link the victims together was like twisting a Rubik's cube. We looked for similar names, schools, jobs, socioeconomic backgrounds—anything and everything, from hair color to how the couple first met. But we kept coming up with nothing. Bubkes.

"Hey, before you call Driesen again, we need to make another call first," I said.

"To whom?" she asked.

As badly as I needed a shower, there was something else I needed even more. Food.

"How about the nearest Chinese restaurant?" I said. "I'm starving. I'm actually getting woozy."

Sarah nodded. "Yeah, you're right. Me, too."

We'd been working nonstop since we arrived at the *New York Times* offices without so much as a Tic Tac.

I dialed Emily LaSalle's extension and asked her where we could place an order. She'd been holed up in her office the entire time, scouring the Internet to see if the Gawker.coms of the world had made the connection yet between her Vows columns and the honeymoon murders. It was only a matter of time.

"Ming Chow's is right down the block, and they deliver," she said. "I recommend the kung pao chicken."

"Great. Do you know the number?" I asked.

"Actually, you can order online from their..." Her voice trailed off. I thought maybe we got disconnected.

"Are you there?" I asked.

"Wait one second," she said.

Actually, it was more like ten seconds, or

about the time it took for her to rush down to the conference room in her sky-high heels. She was half out of breath when she pushed through the door.

"Do you remember when I said I gave you all the information we had on each Vows couple?" she asked.

Sarah and I answered in stereo. "Yeah."

"Well, I just thought of something else," she said.

Chapter 85

THAT WAS IT. The link. Literally.

"Websites," said LaSalle, tugging on her double strand of pearls. "Couples these days have their own wedding websites...some of them do, at least."

Before she could even finish the sentence, Sarah's thumbs were pounding away on her BlackBerry again.

"I'll take the victims," she called out.

I quickly grabbed the MacBook that LaSalle had let us borrow. Divide and conquer.

"I'll take the rest," I said. In other words, the newlyweds who were spared.

I Googled the names of the first couple on

our list, Pamela and Michael Eaton. They were the Vows couple who appeared the week after the Kellers. In addition to their names, I added a few more words you'd expect to see on a wedding website—*gift registry* and *reception*. That oughta do it, I thought.

Nothing was coming up, though. Meanwhile, Sarah yelled out like it was Friday night at the Elks lodge. "Bingo!"

"Which couple?" I asked.

"The Pierces...from the airport," she said. "It says at the top of the site that it was created by Scott Pierce's best man." She scrolled down on her phone, her eyes quickly scanning. "Oh, get this—there's even a section called The Honeymoon."

"Christ—it actually says where they were going?"

"Worse." She read it to me. "The lovebirds will be flying off the next day from JFK to Rome. Guess all those frequent flyer miles they had on Delta really came in handy."

"They might as well have just put targets on their backs," I said.

All I could suddenly think about was my conversation with John Jr. up in his room the night before he left for camp. You never know who's reading about you online, I'd told him. Case in point, no?

Sarah and I kept searching for other websites. We were able to verify the pattern lickety-split: all the victims had a website. Those who didn't were still alive.

There was one exception, but it actually proved the rule. One couple who was spared had a website but, unlike the victims', theirs didn't divulge any details about the honeymoon.

"So now we know," I said. This was exactly how the killer was targeting his victims.

Sarah drew a deep breath and exhaled. "Yes, but now what do we do?"

"I know what I have to do," said LaSalle.

I'd almost forgotten that she and her pearls were still in the room. "What's that?" I asked.

"I have to suspend the Vows column effective immediately," she said.

Of course. It was common sense. The right thing to do. Who could argue with that?

Well, actually, I could.

I got out of my chair, walked over to Sarah, and promptly got down on one knee. She looked at me as if I were crazy. Ditto for LaSalle.

"What the hell are you doing?" asked Sarah.

"Proposing," I answered. "Sarah Brubaker, will you marry me?"

Chapter 86

"GET UP, YOU fool," she said.

I took that for a yes.

It was the way Sarah said it—the "Holy shit, O'Hara, you might be onto something" tone in her voice. I knew instantly that we were on the same page.

Of the wedding section, to be exact.

The idea was a lot of things—risky, dangerous, a candidate for the Hazard Pay Hall of Fame—but it was also something else: the best chance we had to stop this thing. I was sure of it. So was Sarah.

Poor Emily LaSalle, however, wasn't sure what the hell to think.

"I'm sorry, what just happened?" she asked with a hand on her hip.

"You're looking at the next Vows couple," I explained.

It took a few seconds, but she finally got it. After another few seconds, though, her face went from "Aha" to "Oh, wait." There were frown lines everywhere, and she looked overly concerned.

"I don't know if the *Times* can do that," she said. "I mean, that's a decision for—"

"Your publisher, of course," I said. "And trust me, I understand the ramifications."

Whether it was Kennedy during the Cuban Missile Crisis, the Bush White House when the NSA was engaged in domestic eavesdropping, or the Obama administration after the capture of Mullah Abdul Ghani Baradar, a top Taliban commander, there have been occasions during which the *Times* has been asked to delay or "sit on" a particular story in the interest of national security.

However, this was different. Yes, people's lives were in danger, but this request would have the paper printing a story they knew up front wasn't true. Notwithstanding the fact that most staunch conservatives already had a name for that phenomenon—they called it the *Times* editorial page—it was easy to understand how this threshold might be one the so-called Gray Lady wouldn't want to cross.

"Listen, we're getting ahead of ourselves," said Sarah. "Before we can get the paper's blessing, we need someone else's. The father of the bride, if you will."

I knew she wasn't talking about her actual father, Conrad Brubaker, whom she'd described to me as a retired art history professor usually found swinging a 7 iron on the back nine somewhere out in La Quinta, California. She was referring to Dan Driesen, who would surely have an aversion to dangling one of his agents as human bait.

"Maybe I can get Walsh to call him," I said, only to immediately shake my head in contradiction. "On second thought...maybe that isn't the best idea."

Sarah rolled her eyes. "Talk about another blessing we'll need."

She was right. I had a little issue to work out with my own boss. My suspension. Throw in the breaking news of the John O'Hara Killer and I could already hear Frank Walsh yelling at me.

Jesus Christ, it's not enough you've already got one serial killer coming after you—now you want to arrange for another? You don't need therapy, O'Hara, you need a damn straitjacket!

"Yeah, cancel Walsh running interference," I said. "Driesen is all yours."

Sarah turned to LaSalle. "When is the Sunday wedding section viewable online?" she asked.

"Saturday at five."

That gave us less than three days. I glanced at my watch. Sixty-eight hours, to be exact.

"Amazing," said Sarah. "Who would've thought planning a fake wedding could be harder than planning a real one?"

"At least we've got one thing to look forward to," I said, keeping a straight face.

"What's that?"

"The honeymoon, of course."

Chapter 87

"SOMEHOW I ALWAYS pictured Paris," said Sarah. "You know, a hotel room on the Left Bank with an Eiffel Tower view." She gazed around our tiny, rustic cabin with its knotty-pine paneling and let out a slight chuckle. "This ain't Paris."

No, it wasn't. Not even close.

But for Cindy and Zach Welker, a couple of avid environmental types who first met—as the Vows column explained—on intersecting trails while hiking in Telluride, it was perfect. Two weeks in a Lewis Mountain cabin deep in Virginia's Shenandoah National Park. A little secluded bliss in the great outdoors.

"Hey, who knows?" wrote Zach, otherwise known as me, on our wedding website. "We may even venture out of the cabin once or twice during the honeymoon and do some actual hiking."

Of course, the Lewis Mountain cabins weren't really all that secluded, not if you knew what—or whom—you were looking for. Fifteen dollars for an automobile pass at the park entrance and you were in.

Heck, any serial killer could do it.

Or so we—Sarah, I, and the four other agents from the Washington, D.C., field office who were stationed in the brush outside— were hoping. The D.C. agents were rotating with other agents on eight-hour shifts.

That was the only way Dan Driesen would ultimately go along with the plan. He still wasn't entirely sold on it, but he could hardly deny the ancillary benefit of having me surrounded by other agents. The Honeymoon Murderer wouldn't know what hit him, and the John O'Hara Killer wouldn't even know where to look for me.

In other words, my idea wasn't as crazy as it first sounded to him.

Ditto for Frank Walsh, who was willing to

cut enough corners and red tape to essentially suspend my suspension. I had a badge and company firearm again. "Until further notice," he said.

Throw in the tag-team arm-twisting of Driesen and Walsh to get the *New York Times* to cooperate with our fictitious Vows article, and here we were, Sarah and I playing the role of tree-hugging crunchy-granola newlyweds who just happened to be locked and loaded. Birkenstocks and Glocks, I was calling us.

Now the only question was whether or not the plan would work.

Sarah, fully aware of the irony, summed it up best. "After all the time and effort we went through to get here I'd be seriously disappointed if no one tried to kill us."

Chapter 88

"A PARIS HONEYMOON, huh? Sounds nice," I said, pouring myself some more coffee from the stove. We'd just finished dinner and were hanging out in the small sitting area outside the bedroom. As modest as our cabin was, it did, thankfully, have indoor plumbing, a small kitchen, and electricity.

The mosquitoes they threw in for free.

"What about you?" asked Sarah, tugging on the bottom of her sweatshirt from the University of Colorado, Cindy Welker's alma mater. "Where would you want to spend your..."

Her voice trailed off, her face flushing red with embarrassment. She'd forgotten. I

was once married. I'd already had a honeymoon.

"It's okay," I said.

"I'm sorry."

"Really, it's fine. For the record, we went to
Rome."

"Was it great?"

"It absolutely was," I said. "Right up until I
broke my arm."

"You broke your arm on your honeymoon?"

"Yep. I tripped and fell down the Spanish
Steps while eating a double scoop of chocolate gelato."

She started to crack up. For someone so
attractive, she had this really goofy laugh, almost like Arnold Horshack's from *Welcome
Back, Kotter.* I liked it.

"I know—how clumsy, right?" I started
laughing, too. "Damn good gelato, though."

It occurred to me that up till now Sarah and
I had barely talked about our lives outside of
work. Felt pretty good. Natural. I could sense
she thought so, too.

"So tell me about your two boys," she said.

"Ah, my favorite subject..."

I told her about Max and John Jr. while trying to keep the excessive fatherly pride at a minimum. Still, it was hard not to gush, especially given how much I was missing them. When I finally shut up about how great they were, Sarah simply stared at me and smiled.

"What? What's that look for?" I asked.

"I was thinking how lucky they are to have you as a father," she said. "They mean the world to you, don't they?"

"They do, but it's the other way around. *I'm* the lucky one," I said. "Now, what about you? Do you and your boyfriend both want kids?"

She shot me a look. "Nice try, O'Hara. You just want to know if I'm dating anyone."

"Well, we are on our honeymoon, after all. It's only fair that I know."

"In that case, the answer's no. I'm not currently cheating on you with anybody."

I opened my mouth to say something, but she stopped me with a raised palm.

"And please don't tell me how surprising it is," she said. "You know, the fact that I don't have a boyfriend."

"Actually, all I was going to say is that I understand. It's got to be hard for you."

She looked at me, unsure. "How do you mean?"

"You're a female FBI agent. You're trained in hand-to-hand combat and you carry a gun," I said. "Most guys would be intimidated by that."

Her look suddenly changed. She was staring back at me as if I'd just tapped into her innermost thoughts. "How did you know that?" she asked.

"Lucky guess," I said. "But don't get any ideas. I'm still sleeping on the couch again tonight."

She started laughing again. We both did. Then we both suddenly stopped.

The cabin had gone pitch black. Every light around us, even the one hanging over the porch outside, had gone dark.

The power was out.

Chapter 89

I WASN'T SURE which sound I heard first, the window shattering or the shots being fired. But I was damn sure I felt the bullet that grazed my shoulder.

"Down!" I yelled. "Down, Sarah!"

My eyes had adjusted barely enough to see the outline of Sarah hitting the floor with me as more bullets—one, two, three—came through the window, the shards of glass landing all over us. *How the hell is this happening?*

I reached for my Glock and could hear Sarah doing the same. Meanwhile, the shots outside had stopped. Was it over? Or just intermission?

I whispered to Sarah. "You okay?"

"Yeah," she said. "You?"

"Yeah. One nicked me, that's all."

"You sure?"

I pressed my palm against my shoulder. There's bleeding and then there's *bleeding*. Luckily, it was the former.

"I'm fine," I assured her. "Window or door; which one you got?" As in, which one do you want to cover?

"Door," she said.

I raised my arms toward the window, locking both elbows. The only other window, a tiny one, was in the bedroom, but we were clear of it.

"What's he got? M16?" I asked. It was my best guess, given the three-round bursts and slightly higher pitch of the weapon.

"That or an M4 carbine," she said. "Tough to tell, given the distance."

"At least forty yards."

"Maybe more," she said.

"And he cuts the power first?"

"Goggles," we said in unison. The shooter had to be wearing night-vision goggles.

"Shit, where's that flashlight?" I asked. We had two of them in the cabin. But where were they?

"More important," said Sarah, "where is everybody?"

She was right. Where was our backup, the four agents we had around the perimeter? Even with the shooter behind them, they still should've located him by now.

Unless he got to them first.

No. No way. Not all four agents.

Sure enough, the two-way radio at my waist suddenly crackled with static. "Anyone hit?" came a hushed voice.

I grabbed the radio, whispering back. "We're good so far," I said. "He must be wearing—"

"Yeah, goggles," said the agent. "Moving in with the same. Two to a side."

I'd lost track of who was on what shift around the cabin. At least this guy sounded experienced.

"Which one is he?" I asked Sarah.

"Carver," she reminded me. "Agent Carver."

Cavalry was more like it.

Chapter 90

THE ONLY THING worse than the sound of all hell breaking loose around us was the feeling of helplessness that came with it.

All of it happened so fast. The bright beam of light outside our window followed by a barrage of gunfire echoing through the woods.

Four against one out there. I didn't have to be Jimmy the Greek to like those odds. But it was what came after—the stone-cold silence and the feeling of dread sweeping over me—that I didn't like. Not one bit.

There was nothing Sarah and I could do. Agent Carver's radio was off. All the radios were off.

I slid across the floor amid the shards of glass, leaning up against the wall next to the window.

"What are you doing?" whispered Sarah, the subtext being that whatever it was, I shouldn't be doing it.

But I had to look. I had to try to see what was happening. A quick peek, that's all.

Not quick enough.

My head barely made it past the wood trim alongside the window when—*pop-pop-pop!*—I nearly caught one between the eyes. My neck snapped back, pure reflex at the sound of the shots, as more glass rained all over the cabin.

"Shit!" said Sarah.

I immediately knew what she was thinking. I was thinking the same thing, and it wasn't just how lucky I was to be alive.

I grabbed the two-way again, jamming the Talk button with my thumb. "Carver!" I said. "Carver, are you there?"

He didn't answer.

I tried again, and again all I got was silence. I flipped to the other frequencies, the ones assigned to the remaining agents. *Four against one, for Christ's sake!*

Not one of them answered, though. Nothing. Not a peep.

Dead silence.

I could feel the sweat dripping down my forehead, my heart pounding relentlessly against my chest. *What the hell happened out there?*

Then we heard it. The crackling of my radio again, followed by Carver's voice going in and out. He barely had enough strength to push the Talk button, let alone actually talk.

"Three...down," he managed to get out. "Help..."

There were no more words, only the sound of his labored breathing. It was horrible, just horrible. But it only got worse.

Pop-pop-pop!

Another quick three-round burst shrieked over the radio, the ear-piercing feedback leaving little doubt that the shots were fired at close range. A few yards. Maybe even less.

And just like that, Carver's breathing was gone. *He* was gone. All that remained was that same feeling of dread I'd had, only a million times worse. I was drowning in it.

"We've got to get out there," I said to Sarah.

Only it was too late. The sound of footsteps

heading toward us had broken the silence again.

We'd set a trap for the Honeymoon Murderer, but now we were the ones who were trapped.

He was coming in.

Chapter 91

I COULD BARELY see Sarah across the cabin, but I could hear her scrambling over to the sofa. Was she setting up behind it?

No.

"Got it!" she said, slapping something against the palm of her hand. One of the flashlights.

There was no time to discuss strategy. I took it on faith that we were thinking the same thing. If she saw the night-vision goggles over his eyes, she'd blind him with the light. If not, the flashlight would remain off and we'd have a fair contest. No one could see.

All I could hear now were the footsteps

getting closer. The door of the cabin was to my right; the window—or at least what remained of it—to my left. I had my back jammed hard against the knotty-pine paneling, almost as hard as I was gripping my gun.

Breathe, O'Hara, breathe.

A split second—that's all Sarah and I would have. Crouched down low, I felt like a defensive lineman trying to anticipate the snap count of the quarterback. Time it right, we'd win.

But time it wrong?

I kept listening, the footsteps getting louder and louder. Then it was the strangest thing. It caught me so off guard all I could do at first was freeze.

The footsteps stopped getting louder. They were softer now. No; that wasn't the right word.

They were *disappearing.*

He wasn't running at us, he was running past us. And now he was getting away.

Sarah and I both jumped up, bursting out of the cabin with the light of her flashlight leading the way. We couldn't see him; he had too much of a head start. But we knew where he was heading.

About a hundred yards down a dirt trail was a small clearing off the access road where our Jeep was parked. The glove compartment even had a registration in the name of my alias, Zach Welker. We presumed we'd thought of everything.

"Damn!" I yelled as we heard the sound of the engine at the end of the trail. He was already at his car. The son of a bitch probably parked right next to us.

"You have the keys, right?" asked Sarah, midstride. She was booking along ahead of me and barely breathing hard. She was obviously no stranger to a treadmill.

"Got 'em," I said, double-checking they were still in my pocket. I was huffing and puffing. My chest was burning.

In my head I was already behind the wheel, the car chase in full swing. The setup was perfect, a winding and narrow road at night lined with unforgiving trees. I'd cut my headlights and follow his taillights, and if he tried to do the same I'd still have his brake lights to guide me. What he'd have, though, would be the broad side of a pine tree.

Let's see if you drive as good as you shoot, asshole.

Sarah and I reached the small parking lot. Our Jeep was sitting there waiting for us. I pulled out the key fob to unlock the doors when, even in the pitch-black darkness, I noticed something.

Sarah saw it, too.

The Jeep was too low to the ground.

Sarah shined the flashlight on the front tires. Then on the back two. Each was flat to the rims.

I kicked the shit out of the door in frustration while Sarah looked up to the night sky.

"Dammit, not again!" she screamed.

Chapter 92

IT DIDN'T TAKE long for the deal Dan Driesen and the Bureau struck with the *New York Times* to fall apart. *Disintegrate* might be a better word.

The paper had agreed to sit on the story of the Honeymoon Murderer so we could set the trap for him. In return, they were to receive an exclusive on what should've been his capture. *Should've* been.

Unfortunately, life doesn't always go as planned.

Now the story was right there on the front page—in the far right column, above the fold—for all the world to see.

"Don't do it, O'Hara. Don't beat yourself up," said Driesen. Sarah and I were in his office at Quantico. Flags were at half-mast. Spirits were even lower. "It's not your fault."

Sarah had already told me the same thing—a few times over, in fact. I answered Driesen the same way I answered her.

"It was my idea," I said. How could it not be my fault?

The only names mentioned in the article were those of the dead. The number stood at ten; the three newlywed couples plus the four agents. As for the paragraph on Agent Carver, it said he was married with two boys. The older one was thirteen, the same age as John Jr.

While I was getting my shoulder stitched up at Shenandoah Memorial Hospital it occurred to me that the very last word Carver ever spoke was *help*. If only I could have. I knew I'd be haunted by that forever.

Driesen leaned back in his chair, folding his arms. He blinked slowly, his chin dipping toward his chest. I was pretty sure what he was thinking as he looked at me. *What the hell am I going to do with this guy?*

He and I had only met face-to-face a few days earlier, but he'd read my file. He'd been briefed on me. I was John O'Hara, the agent so overcome with thoughts of avenging my wife's death that I got myself suspended by the Bureau—only to then become the target of a serial killer stemming from an old case that had nearly gotten me fired because I slept with the suspect.

But wait. Tip of the iceberg, folks. There's more.

While on suspension I got hired freelance to solve the murder of Warner Breslow's son and his new bride, only to stumble upon yet another serial killer who ended up killing four agents in a plan I devised that went terribly, horribly, and downright appallingly wrong.

Hell, were it not actually happening to me I never would've believed it myself.

The worst part—and this, too, I'm sure Driesen was aware of—was that now, in addition to being obsessed with revenge, I was consumed by guilt. That's a one-two punch from which a lot of people don't get up.

Was I one of those people? Was I down for the count? Lost?

That's what Driesen surely wanted to know.

"Tell me something, John," he said. Before

he could continue, however, the phone on his desk buzzed. His secretary apologized for interrupting, but there was a call she thought he needed to take.

"Who is it?" asked Driesen.

"Detective Brian Harris with the NYPD," she said.

Driesen's eyes narrowed. Clearly, he didn't know who that was. He picked up. "Dan Driesen," he said.

I watched as he listened. Whoever this Detective Harris was, it didn't take long for him to prove that, yes, this was a call Driesen wanted to take. In fact, Driesen reached for a pen so fast he nearly knocked over his coffee mug.

I couldn't see what he was writing, but as he glanced up and nodded with a slight smile I knew one thing for sure.

He was no longer wondering what the hell to do with me.

Chapter 93

SARAH AND I hopped the next Delta shuttle to New York, hailed a cab from LaGuardia to the Ninth Precinct on the Lower East Side, and climbed the stairs two at a time to the second floor to meet Detective Harris. I was still shaking the guy's hand when I cut to the chase.

"Where is she?" I asked.

"Down the hall," he said.

"Was she okay with waiting?" asked Sarah.

"No, but it's not like she had much of a choice," said Harris. "Once she told me what she told me..."

He didn't need to finish the sentence; it was

simply understood. A given. When a potentially huge break in a case comes walking through the door, you basically lock that door behind her. God forbid she changes her mind.

We followed Harris, a compact man with a shuffling gait, down the hall to a small lounge area furnished with a couple of beat-up couches, a half-empty vending machine, and some old *People* magazines. Make that *really* old. The cover of one announced *Lost* as the new hit television series.

In contrast, Martha Cole, the woman sitting on one of the couches, looked even younger than her twenty-two years of age. Mousy hair, a lean figure, a few freckles dotting the bridge of her nose. It would be a while before she ever ordered a drink without being carded.

At that moment, though, it seemed as if she could really use one. Maybe even two. After Harris introduced us I went to shake her hand, only to see that it was already shaking on its own. The rest of her was, too.

Sarah sat down next to her. "It's okay, Martha," she said soothingly. "I know how hard this must be for you, so we'll try to make it as easy as possible. We just need to ask you some questions."

Fact was, all we knew at that point was what Harris had told Driesen over the phone. A young woman had walked in off the street clutching a copy of the *Times*. She asked to speak to a detective, any detective. When asked why, she said she thought she could identify the Honeymoon Murderer.

His name was Robert Macintyre, and he was a former staff sergeant in the U.S. Army. Robbie, she called him.

"I used to be engaged to him," she explained.

Chapter 94

MARTHA COLE DREW a deep breath, exhaling slowly. She was calming down. I chalked that up to Sarah and gave her a quick, approving nod. *Run with it. She's all yours.*

I took a seat on the other couch next to Detective Harris and crossed my legs. Then I crossed my fingers. We were overdue for some good luck.

As promised, Sarah kept it simple. "Martha, when was the last time you saw or spoke to Robert?" she asked.

"About a month ago."

"And when did the two of you end your engagement?"

Martha hesitated. Her eyes welled up, the emotions kicking in. She was doing her best to fight it.

Finally, she answered. "It wasn't a mutual decision. I'm the one who broke it off."

Detective Harris reached into his pocket, then handed Martha a folded handkerchief. Nice to think some guys still carried those around. Very old school.

"Thank you," said Martha, wiping her eyes. As raw and torn as she was, I couldn't help but notice her determination. She continued: "When Robbie came back from the war— Afghanistan—it was like he was going through withdrawal. He missed the action, the constant adrenaline."

Sarah nodded. "Let me guess—you couldn't compete, right?"

"Exactly. Everything was boring to him, including me," she said. "I thought I was doing him a favor."

"You mean by breaking things off?"

She couldn't hold back the tears any longer. Her guilt was too strong. Her anger even stronger.

"*That damn war!*" she nearly shouted. "It wasn't Robbie's fault, do you hear me? He wasn't the same person. The guy who came back wasn't the guy I'd fallen in love with!"

Sarah put her hand on Martha's shoulder, rubbing gently. "We understand, we really do," she said.

"But Robbie didn't," said Martha. "I tried to explain it to him, but it's like he wouldn't even listen."

"How long ago was this?" asked Sarah.

"The end of last year, right after Thanksgiving. We were supposed to get married on Christmas Eve," she said. "When I broke it off he just went ballistic."

"Did he hurt you?"

"No. But I was scared." She paused, her voice dropping. "He owns guns."

"Do you know what kind? Handguns? Rifles?"

"All of the above. His favorite was what he carried in the war. I forget the name, but it was one of those semiautomatic rifles."

Sarah and I exchanged a quick glance. *Bingo.*

"So what kind of missions was Robert involved with in Afghanistan?" asked Sarah. "Did he ever say anything to you?"

Martha worked the handkerchief on her eyes

again as she thought for a moment. "There was this one time," she said. "He'd been drinking and, well, I don't know how we got on the subject, but he started to tell me things."

"What kinds of things?"

"It was sort of like he was bragging," she said. "There was this group he got recruited for, some kind of special weapons unit. He called it the James Bond crew because they trained with all these new gadgets and stuff like that. Poisons, too."

"Poisons?"

Double bingo.

"Yeah," said Martha. "He once joked that I should be careful because he knew all these ways to kill me with certain chemicals. I didn't think it was very funny."

Sarah and I locked eyeballs again. Certainly Robert Macintyre had the means. But the motive was still not 100 percent clear.

The guy gets dumped a few weeks before his own wedding, so he decides to kill newlyweds. Fair enough. Or should I say crazy enough? Assuming he was suffering from PTSD, post-traumatic stress disorder, the bitter disappointment and heartbreak could easily cause him to snap. Violently.

But why kill just the Vows couples?

Were we looking for logic where there simply wasn't any? Insane behavior has its own set of rules.

Patiently, methodically, Sarah pressed on.

"So you read the article in the paper this morning, Martha, and you obviously must have had your suspicions. But what makes you so sure it's Robert?"

I was hurting for this girl as she wiped her eyes yet again. She felt so damn responsible.

"Robbie told me that if it couldn't be us, it shouldn't be anyone."

"I'm not sure I follow you," said Sarah.

Slowly, Martha looked at Detective Harris, then me, then back to Sarah. And that's when she told us.

"The day I broke up with him was the same day we heard back from the *New York Times*," she said. "They wanted us to be a Vows couple."

BOOK FIVE

PAYBACK IS A BITCH

Chapter 95

A DOZEN OFFICERS, Detective Harris, Sarah, and me. As numbers go we were approaching a small army, certainly more than protocol when bringing in a guy for questioning. Then again, this wasn't just any guy.

There was no hard proof, not a single witness, and no direct evidence linking Robert Macintyre to the Honeymoon Murderer. Everything was circumstantial. It all could've been a coincidence.

If so, I'd be the first to shake his hand and apologize.

"The only way he escapes alive back there is if he knows how to fly," said Harris, returning to the front of Macintyre's Brooklyn brownstone, where the rest of us were gathered. He'd just checked the rear of the building, along with two of the officers. Macintyre's apartment was on the fifth floor, the top. "There's a small courtyard back there but no fire escape."

I turned to Sarah. "You ready?"

"Yeah," she said.

The outside of Macintyre's prewar building was definitely showing wear and tear. The stone was chipped and stained, and there were even a couple of cracked windows. I expected the same, if not worse, once we got inside.

Not so, though. It was clean, modern, and quite nice, actually. Brooklyn hip. You would've thought I'd have learned by now.

Things aren't always as they appear.

We left one officer covering the foyer. The rest of us began climbing the stairs. By the fourth floor a couple of the officers—let's just call them big-boned—were seriously cursing the absence of an elevator. About a hundred cops-and-doughnuts jokes came to mind. I kept them all to myself.

"There," I said, pointing at Macintyre's door

when we reached the fifth floor. It was in the middle of the hallway. Apartment 5B.

Silently, Sarah took control of the choreography. She and Harris lined up on one side of the door, I lined up on the other. Fanning out behind us were the officers—two crouched, the rest standing. Guns drawn.

I knocked.

When we didn't hear anything, I reached over and knocked again.

Still nothing.

It was Sarah's hand that reached out across the door this time. She gripped the knob and shrugged. It was worth a shot.

Well, what do you know...

The good news? The door was open.

The bad news? The door was open.

The little man in my head in charge of waving the red flag suddenly got very busy.

What the hell were we walking into?

Chapter 96

IT WAS SO silent in the hallway the squeak of the hinges sounded like a jet taking off.

Slowly, the door opened. No one moved.

I counted to five seconds. Then ten. Finally, I called out. "Robert, are you in there?"

If he was, he wasn't answering.

The nudge at my side was one of the officers handing me the telescopic mirror, or, as I liked to call it, the peekaboo. It sure beat sticking my head out and getting it blown off. Been there, and almost done that, at the cabin with Sarah. I wasn't about to press my luck.

Angling the mirror around the corner of

the door, I could see a narrow hallway in the apartment that had two openings off of it, one on each side, staggered. At the end of the hallway was what appeared to be a small living room. There was a couch, a flat-screen TV, a lamp next to a coffee table.

But no sign of Macintyre. No six-foot broad-shouldered guy with cropped reddish hair and an angled jaw, as he was described by Martha Cole.

I shook my head at Sarah, and she immediately resumed her choreography. She turned to Harris and the officers, flashing two fingers before pointing back to herself and me.

Translation: *We're going in two at a time. He and I will lead the way.*

The girl certainly didn't shy away from the action, did she?

Three...two...one...

Sarah and I peeled around the doorway, our Glocks out front, pointing down the hall. I pulled up before the kitchen; she stopped before the bathroom.

I motioned behind me for the next wave.

Two by two they came in, moving past us. I turned in to the kitchen while Sarah took the bathroom.

"Clear!" I yelled out.

I could hear Sarah yanking back a shower curtain. "Clear!" she announced.

"Clear!" we heard from the living room.

I returned to the hallway, meeting up with Sarah. The rest of the guys were ahead of us, including Harris. I was assuming there was one more room, the bedroom. I was also assuming that it would be more of the same. Clear.

Instead, we heard two officers yell out in unison. "Body!"

Huh?

Sarah and I turned the corner of the hallway, making a beeline from the living room into the bedroom. The officers were all standing around, staring at him in silence. It was as if he were on display, some type of sick and twisted piece of performance art. Call it *The Dead Groom.*

Robert Macintyre—reddish hair and angled jaw—was tied to a chair, dressed in what was once a nice tuxedo. Now it was riddled with bullet holes and soaked in blood. If the gunshots didn't kill him, the knife stuck deep into his heart surely did.

It was not just any knife, either. I leaned in

for a closer look. The sterling silver handle caught the light coming through the window just so.

"Is that what I think it is?" asked Sarah.

"It sure is," I said. A cake knife.

Holy shit, it's her—Martha Cole!

We immediately turned to Harris, who was already reaching for his radio to call his dispatch. He'd connected the same crazy dots as we had.

"Shit. I think we only took her phone number," he said. "We can trace it to get the address, but..."

But what were the odds she'd given us her real phone number? I'd say they were somewhere between slim and nonexistent—same as the Cubs winning the World Series.

It all made more sense now, why she turned down the ride home from the precinct. She told us she wanted to walk instead, to "clear her mind." At the time, who could blame her?

"Wait!" said Sarah.

We all turned to her. Then we turned to see what she was looking at.

The bed.

We were all so focused on Macintyre that

no one noticed the outline of something under the sheets. Until now.

Was it another body? Another murder?

No, it was worse. Much worse.

It was everyone's murder.

Chapter 97

WE GATHERED IN a horseshoe formation around the bed. I was on one end, Sarah was on the other.

"Grab the corner," she said.

We each took hold of the top sheet, then lifted it up and back. I didn't know what to expect, but it certainly wasn't what I saw.

What the…

It looked like oxygen tanks, the kind scuba divers wear. There were a half dozen of them lying down the length of the bed.

"What's that writing on the side there?" asked the officer standing next to me.

I tilted my head to read the small print, only

to be blinded by a ray of sunlight beaming off the metallic cylinders.

"Hey, will someone drop the blinds?" I asked. They were pulled all the way up, every inch of the windows exposed.

"Got it," said another officer. He was a young Italian guy, his jet-black hair combed straight back. As he turned toward the window, his body blocked the sun for a second, just long enough for me to look back at the print along the tank closest to me. Only it didn't say OXYGEN.

Oh, no! No! No! No!

But it was already too late.

The first shot smashed through the window, catching the young officer square in the chest, an explosion of blood and bone.

The second shot split the head of the officer next to Sarah.

"Down! Everyone down!"

But that's what she wanted, everyone out of the way, now that she had us together. These were no ordinary bullets she was firing; they were large-caliber and incendiary.

In other words, just right for exploding a propane tank.

The third shot would've killed us all if it

hadn't been for someone bumping the bed as he dropped to the floor. That jostled the tanks just enough. The shell ripped through the box springs, but didn't hit a tank.

I lunged for the queen-size mattress. I could feel the stitches in my shoulder ripping apart as I lifted as fast and hard as I could.

The tanks went flying, clanking onto the hardwood floor, rolling in every direction.

"Everybody out!" I yelled. "Now!"

The next shot echoed amid the mad dash from the bedroom, but there was no blast. She hadn't hit one of the rolling tanks.

The entrance to the hallway was like a narrow, unforgiving funnel as we tried to clear the living room outside the bedroom. Feet scrambling, arms flailing, everyone was literally running for their lives.

I was last in line, Sarah right in front of me. If we could just make it out of the apartment before the next shot, then maybe, just maybe, we might be okay.

KABOOM!

Chapter 98

THE FORCE OF the explosion knocked me flat against the floorboards, and a fireball swept over my back. The heat was so intense I could feel my shirt melt into my skin.

It hurt so much I wanted to scream, but I was too busy being thankful. A blast like that? The only way I wouldn't be in pain was if I were dead.

"God, that hurt," moaned Sarah.

More good news. She was alive, too. A little better off than me.

I wish I could say it was my intent to shield her. I was thrown right into her and gravity did the rest. She was faceup and I was looking down at her. Our noses were practically touching.

"You okay?" I whispered.

"Think so. You?"

"A little toasty on the back. I'll live."

She didn't say anything more. She didn't have to. I could see it in her eyes. It was really important to her that I was okay.

Off in the distance I could already hear sirens. The curtains in the living room were on fire. So were the couch and rug. There was a chance at least one of those propane tanks hadn't exploded.

Yet.

"C'mon," said Harris. "We've got to get out of here."

The street outside Macintyre's building was chaos central. Fire trucks and more police cruisers were honking their way through traffic, swirling lights everywhere.

Tenants and neighbors spilled out to the sidewalk en masse, looking bewildered and scared. I glanced around, finally catching my breath. *Breathing.* An old woman in a red robe was clutching rosary beads and saying a prayer. Next to her was a young Hispanic mother holding her baby boy.

Sarah was ripping through a description of Cole, sending off a dozen officers to push the perimeter in every direction. The rest followed us as we searched the buildings behind Macintyre's, from basements to rooftops.

Meanwhile, Harris was on his radio, getting officers out to the surrounding subways.

"Over here!" I yelled on the very first rooftop we reached. On the tar paper next to the ledge overlooking Macintyre's apartment, propped up by an attached bipod, was an FN SPR, one of the sniper rifles I knew by name because it was used by the Bureau's Hostage Rescue Team.

"An SPR," said Sarah as soon as she laid her eyes on it. "Talk about irony."

She was right. SPR stood for "special police rifle." It sat there, along with a few scattered casings, taunting us.

"Every door!" shouted Harris. "We knock on every door!"

We were funneling again, this time off the roof and down the stairs, when Harris's radio crackled. Calling in was an officer on the street. He'd found a witness. Or, rather, the witness had found him.

It was a man who lived on the top floor of

a taller building behind Macintyre's. Looking down, he had a perfect view of Martha Cole after the explosion.

"What did he see?" asked Harris.

The officer paused, the radio falling silent.

"You're not going to believe this," he said finally.

Chapter 99

MY FIRST CYNICAL thought was, You wanna bet?

After everything I'd seen over the years—let alone over the past few days—was there really anything out there I couldn't believe, anything left that could still surprise me?

But I had to admit, this sort of did.

Same for Harris. "Say again," he said into his radio.

We listened for a second time, the officer accenting every word. Especially the last ones. "The witness claims he saw a woman running across the roof after the explosion," he said. "She was wearing a wedding dress."

Harris didn't skip a beat. Nor was he taking anything for granted. He was about to broadcast this to every cop in the area code and beyond. The details mattered.

"The wedding dress," he said. "The color— was it white?"

"Yeah," the officer came back with a touch of New York sarcasm. "The bride wore white."

What an image. The more I tried to picture it, the more everything else seemed to click. The whole picture.

"Christ, she was telling the truth, wasn't she? She just flipped it around," I said.

"What do you mean?" asked Harris.

"Martha Cole didn't break off the engagement, Macintyre did," said Sarah, right in step with me. "It's her motive, not his."

Sarah reached for her cell.

"What are you doing?" I asked.

"All dressed up and nowhere to go? I doubt it," she said.

I'd been around Sarah long enough now to know she was following a hunch. It was the look on her face, the way she bit her lower lip. Problem was, I wasn't following along with her.

Until she was done dialing.

"Emily LaSalle, please," she said. "Tell her it's Agent Brubaker and it's urgent."

Chapter 100

IT TOOK LASALLE only a few strokes on the keyboard in her *New York Times* office to come up with what we needed. The woman's files were as meticulously kept as everything else about her.

Sarah put her on speakerphone just in time for all of us to hear.

"Got it," LaSalle announced.

It was the Vows article that never was. The marriage of Martha Cole to Robert Macintyre.

The bulk of the file was the submission Cole had originally made to the wedding section of the paper. The rest were notes made by one of LaSalle's editors, whose job it was to verify the information. Fact-checking was critical, we'd learned, whether to catch actual couples in the act of embellishing their bona fides or to identify the numerous bogus announcements routinely submitted by pranksters—e.g., the wedding of Ben Dover to Ivana Humpalot.

"What am I looking for?" asked LaSalle.

"Only one thing," said Sarah. "Does it say where Cole and Macintyre were planning to get married?"

"You mean the town?"

"No. The actual church."

"Let me check."

Sarah bit her lower lip again in full hunch mode while I watched Harris and the other officers exchange more looks, as if to say, *Wow—could this get any more twisted than it already is?*

My money was on yes.

LaSalle quickly scanned the file on Cole and Macintyre, reading aloud certain bits and pieces as if they were bullets in a PowerPoint presentation.

"Brooklyn residents...met in the army... both sergeants..."

Harris blinked. "Wait: they were *both* in the army?"

"Figures," I muttered.

Learning how to shoot a sniper rifle with deadly accuracy wasn't exactly something you could do in a night course at the New School. But where the hell did Cole learn how to lie so effectively? I would've been more embarrassed over being duped if she hadn't been so damn good at it.

"Okay, here we go," said LaSalle. "It says here it was supposed to be at Saint Alexander's in Brooklyn."

"Shit," muttered Harris. "Do you think—"

"Emily, is there an address?" asked Sarah.

"No, just the name."

"I know where that church is," came a voice.

I turned to see one of the cops stepping forward. He had a face that all but screamed rookie.

"Is it close by?" I asked.

"Maybe twenty blocks," he said. "My sister belongs there."

Suddenly, our best-case scenario was potentially our worst. If Sarah's hunch was right, and that's where Cole was heading…what was she planning to do?

Only thing for sure was that we needed

to warn whoever might be at the church. I hoped it was no one.

So much for hoping.

Again, Harris's radio crackled. So, too, did every other radio in the group. A chorus of quick static followed by the voice of a female dispatcher.

It was a 417, she announced. A person with a gun. "Possible hostage situation," she tacked on.

By the time she gave the address, Sarah and I and everyone else were already half-way out the building, racing to every parked patrol car.

Chapter 101

A DOZEN OR more police cruisers doing sixty with sirens blaring have a funny way of unclogging traffic. Harris drove; Sarah and I held on. We covered the twenty blocks in a couple of minutes flat.

At first glance, the scene outside Saint Alexander's was the epitome of irony. It looked like a wedding, of all things—or the end of one, at least. A gathering of well-wishers was milling about on the steps of the church as if at any second the bride and groom would come marching out through the doors, arm in arm.

"Jesus, we've got to clear everyone out of

431

here," I said as Harris skidded to a stop along the curb. We all knew what happened to the last building Cole had set her sights on.

The people outside were an easy fix: that was simple crowd control. It was the ones inside the church who were the real problem. The words of the dispatcher were still fresh in my head. *Possible hostage situation.*

I stepped out of Harris's unmarked Explorer, nearly getting myself run over by another arriving patrol car. They were everywhere now, coming in droves.

Every cop converged on the sidewalk while Harris, Sarah, and I started up the steps of the church. I was about to shout to get the crowd's attention when a young priest with close-cropped red hair and freckles stepped forward.

"Are you one of the FBI agents?" he asked me.

Strange first question. How did he know that?

"Yes. I'm Agent O'Hara."

"Oh, good," he said. "Thank God you're here."

"Were you inside?" I asked the priest.

"We all were, but she let us go," he answered. He immediately corrected himself. "Almost all of us."

"Who's still inside?"

"Another priest," he said. "Father Reese."

"Anyone else?"

"No, that's it. We were having choir practice when the woman in the wedding dress came storming in. I thought maybe it was some kind of joke at first. Then I saw the gun."

"A handgun or something bigger?" asked Sarah.

"A handgun," he said. "She was carrying something else, too. It looked like a big green soda bottle. But no label."

Ten to one it wasn't 7UP.

"What did she say?" Sarah asked.

"That everyone could leave, except for one person," he turned to Sarah and said. "Father Reese insisted he be the one."

"Was there anything else?"

He nodded. "Yes. A message."

"For whom?" I asked.

"You," he said. "And Agent Brubaker." He turned to Sarah. "I assume that's—"

"That's me," said Sarah.

"Oh, good," he said. "You're both here. She wants to talk to you—both of you."

Chapter 102

"DON'T DO IT," said Harris. "Don't go inside. That's a terrible idea." He pointed to the two alleyways on either side of Saint Alexander's, which separated it from the adjoining brownstones. "There's got to be a couple of other ways to get in there without her knowing. We can have a SWAT team here in less than ten minutes."

"What if we don't have ten minutes?" said Sarah. "I don't think we do."

"She's already murdered over a dozen people and is now wearing a wedding dress, waving a gun around," I said.

That all but put an end to Harris trying to

talk me out of it. "What about you?" I asked Sarah. "Are you in?"

She removed her Glock from her holster and wedged it into her slacks behind her back.

"At least let's check the perimeter for other ways in," said Harris, resigned. "Just in case."

Two teams of four dispersed right and left around the church. In less than a minute we heard back from both.

"Side door, unlocked," whispered one cop through Harris's radio.

"Basement door, down a set of stairs," whispered another. "Also unlocked."

Harris looked at me again. "Change your mind?"

"Sorry."

Harris radioed back to both teams. I couldn't help noticing that his whisper was one part quiet and three parts pissed off.

"Stay put," he told them. "Go in when you hear shots."

He turned around, barking at the remaining cops to push the crowd of onlookers farther back. Down the block I could see the first news van arrive. Within minutes there'd be a lot more.

"You ready?" asked Sarah.

I nodded.

"For the record, the two of you are nuts," said Harris.

"Hey, it could be worse," I said.

"How so?" he asked.

"She could've asked for all three of us."

I gave him a slap on the arm and climbed the last remaining steps up to the church with Sarah. We stopped in front of the doors.

"Are you religious?" I asked.

"Lutheran," she answered. "What about you?"

"Lapsed Catholic. I was an altar boy growing up, though," I said. "That's got to count for something, right?"

We both drew our guns.

"Let's go find out," she said.

Chapter 103

I TOOK ONE side; Sarah took the other. We had become a good team in a very short time, but this seemed like an impossible test.

With our backs pressed against the faded red brick facade of Saint Alexander's, we each reached over and grabbed one of the double front doors, pulling them back slowly.

The initial fear I had came and went. Martha Cole wasn't shooting on first movement.

After a few seconds, Sarah called out to the killer. "Martha, are you in there?"

The crowd noise down on the street made it hard to hear, but I was pretty sure there was no response. Sarah tried again, louder this time.

"Martha, it's Agent Brubaker and Agent O'Hara," she said. "Can we come inside?"

Cole answered this time, her voice echoing out to us. She was deep inside the church. "It better be just the two of you," she warned.

"It is, Martha," Sarah yelled back. "I give you my word."

She didn't ask us to come in unarmed—not that we were about to comply with such a request. Or so I thought.

"What the hell are you doing?" I asked Sarah, who was tucking away her gun.

"She trusts me," she said. "I have to trust her back."

"That's not the same girl who was crying on your shoulder this morning," I said. "That was an act."

"We'll see. Trust me a little on this."

"Okay, but we go in at the same time," I said.

"Nah. Ladies first."

Before I could say or do anything else, Sarah stepped out from behind the door, her hands raised in the air. If there's a fine line between brave and stupid, Sarah had bridged it.

She now had dual passports. I was so mad I could shoot her—if Martha Cole didn't do it first.

She didn't.

I stepped out, joining Sarah at the entrance to the church. Looking all the way down the aisle, I could see Cole standing at the altar, her arm outstretched to the side. She had her gun pressed directly against Father Reese's head.

Slowly, very slowly, we walked toward them.

"That's far enough!" shouted Cole.

Sarah and I stopped. We were about twenty pews back from the altar. Definitely in range, but not an easy shot.

"Martha, just let us get a little closer so we don't have to shout to one another," said Sarah. "The echo in here makes it very hard to talk. I want to hear what you have to say."

Cole laughed. "Who said we were talking?"

"Why are we in here, then?" asked Sarah. "What do you want from us?"

"Soon enough," she said. "Now have a seat."

There was no point pressing the issue. I

took a step to my right and was about to slide into the pew.

"NO!" Cole screamed. "NO, NO, NO!"

I wasn't sure what I'd done wrong, but whatever it was I wasn't going to keep doing it. I froze right where I was, didn't move a muscle.

Sarah, who still hadn't made a move to sit, raised her palms. "Whoa, whoa!" she said. "Martha, what's wrong?"

"That's the *groom's* side," said Cole angrily. "You need to sit on the left...the bride's side. I'm the one who invited you."

Oh. As in, *Oh, shit, this doesn't bode well.*

Chapter 104

SARAH AND I slid into the pew to our immediate left. The *bride's* side. The upside was that we could take out our guns without Cole being able to see us, something we both did instinctively.

The downside was that we were sitting. Sitting ducks, I was afraid. Still, I liked having a gun in my hand.

"Martha, we've done everything you've asked so far," said Sarah. "We came in, we sat down where you wanted us to. Now I have to ask you to do one thing for us. You need to let Father Reese go."

Cole smirked. "Are you left-handed or right-handed, Agent Brubaker?"

"Why do you ask?" said Sarah.

"Because I'm wondering which side of your seat would I find your gun sitting on right now."

"You can come here and take a look for yourself. You won't see a gun," Sarah lied. "Not from Agent O'Hara, either."

I was listening to this exchange, but I was also watching. For the first time, I was able to take a good look at Martha Cole in her white wedding dress, with its square-cut neckline and lace sleeves down to her elbow.

Brand new, the dress was surely pretty. Now it was dirty, scuffed, and soaked with sweat. In fact, Cole looked to be drenched from head to toe. Even her hair looked as if she'd just stepped out of the shower.

What a contrast the priest was. Sure, he hadn't run twenty blocks swathed in taffeta on a hot June afternoon, but with a gun to his head you'd think he'd be sweating all the same. Instead, he appeared to be absolutely calm. At peace.

In fact, I almost got the sense he knew something that I didn't. Of course, that was the feeling I always got with priests, but this was different. More earthbound.

Either way, it was probably a good thing, because Martha Cole had no intention of setting him free. Not yet at least. I hoped she wasn't planning on setting his soul free.

"Do you know what Robbie told me when he proposed?" she asked. "He said that the two of us would be together for the rest of our lives. *Forever and ever*. He was very convincing."

"Martha, I understand how upset you are," said Sarah. "But—"

Cole cut her off as fast as a New York taxi. "He broke my heart, destroyed it," she said. Then she flashed a sick smile. "That's why I put a knife through his."

Sarah shook her head, her voice growing stronger. "The killing has to stop, Martha."

But she wasn't listening.

"I deserved what those other couples had. I *deserved it!*" she screamed.

I could practically read Sarah's mind. *Stay calm, keep the dialogue going, say her name as often as possible to keep her trust.*

"I'm sure you did, Martha, but those couples didn't deserve to die," said Sarah. "They didn't do anything to hurt you."

"We all die, Agent Brubaker. I saw it every day in the war. The only variable is timing."

"But you don't get to decide that, Martha. You don't get to play God."

"But I did, didn't I?"

There was something in the way she said it, the emphatic use of the past tense. The sense of finality.

My mind started racing. So many thoughts, questions, unknowns.

Two in particular.

Where was that strange green bottle the young priest outside had mentioned to us? And what was in it?

I looked up at the large gold cross looming over the altar. It suddenly occurred to me. This wasn't going to be a long, drawn-out hostage situation. In fact, it wasn't a hostage situation at all.

My eyes shot back down to Cole. I stared at her again, from head to toe. She was drenched, all right, only it wasn't sweat, was it?

Oh, Jesus, Jesus…

I could smell it now, the odor finally traveling the distance from the altar to our pew. Isopropanol. Rubbing alcohol.

"Good-bye," she said.

I jumped up from the pew as Martha dropped the gun, revealing a small lighter in her other hand. So quick, so fast, she flicked a thumb.

"No!" I yelled. "You don't have to do this! You don't!"

That's when Martha Cole spoke her last words—the two words there at the altar that she never got to say.

"I do."

There was nothing we could do. Cole pushed Father Reese away and brought the lighter to her dress.

She went up in flames.

Chapter 105

WHY WOULD SOMEONE do what she'd done? That's usually the first question in the wake of a person's suicide. But Martha Cole had told us everything we wanted to know about her motives. Not only why she took her own life but also why she took the lives of people she'd never even met.

It was those lives, especially those of the three newlywed couples, that left us with the real unanswered question. *How? How the hell did she do it?* Slipping in and out of the grounds of the Governor's Club in Turks and Caicos to trap and then poison Ethan and Abigail Breslow in their sauna? Evading security at Kennedy Airport to poison Scott and Annabelle Pierce before their flight to Italy?

And finally, as if bored with poisons, or looking to show the breadth of her expertise, rigging a bomb aboard the boat that Parker and Samantha Keller had docked in Bermuda?

The answers to all my questions came soon enough. Or at least I got the sort of information that makes you nod your head and go, "Well, that might explain it."

Within an hour of Martha Cole's death, her military file had made its way to Dan Driesen, who e-mailed the pertinent information along to us.

"Here," said Sarah, handing her phone over to me once she'd read the message.

We'd just wrapped up our "official" statements to Detective Harris as well as to two detectives from the nearest Brooklyn precinct.

I'd even made a call to Warner Breslow, who was in London on business. I told him the news, bittersweet as it was. The murders of his son and new daughter-in-law were more senseless than he could've imagined. Would knowing who did it bring him any closure, any sense of justice? For a man like Breslow, I was afraid the answer was no.

"We'll talk again when I get back," he told me. "You did a fine job, John. Thank you."

Reading Driesen's e-mail, I couldn't help thinking about all those naysayers and conspiracy buffs who could never quite fathom how Lee Harvey Oswald managed to fire three shots from a bolt-action rifle in roughly eight seconds. *No way—that's too fast! There had to be a second shooter!* Of course, what the conspiracy theorists always seemed to forget is that Oswald wasn't some self-taught dope who was practicing on tin cans in his backyard. Oswald had received the very best training in the world—on Uncle Sam's dime, no less. In the U.S. Marine Corps.

Martha Cole had been a sergeant in the army, having received training in a wide range of disciplines, including weaponry, explosives, reconnaissance, and sabotage. She was smart, athletically gifted, and an adrenaline junkie. This was according to her psych evaluation.

A hundred times out of a hundred, such a profile makes for an excellent soldier. And during her tour in Afghanistan, that's exactly what she was. The problem began when she returned home. The unofficial term is *redlining*. Like a Ferrari stuck in fifth gear, she was unable to downshift back into the mundanity of civilian life. New York may be the city that never sleeps, but it was no match for the 24-7 danger of Afghanistan and the Taliban forces.

Ultimately, her relationship with Robert Macintyre paid the price. After that, her entire life exploded into rage and revenge.

So now we had the why as well as the how. The only question left was, what? As in, *What now?*

Cole was gone, but somewhere out there Ned Sinclair was still plotting my death. Tomorrow I'd worry about him. Tonight, I was too tired, my brain too fried.

Sarah was shaking hands with Harris, saying thanks and good-bye. The second he walked off, I made my way over to her. She smiled. I smiled back. Then I leaned over and whispered in her ear.

She thought it over for a grand total of one split second.

"Absolutely," she answered.

Chapter 106

JESUS, WHAT THE hell happened to you two?

The guy pouring us the shots of tequila never came right out and said it. Nor did any of the other patrons at the bar, who couldn't help staring. Our clothes were ripped and singed, our faces and hands filthy. Basically we looked as if we'd been dragged through hell and back.

It's a good thing we didn't give a damn.

And after about a half dozen more tequila shots, we *really* didn't give a damn.

Sarah and I had grabbed the last two stools at the end of the bar in what was basically the first place we could find near Saint Alexander's that served alcohol. It was a small restaurant called Deuces and Eights, one of those "local joints" with dinner specials written on a blackboard and a bunch of softball-league trophies on display.

"Wow," I said, watching Sarah throw back yet another shot with ease. "I had no idea."

"About what?" she asked, smacking her lips, then wiping her mouth.

"That you could drink like that. You're not even Irish."

She laughed. "Yeah, I know, and I'm a *girl*, too."

"Not like any I know."

"Careful, O'Hara," she said. "That sounded dangerously close to being a compliment."

"Must be the tequila talking."

"In that case, it's time for another."

She waved to the bartender, who was loading the fridge underneath the cash register with more beers, a brown-and-green assortment of Budweisers and Rolling Rocks.

"Are you sure?" I asked.

She folded her arms. "Did you or did you not whisper in my ear that we should both get drunk?"

I scratched my head. "Sounds vaguely familiar. I think I remember something like that."

"Good. Then stop being such a pansy. Drink or give up your seat to someone who will."

"Okay, now you're asking for it."

The bartender arrived, a bottle of Patrón already in hand. He'd seen this movie before. "Let me guess," he said. "Another round?"

I shook my head no. "Make it two rounds," I said. "We had a very, very tough couple of days at work."

While the guy chuckled and poured, I reached into my wallet. I can't say what happened next was the plan all along, but, as with the jack of diamonds in a game of hearts, I knew I had a pretty good card to play.

"What's that?" she asked. "Are you paying the bill?"

"It's not a credit card."

"It sure looks like it," she said, taking it from me. She stared at it—front and back. "There's nothing on it."

She was right: there wasn't. It was black, polished to a blinding shine, and had the thickness of a poker chip. But, as Sarah said, there was nothing on it. Just *inside* it, I presumed.

"Okay, I give up. What's it for?" she asked.

"It's what it does."

"Which is what? What does it do?"

I swiped it back from her. "Only one way to find out," I said.

With that—bang, bang—I downed the two shots of tequila in front of me. I put the card back in my wallet and took out some cash.

Now I was paying the bill.

"Keep the change," I told the bartender, sliding off the back of my stool.

"Wait—where are you going?" Sarah asked.

I was already halfway toward the door and feeling no pain. "The same place you are," I said.

Chapter 107

WE GRABBED A cab back into Manhattan, straight to the Upper East Side. To be precise, 63rd Street and Fifth Avenue. Before the doorman even opened the door for us, Sarah guessed it.

"Breslow?" she asked.

"Your analytical skills are... very good."

As soon as we were in the elevator I told her about Breslow's lawyer—one of his many lawyers, undoubtedly—who had given me the envelope. The note inside read simply, *If you ever need a place to stay...*

"It also listed the addresses," I said.

She blinked a few times in disbelief. "*Addresses? As in plural?*"

"New York, Chicago, L.A., and Dallas. There were about a dozen more overseas. Paris, London, Rome."

"And that card opens them all?"

"Supposedly." I'd yet to use it, a fact that left Sarah even more dumbfounded as the elevator opened onto a small foyer on the penthouse level. I explained that I hadn't needed to stay in Manhattan since Breslow hired me. Or Paris, for that matter.

"Weren't you at least curious?" she asked.

"Maybe I was. But then some crazy female FBI agent showed up at my house one morning. I sort of forgot about it," I said. "Until now."

There was no need to guess which door led to the apartment. There was only one.

"Wait," whispered Sarah.

I was about to wave the card over a little box next to the door. "What is it?" I asked.

"What if someone's in there?"

"Like who?"

"Like I don't know," she said. "Breslow?"

"The same Breslow I just spoke to in London?"

"Okay, someone else. Another person who works for him. Anyone."

"You're right," I said with a straight face. "We should really turn around and head to the Bureau Hotel, which has free HBO."

"Okay, okay," she said.

Again I was about to open the door. Again she stopped me.

"Wait!" she said. "We can't do this."

"He gave me the card, Sarah. Really, it's okay."

"No, I mean *we* can't do this."

"Do what?"

"What I think we're about to do."

"Which is what?" I asked, playing dumb. Better she say it than me. Sure enough...

"Have...sex," she said.

"Who said anything about sex?"

"Well, I just did. You're a guy and we've been drinking."

"Hey, that's sexist!"

"You're right. Sorry."

I smiled. "Does that mean we're going to have sex now?"

That got me a big eye roll and a solid right hook to my good shoulder. She leaned forward. "You know what this is, don't you?"

"A comedy routine? Not a bad one, either."

"It's called near-death attraction," she said.

"It's what happens when two people face a dangerous situation together and survive."

"You left out the tequila."

"That just greases the wheels."

"I love it when you talk dirty."

She punched me again. My good shoulder was no longer so good. "I'm just saying we shouldn't confuse our working together with *being* together," she said.

"You know what? You're right. That would really complicate things," I said as if coming to an epiphany. "We actually should go. We shouldn't go inside and have maybe the greatest time of our lives."

She stared at me before breaking into her goofy laugh. "Okay, despite the fact that was the weakest and most lame-ass attempt at reverse psychology I've ever heard, I'm going to propose something."

"Do we have to get married again?"

As soon as I said it I immediately covered up my shoulder. Thankfully, she spared me.

"No. This is what I propose," she said. "You should kiss me."

"I should?"

"Yes. If it feels right, we go inside. If not, we leave. And never talk about this ever again."

"Wow. That's a lot of pressure on one kiss," I said. "Especially for a guy who's out of practice."

"Already you're making excuses?"

"No. Just trying to negotiate better terms."

She stepped toward me. We were inches apart, her lips right there. She was toying with me and I was loving it, actually.

"Take it or leave it, O'Hara," she said. "Kiss me, you fool."

Chapter 108

I THOUGHT THE ringing in my head the next morning was maybe a nasty little hangover saying hello. Instead it turned out to be Sarah's phone, which she had placed by the bed. It seems that Dan Driesen was calling at the crack of dawn.

With one eye open, I looked over from my pillow to see Sarah leaning up against the headboard, the sheet barely covering her body. She didn't need to put her index finger over her lips as she did, but I couldn't blame her for making sure I had no intention of talking, let alone breathing too loudly.

As for my belting out a crackerjack rendition of "Danny Boy," I was assuming that was off the table as well.

Sarah listened intently. I couldn't hear what Driesen was telling her, but it became very clear when she sighed heavily and uttered only one word.

"Where?" she asked.

Ned Sinclair had killed again.

What balls. Or maybe he just hadn't seen a TV or newspaper since his name and picture were released to the world. Maybe he was simply going about his business like a racehorse wearing blinders. No outside distractions. No awareness or fear of anyone chasing after him. Nothing but the task at hand: my murder.

Sarah peppered Driesen with questions, the first being whether there was any note, any message, any *any*thing found on Sinclair's latest John O'Hara victim. Also, were there any witnesses? Any new leads at all?

Again, I didn't need to hear Driesen to know the answers. The way Sarah frowned spoke for itself. There was no note or message found, no witnesses or new leads. The investigation, so to speak, was clueless.

Which made the next part of the conversation that much harder for Sarah.

"You've got to let me go there," she implored Driesen.

Never mind exactly where "there" was on the map. I'd learn the hometown of the latest victim soon enough.

The point was, it didn't matter if this John O'Hara was from Spokane or Skokie, Saint Louis or Saint Paul—Sarah wasn't going there. I knew it, and deep down she knew it, too. She could argue all she wanted, but Driesen wasn't about to change his mind any more than Ned Sinclair was about to forget what Sarah looked like.

A minute later, after exhausting every possible angle she could think of, she finally waved the white flag.

"Let me know how it goes," she said before hanging up.

I was finally free to open my mouth, but I knew better. She needed to cool down. Maybe a half minute of silence came and went before she turned to me.

"Casper, Wyoming," she said. "He was found about three hours ago."

"Same caliber?"

"Yep. One to the head, one to the heart."

"Driesen's going there?"

"Mainly to address the media. It'll be a world-class zoo," she said. "All the more reason why it would be safe for me to go."

"So what happens now?" I asked.

"I'm supposed to take a vacation," she said. "Two weeks, mandatory."

"And me?"

But I was already pretty sure of the answer. Sarah's look confirmed it.

"Gee, I wonder what's on HBO tonight?" I said.

At least that got a half smile out of her. "Of course, that's where Driesen already thinks you are," she replied.

I surveyed the two of us naked between the sheets. "Good thing he's not a Skype or FaceTime kind of guy."

She smiled again, but I could tell her head was somewhere else.

"What is it?" I asked.

"Something that Driesen mentioned," she said. "In fact, it's something that's always bothered me about this case."

Chapter 109

I LEANED ON my side, waiting for Sarah to explain what she had on her mind. Only she didn't.

Instead, she slid out of bed and slipped on one of the two cashmere robes folded perfectly on top of a nearby chaise. *Nice touch, Breslow. Quite the life you must lead.*

"Where are you going?" I asked.

"To find a map," she said.

A map? Okay, fine.

As she walked out of the bedroom, I threw on the other robe. I'd catch up to her soon enough. First, I desperately needed to look for something else. Aspirin.

Breslow had that covered as well. In a drawer between the double vanities in the bathroom was an economy-size bottle of Bayer. I washed two down with a handful of water, then made the mistake of catching a glimpse of myself in the mirror.

I walked out of the bedroom, looking at the rest of Breslow's apartment in the daylight for the first time. In many ways, it was what I expected: large, tastefully furnished, with a gorgeous view of Central Park.

Still, I couldn't help noticing a sort of subtext, as if Breslow had held back a bit with the wow factor in order to say, *If you think this place is nice, you should see where I actually live.*

I had, of course. Maybe that's why I got the vibe.

"Sarah, where are you?" I called out.

"In here," she said from the library off the living room.

She was standing behind a mahogany desk, staring down at a large open book she'd pulled from the shelves. It was a world atlas. She'd found her map.

"Well, I'm pretty sure you're not planning your vacation," I said.

I was more right than I knew. In fact, at that moment, I was more right than we *both* knew.

Sarah was looking at a map of the United States, finding all the locations where Ned Sinclair had killed. She'd already circled the towns with a felt-tip pen.

"Sorry," she said as I reached the desk. "Couldn't help myself. Think Breslow will forgive me?"

I looked around at what must have been a thousand books on the shelves. "I'm guessing no one's going to notice," I said. "So tell me: what's the problem? What's bothering you?"

"I can't figure out why Sinclair keeps skipping over John O'Haras who are closer to his last murder," she said. "That means there has to be something else. Another pattern."

"Was that the case with the latest one, in Casper?"

"Yeah. Driesen had already checked. He told me there were at least four O'Haras who were closer to his last victim," she said. "Why does Sinclair travel hundreds of miles more than he has to? Just to throw us off?"

"Maybe he scouts those closer O'Haras and determines he can't isolate them, that it's too risky," I said.

"So he moves on down the line?"

"That would easily explain it."

"I know," she said. "That's the part that bothers me, John. It's *too* easy. There's something we're not seeing, a pattern inside the pattern."

"But that's all he's shown us so far. One pattern after another," I said. "All the victims have the same name? Pattern. He kills moving from west to east? Pattern. He leaves behind a clue with each victim? Pattern."

Sarah's eyes immediately went wide. She stared back down at the map.

"Oh, my God!" she said. "That's it!"

"What is?"

She reached for the felt-tip on the desk. "The forest for the trees," she said. "The whole reason he's doing it in this particular way."

"Because he wants to kill me."

"Yeah. But why?"

"It's what you first told me, how you put it all together," I said. "He blames me for his sister's death."

"Exactly. And every clue he left behind on the victims, they were like riddles, right? They all had the same answer."

My jaw dropped as Sarah jabbed the felt-tip pen smack-dab on Los Angeles, site of Eagle Mountain Psychiatric Hospital and Ned's first victim, Ace, a.k.a. nurse John O'Hara. From there, she connected the dots, the locations of his next three victims.

Winnemucca, Nevada. Down to Candle Lake, New Mexico. Back up to Park City, Utah.

It was the letter *N*.

Ned Sinclair was spelling out *Nora*.

Chapter 110

SARAH ALMOST CHANGED her mind during the cab ride out to LaGuardia. She almost changed it again while we were waiting to board the plane.

"I can't believe you talked me into this," she said at thirty-five thousand feet, somewhere over Pennsylvania.

"You've got nothing to worry about," I said. "You can always tell Driesen you were taking your vacation."

"To Birdwood, Nebraska?"

Okay, maybe not. But despite what Birdwood lacked in tourist appeal, the two of us couldn't get there fast enough. Not only was it home to the only John O'Hara within a hundred miles, but on the heels of Candle Lake, New Mexico, and Casper, Wyoming, it was also in a perfect spot to round out the *O* in Nora.

Question was, had Ned Sinclair gotten there faster than we would? Apparently not.

"So how do you propose we work this?" asked Burt Melvin.

He was Birdwood's chief of police and the recipient of the one phone call we made in advance of our trip. After renting a Jeep Grand Cherokee at North Platte Regional Airport, we made the ten-mile drive to Birdwood and met him at his station.

As soon as Melvin had heard the news of the latest victim in Casper, he assigned around-the-clock protection to Hara, as he called him. Birdwood's John O'Hara was Melvin's longtime friend and the owner of the town's hardware store. He was also a Vietnam vet and an avid hunter, which might explain why the guy was adamant about not fleeing his home to hide from some, quote, "deranged bastard looking to meet his maker."

"Where do you have your guys?" Sarah asked Melvin.

"One outside the front of his house, one inside covering the only other way in—a sliding glass door to a patio," he said.

"The one stationed out front, is he in a patrol car or an unmarked?" asked Sarah.

"Patrol car," he answered. "Why?"

I knew why. I also knew Sarah wanted to tread very carefully with her answer. We couldn't come blowing into town, asking an officer to be a guinea pig.

"We can't catch this killer by scaring him away," she said.

Melvin nodded, scratching the edge of his thick mustache. He sort of looked like the great catcher and former captain of the Yankees Thurman Munson.

"What are you suggesting?" he asked warily.

"That Agent O'Hara and I take the front in an unmarked car, and you keep one of your guys inside, like you've been doing."

He chuckled, only to immediately apologize. "I'm sorry," he said, turning to me. "I still can't get over the fact that your name is also John O'Hara. Kinda like running into a tornado instead of away from it, no?"

If you only knew, my friend. If you only knew.

Melvin had no qualms about Sarah's suggestion, if for no other reason than it meant he now had to dedicate only one of his men to this stakeout instead of two. "You're saving me a nice chunk of overtime pay from a budget that's already stretched too thin," he said. He smiled. "How long can you stay in town?"

"As long as it takes," said Sarah.

But we both knew that wasn't true. You can only go AWOL from the Bureau for so long. We'd bought ourselves twenty-four hours—thirty-six tops.

One way or the other we were headed for some kind of reckoning.

Chapter 111

"IF YOU NEED me I'll be in the master bedroom," I said jokingly, climbing into the back of our rented Grand Cherokee. With the rear seat down and a blanket, it actually wasn't so bad compared to some of the fleabag motels I'd stayed in when I was undercover with the NYPD.

I glanced at my watch. Twenty-three hours and counting.

We remained parked diagonally across the street from John O'Hara's house on Stillwater Lane. They sure got the "still" part right. Not only had there been no sign of Ned Sinclair, there was basically no sign of anyone.

Except for real-estate agents, that is. Their signs were everywhere. Half the homes on the block, all ranch-style, all covered in gray, white, or brown shingles, were for sale. Suffice it to say Stillwater Lane had more than its fair share of mortgages in trouble.

All in all, it was a pretty depressing sight, although it did solve a problem for us. Thanks to a real-estate agent that Chief Melvin knew, Sarah and I were able to use a vacant house down the street for bathroom trips and to wash up.

But the sleeping we did in the Jeep. That was a no-brainer. If Ned Sinclair planned on making an appearance, we needed to be close. Real close.

"Try not to snore, okay?" retorted Sarah from behind the wheel.

She'd been busting my chops about the four hours of sleep we took turns getting during the night not being enough for me. I couldn't help it, though. I was beat.

I stretched out in the back. The Birdwood cop with the 8:00 p.m. to 2:00 a.m. shift inside the house was due in a half hour. He was bringing our dinner, too. A little catnap for me beforehand was just what the doctor ordered.

Unfortunately, I'd barely closed my eyes when I heard Sarah mutter under her breath, "He's early."

I sat up, looking out the side window to see a patrol car pull into O'Hara's driveway.

Out stepped Officer Lohman. I remembered his name because he'd brought us Chinese takeout the night before and I had the pork lo mein.

Note to self: never order the pork lo mein in Birdwood, Nebraska.

"Shit, where's our pizza?" I said, seeing that he was empty-handed. Not only was he early, he'd forgotten our large pepperoni-and-mushroom. Had he no shame?

Apparently he had no excuse, either. Sarah and I waited for him to come over to us and offer up some type of explanation. At the very least he needed to confirm what frequency we'd be using on our radios during his shift.

But he was heading straight for O'Hara's house. Immediately, Sarah stepped out of the Jeep. "I'll see what's up," she said.

I watched as she crossed the street, calling

out Lohman's name. When he turned around he looked startled, as if Sarah had surprised him.

But that made no sense; he knew we were there.

Something wasn't right.

Chapter 112

IT HAPPENED SO fast, and yet in some strange and sickening way I felt as if I were watching it in slow motion. Probably because there was nothing I could do to save her.

Halfway between the Jeep and Officer Lohman, Sarah made a desperate grab for her gun. Desperate because Lohman, inexplicably, had already reached for his.

He got off one shot, the blood instantly exploding out of Sarah's shoulder as she fell backward. His second shot got her in the other arm, spinning her around as she hit the pavement face-first.

I should've gone out the back door of the

Jeep, away from his line of fire. I was no good to her if I went down, too. But the adrenaline, the anger, the sheer frustration of watching her get blindsided had me bursting out into the street, running straight at him at full speed.

He got off one shot as I raised my gun, the bullet buzzing so close to my ear I could feel the breeze.

Now it's my turn, asshole.

He knew it, too. With the first squeeze of my trigger he was already on the run, diving behind the grille of his stolen patrol car. When he turned to fire back at me, I unloaded the rest of my clip so fast he dropped his gun trying to duck.

"Here," said Sarah, her voice straining as I knelt down in front of her. She lifted her arm just enough to hand me her gun. "Get him."

But I couldn't even see him. And there was no way I would leave her side.

Shielding her as best as I could, I waited for his next move.

Instead it was someone else's.

The front door of the house swung open. It was the cop guarding O'Hara from the inside.

His gun was drawn and he was confused as hell.

Why is the FBI agent firing at my fellow officer?

Only it wasn't one of his fellow officers.

Even in the uniform, even with the hat pulled down over his eyes, even in the shadows of the setting sun, even with my having seen only an outdated picture of him—I knew.

"It's him!" I yelled. "That's Sinclair!"

I couldn't blame the cop for freezing for a split second, his mind piecing everything together, including the grim prospects for the real Officer Lohman. You just don't steal an armed police officer's uniform and car by saying "pretty please."

But if there was any doubt as to where this cop should be pointing his gun, Sinclair cleared it up right away. He sprang up from in front of the patrol car like a jack-in-the-box, squeezing off two quick shots at the cop before dropping out of sight again. The second shot splintered the wood frame of the front door, just barely missing the cop's chest as he ducked back into the house. For sure, he was radioing for backup.

For sure, Sinclair knew that, too.

The next sound I heard was the door opening on the far side of the patrol car, the driver's side. I couldn't see him, and that was the plan. He was crawling behind the wheel, starting the engine. Ducking below the dash, he jammed on the gas, blindly backing out of the driveway.

My first shot hit the side window, the glass shattering. I next went for the tires, taking out the two closest to me.

But he was still moving, barreling into the street before shifting out of reverse, his tires squealing against the pavement as he hit the gas.

"Go!" I heard behind me.

It was as if Sarah had pooled all her remaining strength to make sure I wouldn't do what I was about to do. I did it anyway. I let Sinclair drive off without chasing him, and stayed to help her.

I pulled out my folded handkerchief, pressing it firmly over the shoulder wound to stanch the bleeding.

"Here," came a voice behind me. The officer from inside the house was handing me a belt. "An ambulance is on the way."

I tightened the belt above the second wound, this one below the biceps. She'd already lost so much blood.

"You're going to be fine," I told her. "Just fine."

She glanced at the Grand Cherokee, her voice weak. "You should've gone after him," she said, barely above a whisper.

"What, and miss playing doctor with you here?"

I could tell she wanted to laugh, but she didn't have the strength. "You big dope," she said.

I lifted her head, cradling it in my hands. Her breathing was slower, more labored. *Where the hell is that ambulance?*

"Hang on, okay? You have to hang on for me," I told her.

She nodded ever so slightly, those beautiful jade-green eyes of hers struggling to stay open.

Until, finally, they no longer could.

Chapter 113

THE NURSE HOOKING up Sarah's fifth blood transfusion at Great Plains Regional Medical Center had no idea that she and her pink smock were all that stood between me and the verbal beat-down that absolutely, positively was coming my way courtesy of Dan Driesen. He'd just walked in the door straight from Casper, his jacket off and sleeves rolled up. He didn't say a word to me, but if looks could kill I would've been toes-up at the morgue.

I couldn't blame the guy for being mad as hell. Up until that moment, my reputation had merely preceded me. Now I'd managed to exceed it in ways that would surely get me suspended again, if not booted from the Bureau forever.

Sure, Sarah was a big girl and had made her own decision to join me in Birdwood, but now she was lying unconscious after thirteen hours and counting, having lost more blood than, quote, "most folks live to tell about."

This according to her doctor, who delivered the line with a face so straight it could cut glass.

"Visiting hours are over in fifteen minutes," announced the nurse as she left the room. She might as well have rung the bell ringside at Madison Square Garden.

Gentlemen, touch gloves and come out fighting.

Driesen circled me for a moment, as if waiting to see whether I'd offer up some lame excuse or, worse, try to argue that I hadn't done anything wrong. But that would just be me leaning into his first punch. That much I knew not to do.

Finally, as I simply stared back at him in silence, he unloaded on me.

"What the *fuck* were you thinking?" he asked.

"I'm—"

"Shut up!" he said. "Do you realize how many ways to Sunday you screwed things up?"

"I know that—"

"SHUT UP!" he yelled. "I DON'T WANT TO HEAR IT!"

I stood up, taking a step toward him. "THEN STOP FUCKING ASKING ME QUESTIONS!" I yelled back.

It was a bad move, but I couldn't help it. Besides, what was one more bad move on the heels of so many others?

Driesen got up in my face so tight I could count his pores. The thought of leaning into his punch was no longer a metaphor. The guy looked as if he actually wanted to take a swing at me.

It was only fitting, then, that I'd be saved by the bell, courtesy of the same woman who'd rung it in the first place.

The nurse and her pink smock stormed back into the room, the rubber soles of her shoes squeaking on the floor like nails on a blackboard.

"That's it!" she snapped. "Visiting hours are over!"

Driesen looked at her for a moment, his

eyebrows angled as if trying to decide how to respond. He opted for calm and apologetic. "I'm terribly sorry," he said. "We'll keep it down."

"You're damn right," she said in reply. "I want you both out of here...*now!*"

For good measure, she pointed toward the door, like a gestapo Babe Ruth calling his home-run shot.

Of course, as the reigning expert in the room on bad moves, I could've told her she should've quit while she was ahead.

On a dime, Driesen scrapped calm and apologetic in favor of outright apocalyptic. In a voice louder than I thought humanly possible, he laid into this short and stout woman so fast and furious that it would've been funny if it weren't so scary.

That's when I knew. Driesen was more than Sarah's boss. He was a mentor—her rabbi, a father figure. We *both* really needed her to be okay.

Score one for screaming like a madman.

No sooner had Driesen let up for a second, if only to catch his breath, than we heard the best sound in the world...a voice I wasn't sure I'd ever hear again.

"Jeez, can't a girl get some sleep around here?"

In unison we all turned to Sarah lying in the bed, her eyes now open. Driesen smiled. I smiled. Even the nurse smiled.

Then Sarah smiled.

She was going to be okay.

Chapter 114

I WANTED TO rush over to her. Hold her. Kiss her. At the very least I wanted to take her hand so I could feel her touch against mine.

All things I couldn't do.

With Driesen in the room I was merely Sarah's colleague at the Bureau who was very happy to see that she was going to survive. All smiles and relief—from a proper and platonic distance.

Sarah's doctor was summoned. As soon as he arrived Driesen waved me over to the corner of the room by the door. There was no more yelling, no more right up in my face. Chalk it up to the overwhelmingly good feeling in the room. Still, as he spoke, there was no mistaking the tone. He was dead serious.

"This is what happens now, whether you like it or not," he began before detailing what would be my open-ended stay at the Bureau Hotel back in New York until Sinclair was caught. House arrest, for all intents and purposes. "Are we clear?"

"We're clear," I answered.

The only freedom I had was once again choosing whether or not to pull the boys from camp to join me.

"Think about it for a moment while I make a couple of calls," said Driesen, reaching for his cell.

He left the room, finally leaving Sarah and me alone. Hospitals are one big revolving door, and there was no telling when a nurse, doctor, or even Driesen would return, so I made it fast. The kiss. The hug. The chance to tell her that she scared the hell out of me. The one thing I didn't need to tell her was that I hadn't felt this way about another woman since my wife had died.

But Sarah had figured that out on her own.

"I recognized him," she said, referring to Sinclair. "But he recognized me first."

"Only by a fraction of a second," I said.

She glanced at her shoulder and then her other arm, both heavily bandaged. "That's all it took."

I squeezed her hand, smiling. "Lucky shots."

Sure enough, without so much as a knock on the door, another nurse strolled in. I quickly let go of Sarah's hand, although this particular nurse was so preoccupied with the bouquet of yellow lilies she was carrying that it hardly seemed to matter. "These just arrived for you," she announced. She placed them down on the windowsill, but not before burying her nose deep into the bouquet, breathing deeply. "They smell terrific."

Sarah looked at the flowers and then back at me as the nurse walked out. There had to be at least two dozen lilies, beautifully arranged.

"Don't look at me; I didn't send them," I said.

She laughed. "It sure wasn't Driesen. Flowers are definitely not in his repertoire."

"Maybe it's standing operating procedure from Quantico," I said jokingly. "One dozen for every bullet you take."

I walked over to the bouquet, spotting a small envelope attached to the lip of the glass vase. Pulling out the card, I read it silently.

"Who's it from?" she asked.

I didn't answer right away. I was reading the card for a second time, thinking. Thinking fast.

Sarah tried again. "John, who are they from?"

I looked up at her, shaking my head. "So much for my Quantico theory," I said.

"What do you mean?"

"They must have screwed up the names. These are for someone named Jessica Baker," I said. "I'll go clear it up with the nurse."

I walked over and gave Sarah a kiss on the forehead. Then I walked out of the room, onto an elevator, and out of the hospital. I didn't go see the nurse. And I made damn sure that Dan Driesen didn't see me.

I hated lying to Sarah, but it would have been worse if she had to lie to protect me. I could practically hear Driesen cursing my name and asking Sarah where the hell I was going.

But she wouldn't be able to tell him. No one would. No one knew where I was going now.

This hunch was all mine.

Chapter 115

THE RAIN WAS relentless, beating down on my windshield so hard that the wipers could barely keep up. If I had been driving, I would've had to pull over. But I wasn't driving.

For the past two days, I'd been parked on an access road within Kensico Cemetery in Valhalla, New York. To get there I'd taken two flights from Birdwood, Nebraska, driven one rental car from Westchester County Airport, and made one stop at the local Stop & Shop to load up on food and water.

The only other place I stopped along the way was a Radio Shack, where I bought a cell phone charger that plugged into the cig-arette lighter. The long-haired clerk roaming the aisle tried to sell me on a backup battery that provided an additional six hours of talk time.

"Good to know," I told him. In other words, thanks but no thanks.

Truth was, I didn't even need the talk time I already had. I couldn't risk being found via GPS, so I was only turning on the phone once every few hours, and only to check messages.

The ones from Driesen tapered off after the first twenty-four hours. As for those from Sarah, I didn't expect any, nor did they come. Some small part of her was surely miffed that I was keeping her in the dark, but the rest of her knew I had my reasons. Soon enough, she'd know them. The only question was whether I'd be right.

After scanning the field of headstones for the gazillionth time, I picked up the card Ned had sent with the flowers. There was no need to read it again; I had it down cold. In fact, I'd known the entire poem by heart since Mrs. Lindstrom's eleventh-grade English class back at Keith Academy.

The woods are lovely, dark and deep.

Ned, of course, didn't sign the card. He didn't have to. He expected us to know the flowers were from him.

But why the poem? And of all poems, why Robert Frost's "Stopping by Woods on a Snowy Evening"?

What promises do you have to keep, Ned?

That answer, I was convinced, was in my other hand.

It was the letter I'd found stashed behind Nora's photograph, in the frame buried at the bottom of the toy chest under Ned's bed. I still didn't know why he had all those DeLorean cars. But I knew why he kept the letter. It was from Nora.

My darling brother, it began.

The tone was big-sister and loving, the entire first page dedicated to questions about Ned's work and life in California. There was little doubt that she truly cared for him. *I'm so proud of you,* she wrote many times over.

Then came page 2.

The focus shifted to her life, the tone immediately dire. *You're the only one I can tell this to, Ned.*

She'd fallen in love with "the wrong man," someone who wasn't what he claimed to be. Everything was a lie. His job, his intentions, even his name.

I'm in danger; I can feel it. Agent John O'Hara is going to be the death of me, Ned.

She didn't elaborate; there were no further details. Only a request in the event her premonition would prove to be true.

Promise that you'll come visit me. And when you do, bring me yellow lilies, like you did after that horrible night when we were children, when we were just little kids. Just kids.

That request was the reason I was still sitting in the car in the pouring rain. I was waiting and waiting for Ned to finally show his face. To keep that promise to Nora.

Chapter 116

THERE WAS A splash of yellow in the distance, moving slowly through the downpour. I leaned forward, my eyelashes practically scraping against the windshield as I blinked and squinted to see who was there. It could be anyone—but it wasn't just anyone.

Ned's head was down, his face obscured by the brim of a Mets baseball cap. Still, there was no mistaking where he and those yellow lilies were heading. Straight to his sister's grave.

I gripped the door handle, giving it a soft and silent pull. It was time to get wet.

Be quick, O'Hara. And stay low. Don't get yourself killed tonight.

The path from the car to the first headstone was a straight dash. Then I zigzagged my way forward, the route having already been plotted and practiced. The rain was my ally now, the sound masking my footsteps. Better still, it was keeping Ned looking down, his head hunched beneath his shoulders.

With one more zag after a zig, I was crouched behind a headstone, my back pressed so hard against the granite I could feel the quartz pieces through my soaked shirt.

Nora's grave was about twenty feet away. Strangely, I could see her face now. I remembered so much about her. About the two of us. With a quick peek I saw Ned and the lilies maybe another thirty feet beyond it. Out came my gun. A count to five or so and he'd be in my range. I counted, then—

"Freeze!" I yelled, springing up.

The lilies slipped through his hands as he looked up at me from under his cap. His eyes were wide with surprise and then even wider with fear. He had no idea what was happening.

And shit! I had no idea who he was.

"Put your hands up!" I barked, edging closer to the man, whoever he was.

You can tell whether a person is a true threat by how he responds to someone else holding a gun. If he's looking at the gun, he's not a threat.

This guy was no threat to me.

"Who are you?" I asked. He was so busy staring at my gun that I had to ask him twice.

"I work here," he said finally.

I looked him over. Sure enough, he was wearing Timberland boots and a jumpsuit, complete with KENSICO spelled out above his heart. A grave digger, probably.

"What's your name?" I asked.

"Ken. I'm just Ken."

"Who are the flowers for?"

"Someone named Nora Sinclair. Her head-stone's right there," he said, pointing. "Who are you?"

I lowered my gun, walked over to the guy, and showed him my badge.

"Oh," he said, making the connection. "You're the one in the car, right?"

I nodded. "Yeah. I'm the one in the car."

"My boss told me I wasn't allowed to ask who you were," he said. "Figures."

His knees no longer shaking, Ken bent down to pick up the lilies. Meanwhile, my mind was already plotting how I'd draw a bead on Ned again through the florist he used to order the flowers. Where did he call from? Did he use a stolen credit card? Would he use it again?

"I'm sorry, what did you say?" I asked.

Ken had said something but I hadn't heard him. He was scooping up the last lily.

"The guy told me he got really emotional standing next to the grave," he said.

"Wait; what?" *What guy?*

"He just handed me fifty bucks to deliver these," he said, standing up. "Easiest money I ever—"

"Get down!" I yelled.

Chapter 117

AT THE SOUND of the shot, Ken's cap went flying. Then he got the message and went down on the ground. Then he was crawling away, then running.

As I dove behind the nearest headstone, I felt a hot sting through my calf. Ned had no intention of missing me twice.

"Drop it!" I suddenly heard.

I'd barely scrambled to my knees, ready for a good old-fashioned standoff, when I turned to see Ned and his Browning Hi-Power Mark III pistol. He must have sprinted from his hiding place in order to reach me so fast.

Slowly, I dropped my Glock to the ground.

After he gave it a swift kick across the wet grass, Ned turned and smiled.

"Well, if it isn't John O'Hara," he said.

I faked a smile in response, spreading my palms. "The one and only."

That made him chuckle. "Good one," he said. "Clever."

"Unfortunately, not as clever as you."

"Very true," he said. "Although I give you credit for getting this far."

The odd thing was, he actually seemed sincere about that. As motivated as he was by revenge, it was as if he still wanted a fair fight. Hence his clues; the way he'd been almost testing Sarah and me.

"How'd you know I'd be here?" I asked.

"I'd be lying if I said I knew for sure. But I guess I knew the same way you did. Math."

I didn't follow.

"It's called a Fibonacci sequence," he continued. "When the next number in a series is always the sum of the two numbers that precede it. Five, eight, thirteen, twenty-one, thirty-four. In a way, it's the premise for all deductive reasoning."

I stared up at Ned, listening to his every word. Take away the gun aimed at my chest and he could've been giving a lecture back at UCLA. Where was the anger? The hatred of me? He was calm. Too calm. I couldn't find an opening.

"It's really a shame," I said, shaking my head. "You know, what might have been."

He rolled his eyes. "Okay, I'll bite," he said. "What do you mean?"

"I know what happened when you and Nora were children, the whole terrible story. Even how your mother took the blame for you."

"So?" he asked. It was his first twitch. His quick blink that told me time didn't heal all wounds.

"So imagine what might have been had your father not been a monster," I said. "How different your and Nora's life would've been."

"Don't forget about your life, too," he said. "Or what remains of it." He motioned to the bloody grass beneath my knee. "How's your leg doing?"

"Don't worry; I'll live," I answered.

He chuckled again. "Another good one," he said. "I bet you made my sister laugh, too. Before you killed her."

Chapter 118

NED STARED DOWN at me. His jaw drew tight, and his arm stiffened behind his gun.

"I didn't kill her," I said. "No matter what you think, it wasn't me."

"You're lying!" he fired back. "No matter who it was, you're the one responsible. If it wasn't for you, she'd still be alive."

Maybe he was right about that.

I glanced at his Browning pistol, the rain beading against its black epoxy finish. "So how come you haven't shot me?" I asked. "Since I deserve it so much."

"You deserve this, too!" Ned wound up his right leg, his instep landing across my ribs.

As I toppled from my knees, rolling on the ground in pain, all I could think was one thing.

So far so good. Better to be kicked than shot dead.

"Gee, I'm sorry," said Ned sarcastically. "Did that hurt?"

I pushed up on my hands so I could look him in the eyes. And then I forced a smile. "Is that all you've got?"

I was pretty sure I heard a rib crack as Ned knocked me again with all he had, which was plenty. He was stronger than he looked. And angrier.

But I was begging for more. "C'mon, mama's boy, show me what you can really do! Nora seduced you, didn't she? She did the same thing to me."

Ned aimed higher this time, his foot coming across my face. *Whack! Thump!* I was back on the ground again, curled in a fetal position. My hands were inches from my ankles.

I could feel the swelling around my left eye, the lid collapsing shut.

Through my right eye I watched as Ned backed up for a running start. It was as if we were playing a game of kickball and I was the ball. His entire focus was on delivering more pain.

That's it, Ned, let it all go. The anger, the hatred...

Your hands.

They'd fallen to his side, his pistol by his waist, pointing down instead of at me. Finally, and for only a split second, the game had changed.

Now I was the one a step ahead, with a math equation of my own.

Two minus one still leaves one.

As fast as I'd ever moved, I reached for my spare—the 9mm Beretta tucked into my shin holster. I grabbed it and fired without really aiming.

The shot hit Ned near his shoulder, in a spot similar to the one where he had hit Sarah. He stumbled back, feet wobbly, reality sinking in. He tried to lift his arm to fire, but I was ready for him. And guess what? I was even angrier than he was.

BLAM!

This shot was truer, ripping through his chest, the force nearly cutting the legs out from under him. But he wouldn't go down.

He was stumbling back, the blood spilling down his body, changing colors in the rain. Deep red, light red, almost pink.

As he raised his pistol again, he opened his mouth to say something. But he'd already done enough talking as far as I was concerned. He'd talked way too much, the sick murdering bastard.

BLAM!

The shot echoed around the surrounding oak trees as I fell onto my back. Then I was staring up at the swirling clouds. I was trying to catch my breath.

Slowly, I made my way over to where he'd fallen. My last bullet had caught him in the heart.

Ned Sinclair was dead.

Not six feet from his sister Nora's grave. And you know what? They deserved each other.

Chapter 119

IN THE AFTERMATH, so to speak, of Ned Sinclair's death, one of my immediate problems solved itself. Squandering the kudos I'd received in the wake of the identification of the Honeymoon Murderer, I'd broken half the rules in the FBI handbook and angered more than a few superiors, not the least of whom was Dan Driesen. But in doing so I'd also shut down a killer who had scared every guy named John O'Hara in the country, including one who just happened to be the president's brother-in-law.

I wasn't fired. I wasn't even put back on suspension. Frank Walsh still wanted me to see Dr. Adam Kline, but after the good doctor heard of the little field trip I made after mending for a few days back home in Riverside, he decided his work with me was done.

"That showed real courage," he told me in what would be my last visit to his office. "You did the right thing. You're good by me."

I wasn't sure about the courage part, but even before I rang the doorbell at Stephen McMillan's house, I was pretty sure about it being the right thing to do.

This was one problem of mine that wouldn't take care of itself.

I sat in McMillan's living room, listening as he delivered his heartfelt apology for causing Susan's death. I had little doubt that every word was as true and real as the tears streaming down his cheeks.

"I know it's no consolation, but I haven't had a sip of alcohol since the accident," he told me.

"You're right," I said. "It's no consolation to me or my kids. But I'm sure it means a lot to your family."

McMillan glanced at a photograph of his teenage son and daughter that was sitting on a small table next to his armchair. He nodded.

The two of us talked for only a minute longer, during which he was either too smart or too scared to ask for my forgiveness. That was something he'd simply never get.

But what I could and did offer him was this: acceptance of what had happened.

I told him I could accept the fact that he fully understood what a mistake he'd made and what a terrible loss it was for my boys and me. He'd made that abundantly clear, and I believed him.

"Thank you," he said softly.

Then, after we both stood up, I did something I never imagined I'd ever do. Not in a million years. Or even longer.

I shook his hand.

"What changed your mind?" asked Harold Cornish once we left the house. As our go-between, McMillan's attorney had been waiting for me in the foyer. "Why did you finally agree to meet with my client?"

I could've told Cornish a very long story about what I'd been through since I'd last seen him on his little visit to my back patio. Martha Cole. Ned Sinclair. And the one thing the three of us had in common, a singular desire.

Instead, I simply summed it all up for him. "Nothing good ever comes from revenge," I said.

EPILOGUE

Chapter 120

"OKAY, FOR THE last time," said Sarah, smiling at me from the bow. "How is it that we're on this boat?"

"It's like I told you. I met a guy on a Jet Ski down here and he owed me a favor."

Sarah folded her arms, waiting me out. It didn't take long. You can only be coy with a pretty girl in a black bikini for so long.

I told Sarah about my first trip to Turks and Caicos, when this whole crazy ride began. And in the case of the Speedo-wearing con man, Pierre Simone, I meant "crazy ride" literally.

With perhaps a little encouragement from

police commissioner Joseph Eldridge, however, Pierre managed to provide a humdinger of a make-good. "I won it in a poker game," he told me on the phone in his French accent, his exact whereabouts undisclosed. "Zee guy had a flush, and I had zee full boat."

I didn't know if Pierre was simply making a joke. I didn't care. For one glorious week, I had a forty-foot-long tall-rig Catalina and the chance to dust off my skippering skills, which I learned as a teenager during three summers at my local YMCA sailing camp.

I also had one hell of a first mate joining me for the ride. Even the scars from her bullet wounds were damn sexy, at least to me.

"I'm grabbing a beer," said Sarah, heading down to the galley. "You want one?"

"Absolutely," I said from the helm.

Back in Riverside, everyone had been home for a couple of weeks. Max and John Jr. raved about their time at Camp Wilderlocke, and Judy and Marshall raved about their Mediterranean cruise. Still, with all their great stories to tell, it was my story of bringing down two serial killers that they couldn't get enough of.

"A doubleheader!" Max called it from underneath his Yankees cap. As for my being Ned Sinclair's ultimate target, he proceeded to offer up the ultimate solution. "You should've just changed your name, Dad!"

That gave everyone around the dinner table that night a good laugh. It also gave me further proof that if family is the true currency of happiness, I was a very wealthy man.

Of course, having Warner Breslow's check in my bank account wasn't too shabby, either. Two hundred and fifty thousand dollars for services rendered.

And in my safe at home was the signed agreement for my bonus.

Breslow had asked me if Max and John Jr. were good students. "Do they do their homework?" he inquired. They had always gotten good grades, but now they had even more incentive to study. Breslow would be paying for both their college educations.

"Ethan and Abigail loved kids," he told me. "For as long as I live, I'll be reminded of that when I think of your two boys."

The tabloids would still write nasty things about Warner Breslow, and some of it might even be true. But I'd like to think I caught a glimpse of the man few other people had ever seen. What I saw was just a father who loved his son deeply.

"Here you go," said Sarah, back on deck.

She handed me an ice-cold Turk's Head beer and we clicked cans, toasting our beautiful sunny afternoon in paradise.

Neither of us owned a crystal ball, and there were still things to learn about each other in the weeks, months, and, I hoped, years that lay ahead. But this much I knew for sure: there was no one else I'd rather be with on that boat. And I had a pretty good notion that Sarah felt the same way.

"So where should we head?" she asked.

I smiled. "Good question."

We both looked around. There was nothing but blue sky, blue water, and endless possibilities for the two of us.

Sarah stepped behind me at the helm, wrapping her arms around my waist. Then she whispered in my ear.

"Let's just see where the wind takes us, John O'Hara."

About the Authors

JAMES PATTERSON has created more enduring fictional characters than any other novelist writing today. His Alex Cross novels—the most popular detective series of the past twenty-five years—include the bestsellers *Kiss the Girls* and *Along Came a Spider*. Mr. Patterson also writes the bestselling Women's Murder Club novels, set in San Francisco, and the top-selling New York detective series of all time, featuring Detective Michael Bennett. James Patterson has had more *New York Times* bestsellers than any other writer, ever, according to *Guinness World Records*. Since his first novel won the

Edgar Award in 1977, James Patterson's books have sold more than 275 million copies.

James Patterson has also written numerous number one bestsellers for young readers, including the Maximum Ride, Witch & Wizard, and Middle School series. In total, these books have spent more than 220 weeks on national bestseller lists. In 2010, James Patterson was named Author of the Year at the Children's Choice Book Awards.

His lifelong passion for books and reading led James Patterson to create the innovative website ReadKiddoRead.com, giving adults an invaluable tool for finding the books that get kids reading for life. He writes full-time and lives in Florida with his family.

HOWARD ROUGHAN has cowritten several books with James Patterson and is the author of *The Promise of a Lie* and *The Up and Comer*. He lives in Connecticut with his wife and son.

Books by James Patterson

Featuring Alex Cross

Alex Cross, Run • *Merry Christmas, Alex Cross*
• *Kill Alex Cross* • *Cross Fire* • *I, Alex Cross* •
Alex Cross's Trial (with Richard DiLallo) •
Cross Country • *Double Cross* • *Cross* (also
published as *Alex Cross*) • *Mary, Mary* •
London Bridges • *The Big Bad Wolf* • *Four
Blind Mice* • *Violets Are Blue* • *Roses Are Red*
• *Pop Goes the Weasel* • *Cat & Mouse* • *Jack
& Jill* • *Kiss the Girls* • *Along Came a Spider*

The Women's Murder Club

12th of Never (with Maxine Paetro) • *11th
Hour* (with Maxine Paetro) • *10th Anniver-
sary* (with Maxine Paetro) • *The 9th
Judgment* (with Maxine Paetro) • *The 8th
Confession* (with Maxine Paetro) • *7th
Heaven* (with Maxine Paetro) • *The 6th Tar-
get* (with Maxine Paetro) • *The 5th Horseman*
(with Maxine Paetro) • *4th of July* (with
Maxine Paetro) • *3rd Degree* (with Andrew
Gross) • *2nd Chance* (with Andrew Gross) •
1st to Die

Featuring Michael Bennett

I, Michael Bennett (with Michael Ledwidge) • *Tick Tock* (with Michael Ledwidge) • *Worst Case* (with Michael Ledwidge) • *Run for Your Life* (with Michael Ledwidge) • *Step on a Crack* (with Michael Ledwidge)

The Private Novels

Private Berlin (with Mark Sullivan) • *Private London* (with Mark Pearson) • *Private Games* (with Mark Sullivan) • *Private: #1 Suspect* (with Maxine Paetro) • *Private* (with Maxine Paetro)

Summer Novels

Now You See Her (with Michael Ledwidge) • *Swimsuit* (with Maxine Paetro) • *Sail* (with Howard Roughan) • *Beach Road* (with Peter de Jonge) • *Lifeguard* (with Andrew Gross) • *Honeymoon* (with Howard Roughan) • *The Beach House* (with Peter de Jonge)

Stand-alone Books

NYPD Red (with Marshall Karp) • *Zoo* (with Michael Ledwidge) • *Guilty Wives* (with

David Ellis) • *The Christmas Wedding* (with Richard DiLallo) • *Kill Me If You Can* (with Marshall Karp) • *Toys* (with Neil McMahon) • *Don't Blink* (with Howard Roughan) • *The Postcard Killers* (with Liza Marklund) • *The Murder of King Tut* (with Martin Dugard) • *Against Medical Advice* (with Hal Friedman) • *Sundays at Tiffany's* (with Gabrielle Charbonnet) • *You've Been Warned* (with Howard Roughan) • *The Quickie* (with Michael Ledwidge) • *Judge & Jury* (with Andrew Gross) • *Sam's Letters to Jennifer* • *The Lake House* • *The Jester* (with Andrew Gross) • *Suzanne's Diary for Nicholas* • *Cradle and All* • *When the Wind Blows* • *Miracle on the 17th Green* (with Peter de Jonge) • *Hide & Seek* • *The Midnight Club* • *Black Friday* (originally published as *Black Market*) • *See How They Run* • *Season of the Machete* • *The Thomas Berryman Number*

For Readers of All Ages

Maximum Ride

Nevermore: The Final Maximum Ride Adventure • *Angel: A Maximum Ride Novel* •

Fang: A Maximum Ride Novel • *Max: A Maximum Ride Novel* • *The Final Warning: A Maximum Ride Novel* • *Saving the World and Other Extreme Sports: A Maximum Ride Novel* • *School's Out—Forever: A Maximum Ride Novel* • *The Angel Experiment: A Maximum Ride Novel*

Daniel X

Daniel X: Armageddon (with Chris Grabenstein) • *Daniel X: Game Over* (with Ned Rust) • *Daniel X: Demons and Druids* (with Adam Sadler) • *Daniel X: Watch the Skies* (with Ned Rust) • *The Dangerous Days of Daniel X* (with Michael Ledwidge)

Witch & Wizard

Witch & Wizard: The Kiss (with Jill Dembowski) • *Witch & Wizard: The Fire* (with Jill Dembowski) • *Witch & Wizard: The Gift* (with Ned Rust) • *Witch & Wizard* (with Gabrielle Charbonnet)

Middle School

Middle School: My Brother Is a Big Fat Liar (with Lisa Papademetriou, illustrated by Neil Swaab) • *Middle School: Get Me Out of Here!* (with Chris Tebbetts, illustrated by Laura Park) • *Middle School: The Worst Years of My Life* (with Chris Tebbetts, illustrated by Laura Park)

Other Books for Readers of All Ages

I Funny: A Middle School Story (with Chris Grabenstein, illustrated by Laura Park) • *Confessions of a Murder Suspect* (with Maxine Paetro) • *Med Head* (with Hal Friedman) • *santaKid* (illustrated by Michael Garland)

For previews and information about the author, visit JamesPatterson.com or find him on Facebook or at your app store.